J. J. DURHAM

An Act of Mercy

an imprint of HarperCollins*Publishers*
www.harpercollins.co.uk

Killer Reads
An imprint of HarperCollins*Publishers*
1 London Bridge Street
London SE1 9GF
www.harpercollins.co.uk

This paperback edition 2015

First published by HarperCollins*Publishers* 2015

A catalogue record for this book
is available from the British Library

ISBN: 978-0-00-813277-4

This novel is entirely a work of fiction.
The names, characters and incidents portrayed in it,
while at times based on historical fact, are
the work of the author's imagination.

Set in Minion by Born Group using Atomik ePublisher from Easypress

Find out more about HarperCollins and the environment at
www.harpercollins.co.uk/green

AN ACT OF MERCY

J. J. Durham was born in a pit village in the north east of England and grew up in a caravan stuffed full of books, cutting her literary teeth on the great storytellers of the 1960's and 70's – Wilbur Smith, Frank Yerby, Mary Renault, Sergeanne Golon, and Lance Horner. She has a degree in English Literature, and has published two previous novels. *An Act of Mercy* is her first historical crime novel, and it features pioneering Victorian detective Harry Pilgrim.

www.jjdurham.co.uk

CHAPTER ONE

'There ain't many things in life I'm afraid of, sir … '

'But … ?' Sergeant Harry Pilgrim glared up at the constable from halfway down the sewer ladder.

He hopped from one foot to the other, peering down at his superior. 'Rats is one of them.'

'Rats?'

'Just so, sir. Fearful scratchy, louse-ridden creatures, sir, and I could no more go down that hole with you than walk on water, sir, even if you paid me a hundred guineas.'

Pilgrim looked at the constable. They both knew he earned just twenty shillings a week.

'I don't have time for this, Wainwright. Pass me the tinder box.'

'Here it is, sir.' The constable's face slackened with relief.

Pilgrim took the box and tested the wheel. It fired readily; spinning sparks into the darkness as he descended the ladder. The rungs were surprisingly dry – it hadn't rained for more than a fortnight – but even so, Pilgrim landed at the bottom with a splash. He didn't look down to see what he had landed in, but up instead, to Wainwright's face, haloed by the night sky like a lugubrious saint.

'If I'm not back in five minutes go to the barracks.' Pilgrim's voice echoed off the arched brickwork. 'Tell Constable Williamson where I am, and get him to wake some of the men to follow me.'

'Will do, sir … and sorry, sir … about the rats.'

Pilgrim sparked the tinderbox again, and lit the wick of the lamp. He raised it up. He was in one of the new parts of the sewer system. The roof was easily high enough for him to stand, but the bricks were already crumbling, and daubed with rust-coloured streaks. It wasn't rust, of course.

Pilgrim grimaced. He was glad that smallpox had robbed him of his sense of smell. He knew he had to hurry. The man he was pursuing was at least five minutes ahead of him now. He pressed on into the sewer; a straight tunnel with no turns or visible exits.

'… seventy-four … seventy-five …' He counted the paces, until he reached a point where the tunnel split into two. He hesitated. His quarry could have gone down either of them. But which one? He lifted the lamp higher, and listened. Nothing. Except the scratch of claws on brickwork. He could make out the huddle of rats on the copings beyond the range of his lamp. It was just as well Wainwright hadn't wanted to join him. On the other hand, if he had, they would at least have been able to explore both routes. Frustration welled. Pilgrim had come so far, but now found himself torn between choosing one of the tunnels at random and turning back.

Then he heard it: the rasp of metal on metal, coming from the left hand branch. He took off his scarf, hung it on a nail that was protruding from the wall of the left hand tunnel, then galvanized into action, wading through the water as quickly as he could. It was impossible not to splash, but he hoped that the man he was chasing would be too absorbed in his own progress to hear the pursuit. Pilgrim ran on through the greasy water. Something caught at his foot. He lurched and stumbled, pitching forwards, then floundered a moment, grabbing for something, anything, that might help to keep his face out of the filth. His fingers closed on something substantial, and he used it to push up onto his feet. Releasing it, he recoiled at the sight of an eye staring up at him. A dead dog.

2

He made an effort to steady the pounding of his heart. At least he hadn't dropped the lamp. He listened. Nothing. All his senses told him he was alone in the tunnel.

'Bollocks.'

He lifted the lamp. More brick, more slime, more black water, stretching away into the darkness. But there, on the boundary of the glow cast by the lamp, he saw something else: rungs set into the wall. He waded towards them and peered up at a manhole cover. If his suspect was no longer in the tunnel, he had to have got out somewhere. Realising he couldn't climb with one hand, Pilgrim took a deep breath and pinched out the wick of the lamp. Blackness swallowed him: a solid thing. He beat down his anxiety by concentrating on the feel of the metal rungs under his hands. One. Two. Three. Four. Five. Hand over hand; he pulled himself upwards, until his head bumped against the manhole cover. He lifted it, and slid it to one side. He blinked.

Moonlight painted the lane as bright as midday in Margate. He made a hasty calculation of direction and distance, and decided he was probably somewhere to the west of St James' Square. Behind Curzon Street, perhaps. Or Half Moon Street. A wealthy area, that wouldn't take kindly to detectives popping up out of the sewer, even at that hour. He levered himself up out of the hole, glad that most of the worthy citizens of Mayfair would be tucked up in their beds.

After a moment's hesitation, he left the cover partly off the hole, considering it worth risking an accident in the hope that the moonlight would guide Wainwright, Williamson, and the other constables to him.

He straightened up and listened. His suspect had to be long gone: the manhole was at the junction of three lanes, and he could have fled in any direction. But he willed himself, with a discipline forged from experience, to stand still. To listen and to look. A shadow detached itself from the larger shadow of a nearby wall, and wound itself around his legs. He resisted the urge to kick it, and peered instead at the surrounding buildings. Several stable blocks lined the converging lanes, overshadowed by the houses behind them. The houses were all in darkness.

Except one. One with lights shining in several windows on the upper floors. Pilgrim headed for it. The gate that gave onto the lane was closed, but not locked. The hinges were well oiled, and it swung open without a sound.

As he picked his way towards the house, he paused, his eye caught by something gleaming on the path. Water. He suppressed a thrill of triumph. His man had come this way: given the recent dearth of rain, there was no other way for the path to be wet. There didn't seem to be a back door, but there was a side entrance, in the shadows of the neighbouring building. It was too gloomy to see the doorway properly, so he bent to touch the step, a parody of genuflection. It was also wet.

He hesitated. He couldn't go crashing into a wealthy household on his own, although he wouldn't have had the same scruples in one of the poorer parts of the city. If Wainwright had gone back to the barracks as instructed, if he had then roused Dolly and the other constables and taken them to the manhole in Cockspur Court, then Pilgrim was looking at a wait of at least forty minutes. Providing, of course, that Dolly had spotted the scarf he had left to mark the left-hand tunnel in the sewer. If not …

With a feeling that the situation was slipping out of his grasp, he worked his way around to the front of the house. And there his anxiety deepened: a Hackney carriage was waiting at the kerb. The nag between the traces had a dejected air, looking no happier to be out in the middle of the night than Pilgrim was himself. Pilgrim guessed it had been there for some time.

He crept into a gap in the shrubbery, just yards from the cab. He had no sooner settled into his chosen spot, however, when a gust of night air found a crack in the glass of one of the carriage lamps, and extinguished the flame. The driver's shoulders slumped, and he slid off the box. Pilgrim heard a flint strike.

4

'Come on, you tokey bugger.' The driver jabbed at the wick, and the lamp flared.

Pilgrim drew back into the shadows so that the driver wouldn't see him, pulling his collar over the lower half of his scarred face. The carriage lamp died again, plunging Pilgrim back into gloom.

'Stay like that, then, you bugger.' The driver continued berating the lamp until he resumed his seat on the box, where he lapsed once more into silence.

Pilgrim's eyelids drooped, and he wondered, not for the first time, what he was doing there. It was one of his golden rules never, ever, to act on tip-offs from the public. In his experience, anonymous leads were unreliable at best, if not downright mischievous. But there had been something about the note he had received that evening, the use of red ink, perhaps? It had been addressed to him, care of 'Mr Charles Dickens, at the offices of *Household Words*'. Pilgrim was not a man given to fancies – far from it – but he had had the strangest sensation when Dickens put the envelope into his hand.

He settled further into his hiding place, pondering the nature of anonymous informants, the use of red ink, and the usefulness of having golden rules if you were in the habit of breaking them. His eyes drifted shut …

He jerked awake again as the carriage door slammed. Had someone climbed inside? The driver shook his reins and urged the horse into motion. Pilgrim resisted the impulse to shout at him to stop; he didn't want to lose the element of surprise. He had no choice but to spur his reluctant limbs into action. Luckily, the horse was no more enthusiastic for the exercise than he was, and barely accelerated above an amble to the end of the street. It slowed down still further to turn the corner, and Pilgrim seized his chance. He put on a burst of speed, and grabbed for the door handle, using his own forward momentum to open the door and swing himself up into the cab.

'What the … ?' The startled passenger, a young man with mutton chop whiskers, leapt off the seat. Pilgrim swung his fist lazily, almost casually, and felt it connect with the man's chin. He slid to the floor, like a puppet with its strings cut.

The driver sawed the cab to a halt. 'What in hellfire … ?'

Pilgrim ignored him, and turned his attention to the packages on the floor. There were six in total, all swathed in brown canvas. The largest was about the same size as a hatbox. Pilgrim knelt beside it, and started to tear at the wrappings. It was indeed a hatbox. He fumbled with the strap. As he did, the box slipped from his grasp and it sprung open, dumping the contents. A roughly spherical object bounced away across the floor of the cab, trailing wet strips of rag behind it. It came to rest under the seat.

He stared at it. It stared back. It took him a long, shocked moment to realize what it was.

CHAPTER TWO

'Can't beat a splendid piece of beef. And the bloodier the better, eh? Builds up the constitution.'

The chunk of flesh quivered so rare on the silver platter that it looked as if it had trotted to the table straight from Smithfield, without detouring to a kitchen.

'So I understand, Mr Phillips.' The Guest of Honour, who much preferred his beef brown, masked his dismay with a smile. Charles Dickens was nothing if not a social creature, and prided himself on his manners.

'Don't mind if I carve it meself, do you?' asked Phillips. 'The servants always make a bloody hash of it.'

'Language, John.' The rebuke from Mrs Phillips was mild, for the guests of her late supper party were used to her husband's eccentricities. She nodded as the footman replenished her wine glass.

The dining room was panelled from floor to ceiling: a surfeit of mahogany and scagliola columns. The gentlemen, wearing white waistcoats, uniformly red-faced and bewhiskered, were indistinguishable from each other. The women, on the other hand, had gone out of their way to be as individual as possible, resulting in a visual cacophony of multicoloured silks, feathers, and paisley shawls. Lady Harcourt-Brown rustled as she leaned towards Dickens, offering a generous view of crepey bosom.

'We have been reading in *Household Words*, Mr Dickens, about the new detective police who have been appointed.'

He kept his eyes fixed on the beef that was yielding to the enthusiasm of his host's carving knife. But the Lady was not to be similarly distracted.

'Do you think they will put an end to the lawlessness on our streets?' she prompted.

'Ha!' It was not Dickens, but her husband, Sir Harold, who responded.

'You do not think so, sir?' They'd caught his attention at last.

'Indeed I do not. In my experience, these so-called detectives are very ordinary people, with delusions of cleverness, who are worth nothing when taken beyond their usual routine.'

'I'm afraid I must disagree with you,' Dickens began. 'The rate of ...'

'It will all come to nothing.' Sir Harold dismissed Dickens, the detectives, and the improved conviction rates of the capital with a wave. As Justice of the Peace for Clerkenwell East, he was well known for being 'down on' anyone unlucky enough to appear before him, and prided himself on that reputation. 'It is never a wise or safe proceeding to put authority in the hands of the lower classes.'

Dickens's gaze flicked to the footmen lining the room. They remained granite-faced, as good servants should.

'If you ask me,' continued Sir Harold, 'there's something underhand about these detectives of yours. All that sneaking about and lurking in corners. It isn't ...,' he cast around for a suitable word, 'English.'

'Nonsense, Harold,' snorted Lady Harcourt-Brown. 'I, for one, feel safer with these gentlemen on our streets.'

'Hear, hear,' said Mrs Phillips.

'I imagine they must possess very specific qualities?' Mr Phillips surrendered the beef to a footman to distribute among the guests.

'Indeed.' Dickens understood his host's question for what it was: his cue to earn his supper. He took a breath. 'You might think that a detective, having been recruited from the ranks, would inevitably betray some evidence of his lowly beginnings, but you would be wrong!' He wagged a finger at his audience. 'A good detective must blend in as easily in the upper echelons of society as among the criminal classes. He must be well mannered and respectable looking, with good deportment – nothing lounging or slinking in his manner. And, of course, he must possess keen observational skills and a quick perception.'

Sir Harold harrumphed.

Dickens continued. 'In my opinion, this city needs an effective police force, in the same way a child needs the guidance of a wise and impartial parent. It offers protection to the vulnerable elements of the population. Which is why I am determined to do all I can for it.'

As he finished, he wondered whether Harry Pilgrim had acted on the anonymous note he had given him earlier in the evening. The detective had received the tip-off with his usual sangfroid, giving him no indication whether he intended to do anything about it. Pilgrim would certainly be able to give some of his acquaintances a run for their money at the cribbage table.

'I understand there is one detective who is particularly successful,' said Mrs Phillips, apparently picking up on his thoughts. 'Sergeant Pilchem, I believe he is called?'

'His real name is Pilgrim. Henry Pilgrim. A veritable prince of detectives.'

Lady Harcourt-Brown's gaze slid mischievously to her husband. 'In that case, perhaps we should invite Sergeant Pilgrim to our next supper party, Harold?'

Sir Harold's face suffused with blood, and his eyes bulged. For a moment – one brief, glorious moment – Dickens thought he might be choking on the beef. But no. It was indignation.

'Over my dead body!'

CHAPTER THREE

Pilgrim tucked into his breakfast: bloody pork chops and coddled eggs. Freshly shaved and wearing a suit, he was almost unrecognisable as the man who, less than five hours earlier, had apprehended the murderer who would be dubbed 'The Hackney Cab Killer' by the second editions of the newspapers. Pilgrim's scarred face was shocking in the morning light; the skin of the lower half of his chin and neck as pitted as orange peel.

He sat apart from the younger, uniformed officers that also boarded at the barracks, letting their banter wash over and around him, like waves around a rock. The dining room was functionally furnished, with no comforts beyond the long scrubbed table and benches, and a motto painted on the wall: 'Be sure your sin will find you out'. Pilgrim eyed it as he chewed. If only it were true, it would save him a world of trouble.

'There you are, sir.' Adolphus Williamson bounced over to sit beside him, carrying his own tray. Pilgrim smothered a smile. Dolly Williamson, with his smooth, scrubbed features and pink cheeks, looked exactly like the toy he was nicknamed after. Pilgrim knew that appearances were deceptive, however: beneath Dolly's cherubic appearance lay a will of iron.

'Sorry we were too late this morning to be of any assistance, sir.' Dolly continued, taking up his knife and fork. 'I said we should have come as we were, in our nightshirts, but Sergeant Tanner wouldn't hear of it. Wish I'd been with you when you stopped that cab, sir.'

'He didn't put up much of a fight, if that's any consolation.'

'Not really.' Dolly pulled a face, and bent to feed a ginger tomcat a piece of his own chop. 'Any scrap's better than none at all. What do we have on this morning?'

'Whitehall, but I need to call in at the *Chronicle* first, to see if there are any rooms to rent.'

'You're moving out of the barracks?' Dolly raised his eyebrows. 'You can't do that, sir, you're a fixture here, just like old Thomas.'

Pilgrim studied the cat that glared back at him with its single remaining eye. He avoided it whenever he could, for it had the temperament of a Glaswegian stevedore.

'Did you know the neighbours have been complaining about him?' He said to Dolly. 'Apparently he's turned cannibal. He's been eating their pet kitty cats. If I don't get out of these barracks soon I might start to do the same.'

'Nonsense.' Dolly bent to stroke the cat, but his gaze remained on Pilgrim. 'You're an old softy, aren't you?'

There were only five detectives in the new detective division of Scotland Yard – two sergeants and two constables – headed by Chief Inspector Charley Field. They all shared an office, apart from Field, but it was empty when Pilgrim and Dolly finally arrived, after a fruitless visit to the offices of the *Chronicle*.

The furnishings reflected the fact the division was newly created: all four desks and chairs were mismatched, gleaned from elsewhere in the force, and a sofa – strictly for visitors – borrowed from Customs and Excise. A map, divided into sections with thick blue ink, hung on the wall: Cross's *New Plan of London*, published earlier that year. There was nothing else in the room to betray its function: no housebreakers' tools, silverware, luggage, or other unclaimed stolen goods, no disturbing drawings of criminal physiognomy. To all intents and purposes it was indistinguishable from an office of shipping clerks. Pilgrim knew it was a source of disappointment to Charley Field, who would have liked something more dramatic to show visitors.

As Pilgrim took off his overcoat, Constable Wainwright lurched through the doorway, shouldering a large mail sack.

'You're here, sir!' he gasped. 'I have your monthly delivery for you, from Mr Dickens's journal.' Wainwright heaved the sack onto Pilgrim's desk and upended it with a flourish. 'It's the biggest yet.'

Pilgrim scowled at the pile of letters. 'Did you have to put them there?'

'But they're from well-wishers, sir.'

'Well-wishers? People demanding that I find their missing cats, or jewellery. Or husbands. For some reason they believe everything Dickens writes about Sergeant Pilchem, but he has nothing to do with me.'

'Go on with you, sir,' said Dolly. 'There's no need to be modest. Everyone knows it's you.'

Pilgrim scowled. 'I wish the Inspector would stop encouraging Dickens.'

'Hear bloody hear!' The words were spoken by Dick Tanner, the other Detective Sergeant, who stood in the doorway. A powerfully built man in his thirties, he had a head like a bullet and hands made for heavy labour. He glowered at Wainwright. 'Where the hell have you been?' He tossed a file onto his desk.

Wainwright flushed. 'To *Household Words*, sir. Inspector Field sent me.'

Tanner glared at the pile of mail on Pilgrim's desk. 'Waste of time, puffing up egos when there's proper work to be done.'

'Couldn't agree with you more,' said Pilgrim.

'Egos that are big enough already, if you ask me.'

Pilgrim ignored the aside, and bent to retrieve some paperwork that had fallen from Tanner's desk. It was a mortuary sketch of a young woman. 'Did you do this, Wainwright?' he asked.

'Sir?'

'This drawing; it's very good.'

Dolly moved to stand behind Pilgrim to inspect the drawing for himself. Wainwright relaxed under their evident approval.

'Inspector Field says I have a gift.'

'He's right,' said Pilgrim.

The young woman in the drawing looked as if she could be asleep, her eyes closed, freckled face relaxed, and lips slightly parted. The gash across her throat had been cleaned of blood, and Wainwright had faithfully recorded each layer of skin and muscle, the seam of subcutaneous fat, and the section of vertebrae that was visible through the incision.

'Who is she?' asked Pilgrim.

Tanner took the drawing from him. 'Another sorry slapper gone to meet her maker. Found on the floor of her lodgings on the Waterloo Road.'

'What's her name?'

Tanner didn't reply. Pilgrim had to prompt him. 'She did have a name?'

'Eliza Grimwood.'

'You got the killer?'

'No one saw or heard anything.'

Dolly grinned. 'Business as usual, then.' He wandered to Pilgrim's desk and picked up one of the letters. 'Aren't you going to open these, sir? I can give you a hand, if you like.'

Pilgrim was saved from having to answer by Wainwright.

'Oh, I forgot to tell you, Sergeant Pilgrim, sir, Inspector Field has asked to see you and Constable Williamson. Right away, he says. He's getting his photograph taken at present, but says as you're to go straight in.'

A flash greeted Pilgrim and Dolly as they entered Charley Field's office. When their vision cleared, they could see the Inspector standing in the middle of the room, fists on his waist and legs akimbo.

'Be with you in a minute, boys,' he said. 'You can't hurry art, you know.'

A barrel-chested figure, in his early fifties, with a ruddy face and military air, he was generally a man of action, unable to stay still for more than a moment at a time. At that particular moment, however, he had no choice, for his head was gripped by a photographic brace.

The legs of the photographer were visible beneath the camera cover, as well as one arm, which was holding aloft a smoking tray. He emerged from under the cover, his hair sticking up in spikes.

'I think we might have that last one.' His tone spoke more of desperation than conviction, and his hands shook slightly as they replaced the plate in the back of the camera with a fresh one. 'Now we'll try a different pose.' He released the springs holding Field's head.

Field shook himself like a dog. 'All done?' he said. 'Capital!'

'But we … '

'Nonsense. I'm sure you've got what you need.' Field grabbed the camera tripod. 'Let me help you with your equipment.'

As the photographer rushed to rescue his camera, Field also scooped up the photographic plates. 'These are yours, aren't they? And this? We wouldn't want you to forget anything.' He bundled up plates, camera, vice, photographer and all, and practically threw them out into the corridor.

Closing the door on the confusion, he turned back into the room and signalled for Pilgrim and Dolly to take a seat.

'Newfangled nonsense,' he said. 'Making people stand about like cattle. It'll never catch on. Still, we have to keep the newspapers happy.' He settled himself in the chair behind the desk, and turned his knowing gaze from Pilgrim to Dolly, and back again. 'I have to say, you don't look at all well, boys. I've seen more colour in gallows-meat. What you need is a spot of country air.'

Before they had a chance to respond, he jumped up, strode back to the door, and disappeared through it.

Dolly looked at Pilgrim. 'What … ?' he began.

But Field was already back, towing a bespectacled man in his wake. He pulled up another chair, and pushed the man into it.

'This is Chief Constable Moxton. Head of the Essex Constabulary and an old friend of mine. He needs our help.' Field turned to Moxton. 'Now, George, tell my boys all about your problem. If anyone can help you, these two can. They're the city's best. Even Mr Charles Dickens will tell you so.'

Chief Constable Moxton's eyebrows rose fractionally. 'Quite a recommendation.'

Pilgrim sensed the barb beneath the words.

'Indeed it is.' Field swallowed it.

'How can we help you, sir?' asked Pilgrim. He nodded at Dolly to take out his notebook.

Moxton took off his spectacles and wiped them. 'Last Friday morning, a little after noon, a large trunk was delivered to the Reverend Bonwell, of Great Barrow ...'

'Is that one 'l', sir, or two?' cut in Dolly. 'In Bonwell?'

Moxton turned his gaze on the constable, replaced his spectacles, and continued as if he had never spoken. 'The trunk contained the body of a young boy, aged about four years old.'

Pilgrim felt Field's gaze flash over him, but kept his own firmly on Moxton.

'Our initial examination,' continued Moxton, 'showed that the boy died of unnatural causes.'

'Did the Reverend know him?' asked Pilgrim.

'No. I have given Inspector Field all of our notes to date. Everything is in the file.' Moxton stood up. 'The investigation is in your hands now, Field. I wish you luck of it.'

Pilgrim and Dolly, taken by surprise at the brevity of the briefing, were slow to rise.

'Adolphus,' said Field, 'would you be so good as to show the Chief Inspector out?' He jumped up and pumped Moxton's hand. 'We will keep you abreast of developments here, George. You may count on it.'

15

Pilgrim and Field watched as Dolly followed Moxton out and closed the door behind them. Pilgrim turned to look at Field.

'Sour old bastard,' said Field.

Pilgrim sat down again. 'So what's the real story?'

Field went to the decanter and splashed some port into a glass. 'Join me?' he asked.

Pilgrim shook his head.

'Sorry, I forgot.' Field carried his drink back to his seat and propped his feet on the desk. 'The Reverend Bonwell, in his wisdom, burned the wrappings on the parcel. But not before the housekeeper had noticed from where the carriage had been paid, God bless her soul. "Euston Square Station". She said as much in her interview.'

'Which made it a Metropolitan case.'

'Exactly so. George wasn't pleased. They don't get many murders in Essex.' Field looked at Pilgrim, his eyes sharp and serious. 'I must be straight with you, Harry, I wasn't sure if I should put you on the case.'

Pilgrim's features smoothed. 'Why wouldn't you?'

'Don't be disingenuous. The boy's not much younger than … '

'I don't have a problem with the case,' cut in Pilgrim, 'but the same can't be said for Moxton. You're making enemies, Charley.'

'You can't make custard without breaking eggs.'

'Do you want me to keep Moxton abreast with developments?'

'Do I hell! The old goat can roast as far as I'm concerned.'

Pilgrim stood. 'Thank you for putting Adolphus on the case. It will help to have two pairs of eyes and ears at Great Barrow, and Dolly is sharp, even though he pretends not to be.' Pilgrim smiled. 'He reminds me of someone I used to know, years ago.'

'The boy will go far.' Field grinned and finished off his port.

Pilgrim nodded and made for the door.

Field stopped him. 'I forgot to congratulate you on your arrest of Johannes Appler last night.' At Pilgrim's blank look he was forced to elaborate. 'The man in the cab? Quite a task you left for the poor Desk Sergeant, with all those stinking packages to tag and record.'

'You've interviewed Appler?'

'Briefly. He claims he was transporting the packages for an acquaintance.'

Pilgrim frowned. 'Of course, he would say that …'

'But … ?' Field eyed him. 'I can sense a "but".'

'There was something about his expression, just before I hit him.'

'Surprise, I should imagine!'

'Something else too. Or, rather, something that wasn't there.'

'Oh?'

'Fear of discovery.'

Field stared at Pilgrim for a moment, then shook his head. 'You're chasing shadows. We couldn't have caught Appler more red-handed. However,' he rubbed his nose, 'if you'd like to speak to him yourself?'

Pilgrim nodded. 'If you think it might help.'

The holding cells were on the ground floor. The Desk Sergeant, an ex-soldier by the name of Phelps, had charge of the keys.

'Pity I was off shift last night, sir. I hear you had quite a time of it. Would you like me to come in there with you?'

'No thank you, Sergeant, I can handle it.'

'So you can, sir, so you can.' Phelps handed the keys to Pilgrim with a gap-toothed grin.

When Pilgrim entered the cell Johannes Appler sat up on his cot. A sickly bruise spread from under the whiskers on his jawbone, right up to his cheek.

'Do not come any closer.' The young man gave Pilgrim a look of frank dislike. 'In Amsterdam I would be charging you with brutality. And I would be permitted to have a lawyer present.'

'You're not in Amsterdam.' Pilgrim drew up a stool, which was the only other piece of furniture in the cell. 'Would you tell me how the packages came to be in your cab?'

Appler rubbed his eyes. Pilgrim realized that he had been crying, for all his apparent self-possession.

'I have already told your Chief Inspector everything. He made notes. What is the point in my repeating it? All I seem to do is to incriminate myself further.'

'You say you didn't kill this girl.'

'I certainly did not.'

'The surest way to prove that is to help us catch the real killer.' Pilgrim persisted. 'Tell me about the packages.'

Appler sighed. 'I agreed to take them to the East India Dock. To repay a debt.'

'To whom?'

'I do not know his name.'

Pilgrim lifted an eyebrow.

'I know it does not look good. I met the man at a gambling club on the Brompton Road, and lost a sum of money to him. He agreed to write off the debt if I took a delivery to the Docks.'

'He brought them to your house?'

Appler nodded. 'Yesterday afternoon. And told me to expect a cab at midnight.'

'What did you think was in the packages?'

Appler shrugged. 'I did not consider it my business.'

'Weren't you at all suspicious? Couldn't you smell them?' Pilgrim hadn't been aware of the stink himself, but it had been much complained about when he had brought them into the station.

'I have a head cold.' Appler took a handkerchief from his pocket, and blew his nose extravagantly, as if to emphasize the truth of it. He sighed. 'I guessed the delivery was dishonest in some way. But I chose to … how do you say … turn an unseeing eye? The debt was considerable.' He tucked the handkerchief back into his pocket. 'I swore to myself that I would not gamble again, that once I had repaid the debt I would go back to Amsterdam.'

'You've given a description of the man to the Chief Inspector?'

'He was a young man, but there was nothing about him that stood out.' He hesitated. 'I do not think he was British.'

'What makes you say that?'

18

'He had an accent.'

'French? German? American?'

Appler shrugged. 'It is hard for me, een Nederlandse, to say.'

Pilgrim gave him a pen and a sheet of paper. 'Write down anything else you can remember. Anything at all. And make a note of all your engagements on the day of your arrest and the four days previous to it.'

As Pilgrim went to the door of the cell, Appler stood up.

'My parents,' he said. 'They do not know I have been arrested. They live in Amsterdam, in the Pijlsteeg.'

'Write down the address and I'll telegraph them.'

Appler stopped him before he went out of the door.

'Could you please try to be as tactful as possible? They are simple, God-fearing people.'

CHAPTER FOUR

The journey to Great Barrow was as slow and unpleasant a trip as was possible, considering it was no more than forty miles and the weather mild. But a cow on the line at Brentwood, and the fact that Great Barrow itself wasn't within walking distance of Chelmsford, made it well past noon when Pilgrim and Dolly climbed down from the pony and trap in front of the Great Barrow Police Station. It was a neatly kept building with flowers in a tub outside. Inside, the well-swept reception hall was empty and silent. No police officers. No lawyers. No sheepish-looking thieves or carousing drunks. No sign of life at all, in fact, except for a moth-eaten gun dog sleeping by the counter that didn't even lift its head as Pilgrim strode to the desk and rang the bell. There was a scuffle on the other side of the door, and it opened to reveal a uniformed Desk Sergeant, with the stiffest, most extravagant handlebar moustache the detectives had ever seen. Dolly stifled an exclamation of awe.

'Sergeant Pilgrim and Constable Williamson,' said Pilgrim. 'We're here on the Bonwell case.'

'Aye, you're expected. Thought you'd be here sooner.'

He came out from behind the desk, stepped over the dog, and headed out of the door.

'Where are you going?' asked Pilgrim.

'You'll be wanting to see the lad's body, won't you?'

They followed him along the main street, which was thick with mud, dodging a pair of geese that cut across their path, and into a ramshackle coaching inn that occupied the corner. With its red pantiled roof and mullioned windows the inn looked idyllic, but the impression was quickly dispelled by the interior. The corridor was dark, low, and smoky, carrying the sounds of eating and drinking from the main taproom. The whiskered sergeant led them away from the noise, towards a stout door at the other end of the passage. He stopped outside it and gave Pilgrim a key.

'He's in here,' he said.

'Why, for God's sake?'

The sergeant had the grace to look sheepish. 'The guv'nor wouldn't have him at the station. "No room" he said. He twisted old Frobisher's arm, that's the landlord, to keep him here.'

Pilgrim caught Dolly's eye as he took the key.

'You'll bring it back when you're done?' asked the sergeant.

Pilgrim nodded, and he stomped away along the passage.

The door opened into a small airless room, obviously a store-room of some kind, with a high barred window and stone floor. It was cool, but not cool enough. Dolly clapped his hand to his nose. On the table lay a shape, covered with a sheet.

'I can't believe they put him in here,' said Dolly. 'Can you really not smell him, sir?'

'No. You can leave him to me, if you like.'

Dolly shook his head. 'No point me being here if I don't help, is there?'

Pilgrim drew back the cover on the table. The boy who had been delivered to the Reverend Bonwell lay underneath it, his eyes open. He was dressed in a smock and a spotted neckerchief, with a straw hat resting on his chest. With his wispy hair and round cheeks still unaffected by death, he was obviously little more than a baby. Younger, certainly, than Moxton's estimate. Pilgrim's guess was no more than three years old.

'Help me undress him,' he said.

They started at the bottom. Dolly unlaced the thick-soled shoes and inspected them, one at a time, while Pilgrim peeled off the stockings to look at each of the boy's feet in turn. He turned the small feet gently in his hand. They were rimed with dirt but otherwise unmarked, without blisters or calluses. The flesh was spongy under his fingers, well past the stages of rigor mortis and bloat, and into active decay, which meant the boy had been dead for quite a few days. But not, thought Pilgrim, as long as a week.

He passed the stockings to Dolly, and moved on to the hands. He inspected the fingers one by one, scraping the dirt from under the fingernails and peering at it. There was nothing out of the ordinary: no blood, or any tissue. He turned his attention to the stockings and shoes, noting the darns on the stockings, and the worn soles of the shoes.

'You're going to have to help me with this, sir.'

Together they eased the boy's coarse smock over his head.

'There's our cause of death,' muttered Dolly.

Black and yellow bruises ringed the boy's throat, obscene against the white skin. Pilgrim brushed his fingers against them.

Dolly investigated the smock minutely, while Pilgrim removed the boy's vest and drawers.

Pilgrim looked down at the corpse, naked on the table, and felt reality slip. For an instant he was no longer standing in the storeroom of the inn, but a sparse living room with a fireplace. The boy laid out on the table was bigger, the limbs just starting to stretch into childhood proper, his head not fair, but a mop of brown. Pilgrim could see every hair etched clearly, every freckle on the skin. The features were so familiar, so sharp, he could reach out and touch them. The vision was merciless in its detail, robbing him of breath.

He glanced at Dolly, but the constable was oblivious, engrossed in his examination of the smock. As Pilgrim reached for the vest, he noticed his hand was shaking. He stilled it by sheer force of will. This was not the time for sentimentality. He stared at the vest for a moment without really seeing it. Then he peered closer. 'That'll do,' he said.

'What?'

'Laundry mark.' Pilgrim showed Dolly a faded symbol, drawn in ink on the seam.

'Looks like an "F",' he opined.

'We'll keep this.' Pilgrim was gripping the vest so hard his knuckles were white. 'And the neckerchief. Let's finish here, and find somewhere to wash up. We have to pay our respects to the clergy.'

In the fading afternoon light St Margaret's rectory looked like a child's drawing; four-square and perfectly symmetrical, with five windows to the front and a big black door.

Pilgrim pulled on the doorbell for a third time, and glanced at Dolly, who was sniffing the lapel of his jacket.

'What's the matter?' he asked.

'I still smell, sir. We both do.'

'Can't be helped now.'

The door opened.

'Yes?' An old woman with skin like a lizard peered at them.

'Detective Sergeant Pilgrim and Detective Constable Williamson, to see the Reverend Bonwell.'

'You'd better come in.' She ushered them through the hallway into a parlour, without taking their coats. 'I'll tell the Reverend you're here.'

'And Mrs Bonwell, if you please,' said Pilgrim.

She threw them another dark look, then went out and closed the door behind her.

'Anyone would think we were after the silver,' muttered Dolly. He took a seat in one of the overstuffed armchairs.

After a glance around the room, Pilgrim strolled to a side table crammed with photographs. They showed stiffly dressed, hatchet-faced, people in formal poses. It was difficult to imagine a less amiable group of people. He picked up one – a family grouping. The Reverend, identifiable by his collar, was seated in the centre, with a woman, presumably Mrs Bonwell, standing behind him.

They were flanked by two children: girls of about five and three. Pilgrim studied the photograph more closely. There was something odd about it. The children were not quite to scale, either with their parents or each other, and their figures were paler, their features blurred. The effect was disturbing, ghostly.

He spotted a large family bible, and was about to open it when he heard footsteps approaching the door.

'Follow me,' snapped the housekeeper.

Her eyes narrowed as she saw the bible in Pilgrim's hand. He replaced it on the table and followed her.

They were met in the study by the Reverend and his wife, positioned exactly as they had been in the photograph: the Reverend seated and Mrs Bonwell standing behind him. Bonwell had a lantern jaw and thick black hair. He met Pilgrim's gaze directly, unlike his wife, who stared down at the carpet. Pilgrim and Dolly took the seats indicated by the housekeeper – two chairs directly in front of the Reverend. As Dolly pulled out his notebook he couldn't resist another sniff of his jacket.

'I understand you are from the constabulary.' The Reverend Bonwell had a deep voice, suited to sermonising.

'We are from the Metropolitan Police, sir. As you know, the trunk was sent from Euston Square Station.' Pilgrim turned to the woman. 'Mrs Bonwell took delivery of it, I understand?'

'She did,' said the Reverend.

'Can you describe the wrappings, madam? Or the label?'

'I would be grateful if you could address your questions to me,' said the Reverend. 'My wife's nerves are not strong. As I have already said, at some length, to the other police constables, I myself removed the paper from the package. There was nothing remarkable about it.'

'And the handwriting on the label?'

'Unremarkable.'

'I understand you threw the label away? Did you not think it might have provided valuable evidence?'

'My wife disposed of it. She has many qualities, but the ability to think like a policeman is thankfully not one of them.'

Mrs Bonwell flushed, and pulled her sleeves over her bitten fingernails.

Pilgrim considered her. 'Do you know anyone in London?' he asked.

'No one at all,' replied the Reverend.

Mrs Bonwell swallowed so hard that Pilgrim could see the movement of her Adam's apple above her collar.

'Perhaps, Mrs Bonwell, you have friends or family …'

'My wife has no family: none living. Address your questions to me.'

Pilgrim obliged. 'You really have no idea why someone might have sent the boy to you?'

'My dear Constable … '

'Detective Sergeant,' corrected Pilgrim.

'My dear Detective Sergeant, how can I possibly begin to imagine what goes on in the mind of such a person? The criminal classes are so far below me, both in understanding and sensibility that I am at a loss when dealing with them. A complete loss. But of course, a man such as yourself, a police constable … '

Pilgrim flushed. 'A man like myself, a Detective Sergeant, finds it hard to believe that someone completely unconnected to you would send the boy for no reason at all.'

'The Lord works in mysterious ways.'

Pilgrim curled his lip.

If the Reverend was aware of his disdain, he gave no sign. He smiled and rose. 'If that is all? I was about to go out. Parish business, you understand. I really cannot help you further.' He went to the door and opened it. 'Why I should be the target of such an outrage is a mystery.'

Pilgrim and Dolly nodded to Mrs Bonwell and followed the Reverend into the hallway, where the housekeeper helped the Reverend into his coat and opened the door.

'Good day to you.'

The detectives followed the Reverend out, and watched him stride off down the lane.

Dolly flipped open his notebook and sighed at the still blank page. 'Well that was time well spent.'

'I think so.' Pilgrim tugged his hat back on, his expression serene. 'We need the boy on the same train as us. You might have to grease the Station Master's palm to make sure of it.'

'But … '

'I can't do it,' said Pilgrim. 'I've lost my pocketbook.'

Dolly managed to secure a berth in the luggage carriage of the train, although he was obliged to be economical with the truth when it came to the actual contents of the large packing case he stowed there. He made sure all the straps were secure, and the lid well nailed down, before making his way to the First Class passenger carriage.

Pilgrim glanced at him over the top of his *Evening Chronicle* as he entered. A steward was lighting the gas lamps, bouncing buttery light off polished wood and brass. The train guard on the platform blew his whistle, and the steward went out, leaving the detectives alone.

'I've never travelled First Class before,' said Dolly. The whistle blew again, and the train gave a jolt as it began to move. Dolly reached into his pocket. 'Before I forget, sir, I've been meaning to give you this.' He handed Pilgrim a piece of paper. 'My cousin is taking in lodgers. She's a widow. Very respectable. And she lives in Holborn, so it's only a hop and a skip to Whitehall.'

'Your cousin?'

'Mrs Charlotte Piper.'

'Thank you.' Pilgrim put the paper in his pocket without looking at it, and passed the *Chronicle* to Dolly.

Dolly opened the newspaper, and gasped.

'Will you look at that! It's the Chief Inspector! This must be the piece Mr Dickens was writing.' Sure enough, Charley Field straddled the page like a colossus, under a headline that bellowed 'New Detective Force Foils Hackney Cab Killer.' 'Shall I read it to you, sir?' Without waiting for an answer, Dolly cleared his throat and began to read.

The mutilated body of a human being, stated to be that of an adult female, was discovered in a Hackney carriage on Saturday night in the West End of the City. The shocking circumstances were outlined to this journalist by none other than our very own Detective Chief Inspector Field:

'On Saturday night Detective Sergeant Henry Pilgrim, of the Metropolitan Force had reason to stop and search a four-wheeled cab leaving residential premises on the east side of Curzon Street. The vehicle contained only a single passenger, and a number of parcels. When Sergeant Pilgrim respectfully requested the man to reveal the contents of the parcels, the smallest was found to contain the decomposed head of a woman. The remaining parcels, which were larger, had in them the trunk of a woman, apparently about 20 years of age, and two arms and legs. The murderer has given his name to the police as Johannes Hendrik Appler, 26, residing at 14 Bolton Street. He is charged with having in his possession the mutilated body of an adult female, at present unknown, which has been unlawfully killed by him. The mutilated remains were removed by the police and handed over to the coroner's office. They are now lying in St Bartholomew's Mortuary.'

This deed of unprovoked savagery on behalf of Mr Appler that would scarcely be effected by a bestial horde of Red Indians, or the Maoris of New Zealand, is abhorrent in an age as civilized as ours. How inconceivable then, that such a crime could be carried out in the heart of our own comfortable Metropolis, and how reassuring that we may now rely upon that most admirable Instrument of Justice, our new Detective Police Force.

*

When he reached the end, Dolly grinned at Pilgrim. 'That's grand. You're famous, sir. Properly famous. Mr Dickens has used your real name this time, not Sergeant Pilchem, like he does in the *Journal*.'

Pilgrim stared out of the window, but could only see the blur of his own reflection.

Dolly frowned. 'Don't you like Mr Dickens? He's much admired, generally.'

Pilgrim sighed. 'I have nothing against him. As a novelist. But I do take issue when he starts mixing fiction with fact.' Pilgrim paused. 'What if, for the sake of argument, our Hackney Cab Killer isn't?'

'Sir?'

'What if we have the wrong man?'

'But … '

'Appler claims he was transporting the packages for an acquaintance. Someone he owed money to.'

'Cock and bull. He's just trying to wriggle out of the noose.'

'But what if he's telling the truth? What if the letter Dickens passed on to us was from someone trying to frame Appler? Appler hasn't gone to trial yet, his jury hasn't been chosen. But now, thanks to Mr Dickens, he's as good as hanged.'

Dolly subsided onto his seat, the newspaper forgotten.

'Dickens has it wrong, Dolly. We're not an Instrument of Justice – that's up to the judges. It's our job to discover the truth, to discover what is hidden, and drag it into the light. Nothing more.' Pilgrim sighed. 'God knows that can be hard enough, without help from novelists.'

CHAPTER FIVE

Charles Dickens contemplated the shadows gathering on the ceiling. They eddied and swirled as clouds passed over the moon outside, creating fantastical shapes and figures. He could make out a face with a nose like an eggplant, and another with a long neck and bare, curving breast. His hand twitched, tempted to stray to his groin, but he forestalled it. One of his restless moods was upon him, and he knew from experience that onanism would do little to soothe it.

The house on Devonshire Terrace was quiet, with no sound at all from Catherine's room across the hall, and none from the nursery above, apart from the usual creaks and groans from settling floorboards and joists. It was one in the morning, and every nerve, every sinew in his body was itching to be up and out of bed. He sighed and scratched his thigh. He had just published the novel he thought of as his crowning achievement, had poured into it every drop of his energy, all the triumphs, and disappointments of his younger self. *The Personal History of David Copperfield* had been well received, as he had known it would be, and he was satisfied. For now. Unusually for him, however, he had yet to begin another novel. He had many ideas bursting in his head, but none was compelling enough to put onto paper. So he had kept himself busy with his new journal, *Household Words*.

It had long been his ambition to create a regular journal, one that entertained and informed its readers, and included contributions of other writers he admired. It had taken hard work and determination to launch it, but now it was underway it seemed to have acquired its own momentum. It would not take up so much of his time. He was proud of what he had achieved so far, and particularly proud of his articles on the new Detective Police. He liked to think that his goodwill had helped the new division overcome some of the initial prejudices of the middle and upper classes.

He lay for another few minutes thinking of nothing in particular, sighed and swung his legs out of bed. There was no point fighting it when the restlessness was upon him, it only left him irritable and enervated in the morning. What he needed was a walk!

He dressed himself by the light coming in through the window, and then made his way downstairs. He tiptoed along the Turkish runner in the hall, pausing only to unhook his overcoat from the peg by the door.

He closed the front door behind him, and stood on the step to take a deep breath of London air. Coal smoke, sewage, and the tang of salt from the docks. There was no finer smell on earth!

The night was moonlit and sharp, and stars sprinkled the sky like sugar frosting. He gazed up at them and his chest swelled with happiness: he felt as if anything was possible! He set off at a brisk pace, in no particular direction, and let his mind wander with his feet. Somewhat to his surprise, the first thing that popped into his head was Johannes Appler. He had played a key part in Appler's capture, having passed on the note that revealed Appler would be using the sewer at Cockspur Court to dispose of his victim's body. It was with a certain amount of surprise that he had learned about Appler's arrest from Inspector Field, although, naturally, he had been delighted to write about it at the request of the Editor of the *Chronicle*.

But …

But … there was something about the business that remained highly unsatisfactory. According to Field, Appler was denying any knowledge of the crime, in the face of evidence that would make any man crumble. Any guilty man. And there was something about the note itself – the use of red ink, perhaps – that seemed unnecessarily dramatic. Who had written it, and what were his motives for betraying the young Dutchman?

He stopped, so abruptly that the couple walking behind cannoned into him.

'Watch out, guv'nor!' snapped the man. The woman giggled. They both turned as they stepped around him, assessing his clothes.

Dickens realized he had strayed, unthinking, into the edge of St Giles, a part of the city he was usually careful to avoid at night. He turned in the other direction, back towards Marylebone, and set off again at a brisk pace. As he did, he became aware of a sound behind him, an echo of his own footsteps, but slightly faster and less substantial. Was there someone behind him? It sounded as if someone had stopped at the same time as he had, and started again in tandem. To test the hypothesis he stopped abruptly. The echo also stopped, but not immediately. For a few paces he heard the footsteps sound clearly on their own. He turned around.

At first he could see no one on the street behind him, but then he discerned a dark shape in the shadows by the railings. Tall, but decidedly feminine.

'Can I help you, my dear?'

She stepped into the light. The face beneath the straw bonnet was pale, apart from two rouged spots, and the eyes were large and expressive. She clutched at her shawl with mittened fingers.

'Are you Mr Dickens?'

He nodded. She seemed at a loss how to proceed.

'May I be of assistance?' he prompted. Now he had the chance to look at her more closely, he could see her dress was of decent quality, but was thick with mud around the hem. The shawl was the kind that could be bought on a market stall for a few coppers, and was often worn by a certain type of female. She saw his scrutiny, and lifted her chin.

His interest stirred.

Two men stepped around them on the pavement, glancing first at Dickens and then at the girl, and coming to their own conclusion. One grinned at Dickens as he passed.

'What is it?' demanded Dickens, more briskly than he had intended.

'I heard you have a place, a refuge, for … homeless women.' She licked chapped lips. 'I wondered … that is, I wanted to ask you …'

'I'm sorry, but we take girls on referral only, from a magistrate, or a doctor. The Magdalen Hospital is on St George's Fields; why not ask there?'

Her eyes flashed contempt. She didn't stir.

He frowned. He had no wish to be discourteous, but he couldn't stand about in the street all night. He was about to say so, when the matter was taken out of his hands: the girl's eyes rolled up in her head, and she dropped like a stone onto the pavement.

He looked at the fallen figure in astonishment, and not a little dismay.

'What's happened here, then?' A burly youth dressed in a dirty overcoat and apron – a labourer on his way home from his shift – stopped beside Dickens and bent to inspect the fallen girl.

'She's fainted,' said Dickens. 'From hunger, I imagine. How would you like to earn a shilling by helping me put her in a cab?'

The youth scowled at him. 'You ain't abductin' her?'

'Of course not!' When the youth continued simply to stare at him, Dickens felt his temper rise. 'If you're not prepared to take my word for it, I'll have no choice but to leave her where she is. Do you want that on your conscience?'

The youth weighed his words, saw the practicality of them, and nodded. 'I saw a growler back on Baker Street. Wait here while I fetch it.' He took off at a jog, hobnails sparking on the pavement.

Less than five minutes later Dickens had bundled the still sense-less girl into a Hackney cab, and the young workman was able to continue on his way, jingling his pocket happily.

'Where to, guv'nor?' called the cabbie from his box.

'Shepherd's Bush.'

'Well, Mrs Wallace, what do you think of my latest find?'

Dickens sat back in the parlour of Urania Cottage, and resisted the urge to pat his stomach. He had slept soundly in the bedroom kept for his particular use, and had enjoyed a hearty breakfast of eggs and muffins. If the shirt beneath his colourful waistcoat was a little crumpled, and smelled a little sour, he was content to put up with it until his return to Devonshire Terrace.

Mrs Wallace, a handsome woman of indeterminate age, gave him a reproving look. At first Dickens had been indifferent to her appointment as Head Matron of Urania Cottage, but now he found, somewhat to his surprise, that he wouldn't want to be without her steady, unspectacular influence.

'I'm not sure I approve of plucking girls off the street, Mr Dickens.'

'I could hardly have left her there.'

The door burst open.

'Missus! Isabella has my comb and she won't give it back! I can't pack it unless she gives it back!' The intruder was a fresh-faced girl of seventeen, her wrap agape, and her hair in curl papers.

'Can't you see we're busy, Annie?' said Mrs Wallace.

'I beg pardon Missus, Mr Dickens, sir.' She bobbed him a breathless curtsey, unembarrassed by her *déshabillé*. 'I didn't mean to cut in, like.' She turned back to the Matron. 'But it's the only bloody comb I have!'

'Don't curse, girl.' Mrs Wallace shooed her out. 'How will you ever find a husband in the colonies, using words like that? Go on with you, I'll be up in a moment.'

The door slammed, and they heard an unladylike bellow on the other side of it.

33

'The missus is coming! Now you're for it, Isabella Bloody Gordon!' They heard the thump of Annie's feet back up the stairs.

'I'd forgotten that Annie and Martha were sailing today,' said Dickens.

'We're up to our ears in drama and packing cases. Your new girl will think she's landed in Bedlam.'

'Is she awake yet?'

'Awake, washed, and dressed. I've given her one of our gowns. Her own was soaked through.'

'What do you think?'

'Well, she hasn't said much, but she seems well mannered enough. She tells me her name is Rebecca Wood, and she seems keen to stay. I suppose there will be room now.'

'I will interview her this morning, as I'm here.'

A thump shook the ceiling, followed by a wail.

'Missus!'

The Matron looked heavenward and sighed. 'Give me a few minutes, sir, and I'll bring the girl down.'

He stretched his toes to the fire. A visit to Urania Cottage never failed to warm his spirits, even when the girls were acting up. Their behaviour was always at its worst in the winter months, when they were cooped up for so many dark hours indoors, but that was due to high spirits rather than outright badness. He was glad to be able to help 'his' girls. There were so many of their kind in the city, women obliged to sell themselves for a bed for the night, or to keep their families out of the spike line. His pulse quickened when he thought of the humiliating workhouse queue, where a family would be forced to stand for hours. And for what? To be separated from each other, and put to labour for a bowl of thin skilly and an even thinner mattress. He had seen the workhouses for himself, at close hand. When he had passed on his discoveries in *Oliver Twist*, some of his readers had wept for pity.

Tears were easily wrung, but pockets proved a little harder. He had no intention of abandoning his campaign to help the poorer elements of the city, but there were times he was discouraged by the relentless effort necessary to achieve so very little. No matter how many times he wrote of the plight of the poor, no matter how many petitions he signed, refuges he set up, or funds he raised, the spike lines outside the workhouses grew longer every year, and more and more unfortunate women were obliged to put themselves in danger.

He glanced at the newspaper that lay on the table, still open at the article that had caught his eye at breakfast – yet another prostitute, found slaughtered on the floor of her lodging house, just like his own poor Nancy. How his readers had thrilled to Nancy's death! How they had sighed over it, and raged against Bill Sykes and the circumstances that had forced her to such a life. But they had soon forgotten their grief. Nancy was merely fiction, after all, and Dickens was coming to the regretful conclusion that fiction had no lasting effect.

But his work at Urania Cottage was different. He found it both heartening and delightful to think what his young charges had once been, and to imagine a different future for their children. His optimistic thoughts were interrupted by a knock at the door, followed by the reappearance of Mrs Wallace, accompanied by his nocturnal petitioner. He got to his feet and nodded to one of the chairs.

'Sit down, my dear.'

Her cheeks had been scrubbed of rouge, and she was dressed in one of their bright blue gowns – a uniform, of sorts, but much more cheerful than the black and white worn by the women at the Magdalen Hospital for the Reception of Penitential Prostitutes. He had personally insisted on having something brighter for the girls at Urania Cottage. There was nothing more depressing than pretty birds with drab plumage.

'Did you sleep well, Rebecca?'

She looked blank.

'It is Rebecca, isn't it?'

'Yes, sir. And yes, thank you, I slept very well.'

35

His interest was piqued. She was well-spoken, even more so than he had realized the night before. 'You came looking for me last night,' he continued, 'so I imagine you had heard of our work here?'

'I read about it in the *Evening Chronicle*, and your *Journal*.'

That was unusual. Only one or two of the Cottage residents could write their own name, and none could read a newspaper. He estimated Rebecca was older than the other girls too, perhaps around twenty, or thereabouts.

He cleared his throat. 'I set up Urania Cottage, with our patron, Miss Burdett-Coutts, in order to help rehabilitate young women such as yourself. It is not a fashionable concept that a woman once fallen into sin can be lifted up again, but it is something we believe in here, most fervently. Our emphasis here is not on repentance, but hope. Not in looking back, but forward, to a better life.'

'I could wish for nothing more.' Her large eyes were fierce.

'Don't have family somewhere? A mother? A father?'

Her lips thinned.

'I must ask,' pressed Dickens. 'But once you have told me, you have my word of honour it will never be spoken of again.'

'My father was a factor, sir, on an estate near Chelmsford. He's dead now. My mother died a long time ago. I've been in service ever since I came to the city, but I lost my position, when ... ' she broke off.

'I assume you have been earning your living on the streets?'

She flushed and lifted her chin. 'If you can call it that ... I did it twice, because I had to.'

Dickens nodded. 'It's fortunate you found us so quickly. Is that not so, Mrs Wallace?'

'Yes, indeed, sir.'

'There is another thing I must ask you.' He met the girl's gaze, unflinchingly. 'If there is any chance at all of your being in a ... delicate condition, I'm afraid we cannot accept you. We cannot accommodate another generation here at the cottage.'

'I'm not pregnant.'

'Good. There are also certain further conditions to accepting a place with us. We will keep you only for a year, to prepare you for a new life, in a new country. In short, we expect you to emigrate. Do you understand what that means?'

'Transportation?'

'No, no, my dear, nothing like that. This is not punishment. This is the chance to begin again, free of stigma: to find yourself a husband, to start a family.'

She paled.

'You would have to leave everything behind.' He took care to labour the point. It was important for all the girls to realize the significance of the step they were taking.

'There is nothing left for me here.'

He nodded, satisfied.

Mrs Wallace leaned forward. 'While you stay with us, we expect you to adhere to a certain code of conduct.'

'You want me to go to church?'

'Well …' Mrs Wallace glanced at Dickens, thrown by the question. 'All our girls attend church on Sunday, and we always have prayers in the evening, at bedtime.'

'I won't do that.' The girl's face was set, stubborn.

'But, surely … ' began Mrs Wallace.

Dickens interrupted her. 'I don't think that would necessarily be a problem. I don't hold with sermonizing. As good Queen Bess once said, I do not wish to "make windows into men's souls".'

Mrs Wallace seemed for a moment as if she might take issue. She opened her mouth … and closed it again.

Rebecca Wood glanced at her. 'If that is the case, I would like to stay.'

'Excellent.' Dickens beamed. 'It's decided, then. Now run along and get some breakfast.'

They watched the girl rise and go gracefully out of the door. When it had closed behind her, Dickens turned to the Matron.

'What do you think?' he asked.

'If Rebecca Wood is her real name, I'm a Dutchman.'

'What makes you think that?'

Mrs Wallace shrugged. 'Feminine intuition. But she'll have to give us her real name if she's going to stay.'

'Ah well, there's plenty of time for that. What do you think of her disposition?'

'The girl has backbone, which is a good thing. But if I've learned nothing else these last three years, it's that you can never tell how they'll turn out.' She began to clear the table, putting the dirty crockery onto the tray. She picked up the newspaper, and sighed. 'Another one dead.' She skimmed the words on the page. 'A governess, engaged to her employer, who "fell into sin" when he abandoned her.' She snorted and dropped the paper back onto the table. 'More fiction than anything you write, sir.'

'Her friends apparently called her "The Countess" on account of her good looks and regal bearing.'

'I daresay she was handsomer than most. Poor souls, old before their time, missing teeth, too addled with drink to care about anything other than where they're going to find a fourpenny piece to buy a bed for the night.' She gathered the rest of the breakfast things and straightened up, indignation glowing in her cheeks. 'It's a pity the newspapers feel they have to make a sensation out of the poor woman's death.'

'It's their job, Mrs Wallace.' Guilt stirred, as he remembered his piece on Johannes Appler's arrest.

'Aye, well, in my opinion they should be less concerned with selling newspapers than in telling people the truth about the world. But I imagine your detectives will get to the bottom of the matter.'

'I imagine they will.'

'They're a good thing, your detectives.' Mrs Wallace sniffed and nodded decisively. 'A very good thing.'

Dickens rubbed his chin. She had given him an idea.

*

'You want to write about me?' It wasn't so much a question as an expression of astonishment.

'If that's agreeable,' said Dickens. 'Inspector Field has been boasting of your investigative skills.'

'He has?' Dick Tanner glanced at Charley Field, who was leaning against the bookcase of his office.

Field nodded. 'Mr Dickens has asked if he might spend a little time with us, observing them at first hand.'

Tanner puffed out his chest.

Dickens sat forward. 'I'm particularly keen to see you at work on the Eliza Grimwood case.'

Tanner's chest deflated. 'Are you sure, sir? I mean … it's a very unwholesome sort of crime. Wouldn't you prefer burglary?'

'I have read about the Countess in the newspapers, and her murder sounds intriguing.'

'Bloody journalists,' Tanner sneered, then caught Field's eye. 'Begging your pardon,' he said to Dickens. 'I don't mean you, sir. But other journalists have not got a grasp of the important aspects of the case at all.'

Charley Field narrowed his eyes. 'Perhaps you'd like to tell us what those aspects are, in your opinion.'

Tanner nodded. 'She was a better class of,' he broke off, suddenly aware that his usual terminology wouldn't serve, 'unfortunate, from the usual, which means she did her trans-actions in private. It's almost impossible to get a picture of her movements that evening. An associate of hers, Catherine Edwin, says she saw Grimwood with a man in the Strand. A well-dressed foreigner, she says. But Black Kate's not known for her honesty, and, apart from her, no one saw Grimwood at all after six o'clock.'

'You searched her room?' asked Dickens.

'We scoured it cleaner than a parson's …' Field coughed. Tanner reddened. 'We searched it thoroughly, but found nothing. No murder weapon, and no trace of a visitor. Only a pair of gentleman's gloves under the pillow that might or might not have anything to do with the murderer.'

'Do you have the gloves?' asked Dickens.

'In my office, sir. Shall I fetch them?'

'I'll come along with you and take a look. If I may?'

Tanner and Dickens both looked at Field, who nodded.

Dickens followed Tanner out of the room, and allowed his smile to slip. He had already made up his mind to dislike the detective. It was a fault of his, he knew, making judgements of character too promptly on first meeting people, often basing his prejudices on little more than the way they might phrase a sentence, cock an eyebrow, or meet or not meet his eye. As a fault, however, it had served him well, for once his judgement was made he seldom needed to revise it.

And he didn't care for Tanner at all. He found the detective's voice grating. He didn't like the way the man puffed himself up, and voiced his opinions about women and journalists so readily, even if he occasionally shared some of those sentiments himself. Now that he had made up his mind to write as plainly as possible about the Countess's murder, he wasn't about to change his mind about Tanner.

But it was a pity Harry Pilgrim wasn't in charge of the case.

CHAPTER SIX

Police detectives were only supposed to enter Whitehall through the rear entrance, the stable yard grandiosely called Great Scotland Yard. There was nothing great about it. In the summer it heaved with horses, cabs, and carriages, with ostlers, Horse Guards, and equestrian messengers whose job it was to make the wheels of government turn more smoothly. Any pedestrian who wanted to make his way through the arched thoroughfare from the main street was forced to risk life and limb. In the winter it was little better, for when the temperature dropped below freezing the cobblestones of the yard turned glassy with horse piss, treacherous to man and beast alike. As a consequence none of the detectives ever obeyed the edict, but entered instead through Whitehall Station, the headquarters of A Division, which had its imposing entrance on Whitehall Place.

Pilgrim made his way across the reception hall. As usual, it was thronged with the uniformed police of A Division and their belligerent charges. He spotted a glum-faced Constable Wainwright, coming down the staircase towards him, whose neat appearance was only slightly undermined by a splash of blood on his collar from where he had cut himself shaving.

'Dolly says you have a visitor, sir,' he said to Pilgrim as he passed. 'She won't talk to anyone but you.'

Pilgrim made his way up to the office with a growing sense of unease.

A young woman got to her feet as he walked through the door. Tall and clean featured, with red hair piled under a feather-trimmed bonnet, she carried herself proudly, despite the cheap shawl and low-cut bodice that proclaimed her profession.

Pilgrim glanced at Dolly. He was seated at his desk, his eyes round with curiosity. 'Give us a moment, would you?'

'Sir.' Dolly tried to mask his disappointment as he left the room. Pilgrim closed the door behind him.

'Frances,' he said.

'Uncle Harry.'

He motioned for her to sit down. 'This is a surprise ... a pleasure, of course.'

'Don't flannel me.'

He flushed. 'You're ... ?'

'Well, well enough.' She took a deep breath, and looked him squarely in the eye. 'You must be wondering why I'm here. Truth is, I'm wondering why myself. I have a friend. A good friend, Martha Drewitt. She went missing, over a week ago. I've looked for her everywhere I can think of ...'

'Frances...' he tried to interrupt.

'Martha would never just up and leave, without telling me. I know, I know that something has happened to her.' She thumped her chest. 'I can feel it, here.'

'I can't help you. Even if I had the time ...,' he tailed off. 'Finding missing women isn't my speciality, as you know.'

'You've still had no news of her, then?'

She was no longer talking about Martha Drewitt. He shook his head. 'You?'

'Not a word. When Ma died last year I thought she might have heard, might have got in touch, but ... ,' she stopped, and her expression hardened. She stood up. 'Well at least I can say I tried. For Martha.'

42

He watched her walk to the door, his expression betraying no hint of the struggle inside. He wanted to help her, but common sense and self-preservation argued against it. She had her hand on the doorknob when he spoke.

'I don't suppose you have a photograph of Martha?'

'As if!'

'Could you give us a description?'

'Will it help? Does that mean you'll look?'

He nodded, common sense smothered into silence. 'Wait here.'

He found Wainwright in the main hall, helping Sergeant Phelps process a couple of burglars. Wainwright was writing a list, as the sergeant pulled various items from the thieves' pockets.

'... three gent's watches, one pinchbeck necklace, six, no, seven, silk handkerchiefs.' He placed them on the counter, next to a paper packet. Pilgrim peered into it.

'What's that?' he asked.

'It was gingerbread,' said Wainwright dolefully. 'My landlady gave it to me, but I made the mistake of bringing it down here.'

'Don't look at me, lad,' sniffed Phelps. 'I never touched it, I'm sure.'

'Can I borrow the constable for a little while, Sergeant Phelps?'

'Be my guest, Detective Sergeant.'

'Bring your sketchpad, Wainwright.'

'Of course, sir, certainly, sir.'

The young policeman's eyes lit up with curiosity.

Curiosity turned to embarrassment when he was introduced to Frances. His long face flushed so hard that even the tips of his ears went pink.

'This is Wainwright,' Pilgrim explained to his niece. 'He has a gift for capturing a likeness. Describe your friend to him as best as you can.'

Wainwright stared at Frances. 'I don't know as how I'd call it a gift, precisely,' he stammered. 'And I'm used to having the subject plain in front of me.'

'Just do your best.' Pilgrim felt a flash of irritation. 'Why not sit at Tanner's desk, by the window? The light's better there.'

Wainwright nodded and did as he was told, pulling Tanner's chair out for Frances to sit on. He drew up another chair and opened his pad. He pulled out a piece of charcoal, fidgeted indecisively with it, and then took a deep breath. 'I might as well just start then, shall I? With the shape of the face. You can put me right as we go along.'

Pilgrim nodded. 'I'll leave you to it.'

He went out and closed the door, then leaned against it. He felt the weight of eyes on him immediately, however, and turned to see Dolly watching from the other side of the corridor. 'I thought you were going to visit laundries with that vest?' he snapped.

'I'm on my way now, sir.'

'Then go.' Pilgrim hesitated. 'No. On second thoughts, stay here and keep an eye on that door. If Sergeant Tanner comes anywhere near it, find an excuse to send him in the other direction.'

'Yes, sir.'

Pilgrim found an empty office, went inside, and closed the door. He leaned against it and shut his eyes. Frances was a shock. The last time he had seen her she was a skinny eleven year old, with missing teeth and scabbed elbows. The intervening years had been kind, in one way at least, transforming her into a beautiful young woman. An uncanny replica of her aunt: his wife, Bess. When he had seen Frances in his office he had thought for one heart-lurching moment that Bess had come back to him. He took some deep breaths, and went back out into the corridor.

A group of men had gathered at the office door. Dolly was standing in the path of Tanner and Charles Dickens, blocking their way.

'You really don't want to go in there, sir,' he was saying to Tanner.

'Why not?'

'There's a terrible ... smell.'

'A smell?'

'The most dreadful smell of ...' Dolly cast around for a suitable scent.

Tanner pushed him to one side.

'Stop wasting my time.' He threw open the door and strode into the room. Dickens followed him.

Pilgrim lengthened his stride. As he reached the door, Dolly turned to him with a mute apology.

'What's your sort doing in here?' said Tanner, inside the room.

Frances and Wainwright, who had been sitting with their heads close together over the sketchbook, got to their feet.

'What sort would that be?' asked Pilgrim.

Dickens glanced from Pilgrim to Tanner and back again, and stepped between them. 'My dear Sergeant Pilgrim! What a pleasure to see you. Sergeant Tanner was just acquainting me with the details of the Grimwood case.'

'Was he?'

Tanner's face suffused with blood. 'You're not the only Detective Sergeant on the force.'

Pilgrim ignored Tanner and turned to Dickens.

'This is my niece, Frances.'

'Delighted to meet you, my dear,' said Dickens. He beamed at Frances.

'She's giving a description of a missing friend to Constable Wainwright,' said Pilgrim. 'He helps out on occasion in the mortuary, as an artist.'

'An artist, eh?' Dickens took the sketch of Martha Drewitt from Wainwright. It showed a young woman, a little too round cheeked and heavy browed for beauty, but with a graceful neck and an abundance of hair. 'Is it a good likeness?' he asked Frances.

'If it ain't, it ain't my fault,' muttered Wainwright. 'I'm used to drawing from life, in a manner of speaking.'

'The features are right,' said Frances, 'but it lacks Martha's vitality.'

'That's something I ain't had a lot of practice at,' said the artist, glumly.

'Even so,' said Dickens, 'this is excellent, most accomplished. But I'm afraid you artists will very soon be out of a job, if photography takes off the way people say it will.'

'It'll never happen, sir. Oh, that photography's all very well for takin' images of corpses, and suchlike, but it ain't art. When it comes down to it, it's not much more than a ruddy fairground trick … beg your pardon, Miss.'

Everyone fell silent.

'The gloves,' prompted Dickens, 'you were going to show me the gloves, Sergeant Tanner.'

'Yes, sir, of course. They're right here in this drawer.' Tanner took out a pair of opera gloves and showed them to Dickens. 'See, they have letters inside them, a "T" and an "R".'

'So they do.' Dickens took one and sniffed it. 'Sulphur and rosin. These have been cleaned recently, if I'm not mistaken. You might want to continue your investigation with glove cleaners, Sergeant Tanner. I'd say there can't be above eight or nine regular glove cleaners in the city.'

Pilgrim took the sketch, and steered Frances by the elbow towards the door. 'Thank you, Wainwright.'

'A pleasure, sir,' said Wainwright, 'and I'd appreciate the chance to take your likeness, Miss, if you're ever back here. I'll do it gratis.'

Frances nodded at him, and then at Dickens.

'Goodbye, my dear,' said Dickens.

Pilgrim guided her out of the room, aware that the men's eyes – even Dickens's – were drawn to her backside under the tight skirt. As they passed, Pilgrim put his mouth close to Dolly's ear. 'You're a terrible liar, Williamson.'

Pilgrim and Frances paused at the top of the main staircase, obliging other people to step around them.

'You can reach me at Gloucester Street,' she said.

'I can't promise anything.'

'I'm only asking you to try.' She started down the stairs.

'Frannie,' he stopped her. 'I miss Bess too. I know it's my fault …'

'Yes,' she cut across what he was going to say, 'it is.'

He watched her make her way down the rest of the stairs, not taking his eyes from her graceful figure until it passed out of the main doors and melted into the crowds on the street.

Then he turned and headed to the reception desk.

'I need the keys to the cells, Sergeant.'

'Right you are, sir.' Phelps stooped to get them from the hook under the counter, and sighed. 'They ain't here. If I've told those youngsters once, I've told them a hundred times – bring the keys back to me. One of the buggers will have them in his pocket. It's a good thing I have a spare set.' He disappeared into the cubbyhole that served as an office, and emerged a moment later with a heavy bunch of keys.

'I'll come with you if you don't mind, sir. I'd better check the keys haven't been left in one of the locks. I'll have someone's bleedin' guts for garters.' Phelps sailed through the barred doorway to the cells on a wave of indignation. Pilgrim followed. Phelps' gaze swept the locks as they went down the corridor. When they reached Appler's cell, however, he stopped, and his face took on a strange expression.

'What?' asked Pilgrim.

'Is it Mr Appler you want to see, sir?'

Pilgrim nodded.

'I think you'd best let me go first.' Phelps unlocked the door, but before he could open it, Pilgrim moved him firmly out of the way.

Appler lay in the centre of the cell; face down in a pool of blood, one arm stretched above his head. There were great smears around his arms and legs, where he had thrashed about in the gore, and a cut-throat razor lay a few inches from his outflung hand. The blade was black and clotted.

When they had caught their breath, Pilgrim pulled Phelps back out into the corridor. 'How did you know?' he asked.

'The blood, sir. I could smell it. I spent long enough on the battlefields of Afghanistan to know it anywhere.'

47

Pilgrim swallowed. Somehow Phelps' revelation that blood had its own scent was even more appalling than the carnage in the cell.

He cleared his throat. 'You'd best fetch Inspector Field,' he said, 'but make sure Mr Dickens is off the premises first.'

Phelps shot away down the corridor, and Pilgrim went back into the cell. He looked around. There was a bowl of water on the chair beside a mirror, a shaving brush, and a towel. Prisoners were generally permitted to shave, unless they were considered a risk to either themselves or their gaolers. With Appler, there had been no reason to think either was the case. Pilgrim put a finger into the water in the bowl. Stone cold. As he wiped his finger on his shirt he noticed a crumpled ball of paper lying on the cot. He picked it up and smoothed it out, recognising the notepaper he had given to Appler. He had evidently started to list his movements on the days prior to his arrest, and had written a few lines – '5th February – Rose late. Paid a call on Bookmaker – P. Beddowes of Turk St at 11 o'clock'. But there was nothing else, save a single word scrawled across the page: 'verloren'. Pilgrim knew no Dutch, but had a little German. He recognized the word: 'lost'.

What had made Johannes Appler surrender to despair? Guilt? The realization that the evidence against him was overwhelming? Or the shame of having to face his parents? Whatever the reason, no one would know it now. Appler was lost indeed.

Pilgrim pushed the paper into his pocket.

He met Field and Phelps halfway down the corridor.

'Has Dickens gone?' asked Pilgrim.

'I sent him packing.' Field's face was grim. 'This is an ugly business, Harry.'

'You haven't seen the half of it yet. We need to find out who brought Appler the shaving bowl, and when.'

'I can tell you that, sir,' said Phelps. 'Young Anderson was on slops duty. He must have taken it in about eight this morning. Can't imagine why he never went back for it, though.'

'Find out,' snapped Field. 'But play it close to your chest, for now. I don't want everyone and his ruddy dog knowing.'

'I hear your Hackney Killer has topped himself,' said Tanner. 'Good riddance.'

Pilgrim ignored the comment. There was no point asking Tanner how he knew. They had tried to remove Appler's body and clean his cell as discreetly as possible, but policemen were incurable gossips. No doubt it was also common knowledge that Constable Anderson had been prevented from going back into the cell for the shaving bowl by a sudden attack of the flux. The delay had given Appler more than enough time to pluck up the courage to kill himself.

Tanner was alone in the office. There was no sign of Dolly, who had presumably taken himself off to the laundries with the vest. Pilgrim pushed his pile of fan mail aside to sit on his desk, and scrutinised Wainwright's sketch of Martha Drewitt. It didn't improve his mood. He glanced sideways at Tanner, who was trying to pick a lock on a small travelling valise covered with decorative luggage labels.

'How is your investigation on Eliza Grimwood coming on?' asked Pilgrim.

'Well enough.'

Pilgrim got up from his desk, and took the lock pick from the other man. He opened the valise with a twist of his fingers. 'Have you asked Ben Thompson at the Spreadeagle whether he saw her that night?'

'Of course I have. Don't try to teach me to suck eggs.' Tanner looked into the valise. A collection of spoons and three goblets nestled in cotton wadding.

Pilgrim picked up one of the goblets, engraved with a heraldic design, and weighed it in his hand. 'Silver,' he said. He looked at the valise. 'Where did you get this?'

'Anderson found it on a stairway at the back of the Old Mint. Some fence's stash, probably.'

'Probably.' Pilgrim tossed the goblet back into the valise, and handed Tanner the sketch of Martha Drewitt. 'I have a girl missing from the Waterloo Road.'

'So?'

'Is it possible there's a connection between her and Eliza Grimwood, or the killer?'

'Possible, but not likely.' Tanner faced him with a sneer. 'What would you have me do; keep an eye on every slack cunny in the East End? The silly drabs go missing all the time.' He thrust the sketch back at Pilgrim. 'Tell you what, Sergeant Pilchem, why don't you keep it? I know you have a soft spot for a trollop like that.'

Pilgrim punched him.

CHAPTER SEVEN

'Bugger and galloping hell's flames, Harry. I know Dick Tanner's not the easiest man to get on with, but I can't have my detectives brawling like navvies.' Charley Field glared at Pilgrim, who was sporting a bruised chin and rapidly swelling eye.

'Do you think Tanner will make a formal complaint?' asked Pilgrim.

'Shouldn't think so. He's a political animal.'

'Unlike me.'

'Unlike you. What the hell were you thinking?'

Pilgrim said nothing, but Field was not to be shaken off.

'Was it Appler? Must've been a shock, finding him like that.'

'No.'

'Is it the boy?' Field persisted, like a terrier with a rat. 'Is the Bonwell case getting to you?'

'No.'

'I can put someone else on it if you want.'

'It's not the Bonwell case.'

Field's expression grew sly. 'Adolphus told me you had a visitor.'

'Did he?'

'An auburn-haired charmer. Adolphus was very specific.'

Pilgrim sighed. 'It was Frances Reilly: Bess's niece. She wants me to help her find a missing friend.'

'You're not going to do it?'

'Is that an order?'

'Don't be bloody-minded. You can't allow yourself to get dragged back into all that. Everything's changed since those days.'

'You certainly have.'

'Yes, I have,' agreed Field. 'And I'm damn proud of it. Be reasonable, Harry. You have to put the past behind you.'

Pilgrim stared at Field for a long time.

'You're right, of course,' he said at last, 'about Frances. I'd already changed my mind about getting involved. I'm taking the train back to Great Barrow on the Bonwell case.'

'I'm pleased to hear it,' said Field, 'but don't hang about. There'll be an inquest into Appler's death. Things could get sticky.'

'I think he was innocent.'

Field sighed. 'Innocent. Guilty. It's irrelevant now. The case is closed.'

'What about the dead girl?'

Field considered the question as he walked over his copy of Cross's *New Map of London*, identical to the one in Pilgrim's office. 'Last year,' he said, gazing up at it, 'there were thirty-two murders in the metropolitan area. Thirty-two murders, eighty-four assaults, sixty house breakings, nine suicides, and twenty-eight rapes.' He paused. 'True, most of them were carried out by cretins, which made them easy to solve, but that still leaves a hellish workload.' He swung around to face Pilgrim. 'It's an unending tide of shit, Harry, and we're the only things stopping it from swamping this sorry cesspit of a city. Until the Commissioners see fit to appoint more than five of us, I have to choose the battles we fight.'

There was a beat of silence.

'And no one has reported the girl missing,' said Pilgrim, flatly.

'That's about the measure of it.' Field caught Pilgrim's expression and sighed. 'I'm not saying it's the way it should be. It's just the way it is.'

*

The Reverend Horace Bonwell emerged from his front door, straightened his hat, and strode off down the frosty lane without seeing Pilgrim, who was standing behind one of the yew trees that flanked the rectory. Pilgrim wasn't hiding, precisely, but he wasn't sorry the minister hadn't seen him. He waited until Bonwell had turned the corner towards the main street, then bounded up the rectory steps and pulled the bell. It jangled somewhere inside the building.

After a minute the door opened. Mrs Walsh glared suspiciously at his swollen eye and scabbed chin.

'The Reverend's out,' she said.

'Is he?' said Pilgrim. 'No matter. I've lost my pocketbook.'

'Your … ?'

'I think I may have left it here, the last time I called.'

'I haven't seen it.' The housekeeper considered him. 'Wait here.'

She vanished back into the house, leaving the door ajar. Pilgrim waited a few moments then followed her. He caught a fleeting glimpse of her skirt as it disappeared into the study, and then he headed for the parlour. He went directly to the bible, and opened it.

There was a family tree on the flyleaf, drawn in black ink in a neat hand. Below the marriage of Horace Bonwell and Alice Drake were two names – Patience and Faith – both marked 'died in infancy'. He traced his finger up again, to the sibling line of Alice Drake, and stopped. Here was something interesting! Another name had been deleted. Not marked 'deceased' but simply scored out with one careful line. Stella Agnes. He tapped his finger on the page and closed the bible.

He could hear women's voices. He followed the sound into the hall, and saw that the study door still stood ajar. The voices were raised, not loud enough for him to make out what they were saying, but loud enough for him to discern a note of panic. He pushed the door open.

'Any luck?' he asked cheerfully.

The two women froze, surprised in their search for the pocketbook. A flush crept up Mrs Bonwell's throat and into her cheeks.

'I said to wait,' snapped the housekeeper.

Pilgrim ignored her, and nodded instead to her mistress. 'So sorry for the inconvenience, Mrs Bonwell. May I help you look?'

He made a show of searching the floor, and then of inspecting the chair he had been sitting on during his last visit. He put his hand down the side of the cushion, and, after a second's pause, pulled out his pocketbook, with the air of Little Jack Horner pulling out a plum.

'Here we are. I knew I must have left it here somewhere.' He made as if to leave, but then hesitated at the door. He turned to Mrs Bonwell. 'I've had a long journey to get here, and it will be a long journey back. I was wondering ... some refreshment? Tea, perhaps?'

Dismay flickered over Mrs Bonwell's face, but it was vanquished by good manners.

'Of course,' she said. 'We'll take it in the parlour, please, Mrs Walsh.'

'I'll put the pot on, ma'am. It shouldn't take long.' The house-keeper cast him a venomous glance.

Mrs Bonwell showed him into the parlour, where they sat in silence, apart from the ticking of the black marble clock on the mantelpiece. The room was oppressive, shaded from the fading effects of the sun with velvet drapes pulled almost completely over the window. The silence stretched. Pilgrim's gaze flicked to the photographs on the table.

'Do you and your husband have children, Mrs Bonwell?' he asked.

'The Lord saw fit to take them from us.'

'It's a hard thing, to lose a child.'

'It was God's will.'

He clenched his hands on his lap. The silence spun out again. He settled himself more comfortably into his chair, while she perched on the edge of her cushion as if it was made of knives. The clock ticked. Under his steady gaze Mrs Bonwell started to fiddle with the crucifix at her throat.

She actually jumped when the housekeeper entered with the tea tray.

'Thank you, Mrs Walsh. I'll pour.'

The housekeeper left.

Mrs Bonwell busied herself with the tea things, her hand trembling as she handed a cup to Pilgrim. As he took it, his gaze dropped to her wrist. There were several distinct marks around it: fingermarks. She tugged down the cuff of her blouse without meeting his eyes.

They sipped their tea. Silence stretched again.

Finally it snapped: Mrs Bonwell clattered her cup down onto the saucer.

'My sister ...' she began. She stopped and started again. 'You asked, when you last came, whether we knew anyone in London.' She hesitated. 'My sister is in London. At least, I believe she is. She ran away, years ago. Horace ... he forbids me to speak of her.'

'What makes you think she is in London?'

'She sends me a note, every now and then. Christmas. My birthday. I tear them up before Horace can see.'

'Did you see the label on the parcel?'

She nodded.

'And the writing on it?' he asked.

'I can't be sure, but yes, it was similar to Stella's.'

'Her surname is Drake?'

Mrs Bonwell raised her eyebrows. 'Unless she has married, but how ... ?'

'Can you describe her to me?'

She hesitated, her eyes searching his. She rose, and went to the sewing table that stood next to the window. She delved into one of the silk-lined pockets, and came out with a piece of card that she passed to Pilgrim. She seemed calmer for having made the decision to help him.

'It was taken on her sixteenth birthday. She may have changed.'

The photograph showed a handsome girl with expressive eyes, and dressed in a high-necked gown, beside a display of flowers. A mischievous smile undermined the formal pose.

'Why did she run away?' he asked.

'There was a young man. It caused quite a scandal. Father had died the year before, and Horace was her legal guardian. You can probably imagine ...'

'Yes, I can,' said Pilgrim. The thought of the Reverend Bonwell on his high horse was not a comfortable one. 'Was there a child?'

She wouldn't meet his eyes. 'I believe so.'

He released his breath, unaware he had even been holding it. 'Male or female?' he asked.

'I have no idea.'

'When was this?'

'Four years ago.'

CHAPTER EIGHT

St Bartholomew's Hospital had long occupied its site to the west of Smithfield, its classical facade dominated by a bullying statue of Henry VIII. Inside, the baroque reception rooms surrendered to a warren of smaller rooms and corridors. After descending a stone staircase and passing countless drab-painted doors, Pilgrim and Dolly at last found themselves admitted to the Coroner's Office.

It was a gloomy room, lined with shelves laden with dozens of jars, filled with gelatinous samples. A human brain and a human foetus floated among them. The other contents were thankfully unidentifiable.

'Sorry to keep you.' Dr Hector Fairweather wiped his hands on his bloody apron. With his limping gait, bald head, and bristling moustache, he always reminded Pilgrim of a walrus he had once seen at the Zoological Gardens.

'Hector.' Pilgrim signalled for Dolly to step forward. 'This is Constable Williamson, one of my new detectives.'

Fairweather nodded at Dolly. 'You'll forgive me if I don't shake hands, lad.'

They were distracted by a noise coming from the corner of the room: the clink of glass on glass. Pilgrim and Dolly turned to find the source: a young man they had not previously noticed was sitting at a table laden with a number of large specimen jars. The young man gave them a baleful stare over the top of his spectacles.

'Pay no attention to young Townsend,' said Fairweather. 'He's helping us to catalogue our collection of matrices.'

'Matrices?' prompted Dolly.

'Wombs.'

Dolly cast a horrified glance at the jars.

'Come on through.'

Fairweather led the way into the mortuary examination room. The wooden peg that stuck out from the bottom of his trouser leg kept pace with his boot, step for step, and made a hollow sound whenever it struck the floor. Dolly's attention was riveted by it.

The examination room was tiled from floor to ceiling and had a drain in one corner. A slab, rather like an altar, occupied the centre of the room, bearing a shape covered with a blood-spotted sheet. As they drew closer, Dolly's face registered his distress.

Fairweather took a lid off a jar, and offered it to him. 'Camphor,' he said, 'it'll help with the smell.'

Dolly smeared his finger in the jar and glanced at Pilgrim for some clue what to do with it. Pilgrim rubbed his own finger under his nose to demonstrate. Dolly followed suit, and his expression betrayed his relief. Fairweather offered the jar to Pilgrim, and then pulled it back.

'I forgot,' he said. 'Smallpox, wasn't it? Quite common to lose your sense of smell that way.'

Fairweather pulled the sheet down to the boy's shoulders. The marks around the throat were more noticeable than they had been before, but were upstaged by the crudely stitched incision that now ran from the boy's sternum to his groin.

Fairweather caught Dolly's expression. 'No point wasting time on fancy needlework,' he said.

'He was strangled?' asked Pilgrim.

Fairweather nodded. 'Apart from the obvious trauma to the throat there is cyanosis, and considerable petechial haemorrhaging, particularly under the eyelids. The killer throttled the boy, probably with the kerchief. He didn't exert enough force to do it cleanly, however. The trachea is still intact.'

'It was a woman.'

They turned to see Townsend, who had followed them into the mortuary. He blinked at them through the thick lenses of his spectacles. 'She wasn't strong enough,' he added, with a distinct transatlantic accent.

Fairweather nodded. 'That would account for the trachea, I daresay.'

'A man wouldn't have made such a botch of it.'

Fairweather glared at him. 'Don't you have anything to do? I'm sure Dr Cuthbertson can find a use for you.'

Townsend slunk out of the room, giving the detectives another baleful glare over the top of his glasses as he went.

Pilgrim was still studying the corpse.

'Do you think he suffered?' he asked.

Fairweather shook his head. 'I would say he probably lost consciousness early on. I doubt he would have felt the injuries to his neck. Some small mercy, I suppose. What do you want me to do with him?'

'It'll be another parish burial. And it had better be soon.'

'Yes, it's been a week or so. You really can't smell him at all?'

'No.'

The doctor pulled the sheet back over the boy. 'There are times when I wouldn't mind a dose of smallpox myself.'

'Have you had any luck with the laundries?' asked Pilgrim, as he and Dolly emerged from the mortuary.

''Fraid not, sir.' Dolly rubbed the camphor from under his nose, leaving a mark on his sleeve like the track of a snail. 'But I've only managed to visit half a dozen so far. Did you know there are more than a hundred and eighty laundries in London? I've organized some of A Division to help, but it'll still take us days to get round them. Do you think we should be starting at Euston and working outwards?'

Pilgrim shook his head. 'It's the only station with trains to Essex, so it doesn't necessarily follow that the killer lives nearby. Start with all the districts that begin with "F" – Fenchurch, Finsbury, Fulham …' he hesitated. 'Of course, the "F" might not be a district. It could be a name, in which case … '

'We're well-buggered. Beg your pardon, sir.' Dolly's gaze slid away, and he shuffled his feet.

'Is there something else?'

'Dr Fairweather.' Dolly coloured. 'There's a rumour in the barracks that he cut off his leg with a sabre when it got trapped under his horse at Waterloo. Is it true?'

'No.' Pilgrim saw Dolly's look of relief and smiled. 'It wasn't a sabre. It was a bayonet blade.'

CHAPTER NINE

Dickens encountered Rebecca Wood by chance in the hallway of Urania Cottage. She was carrying an armful of sheets.

'How are you settling in, my dear? Do you have everything you need?'

'Yes, sir.' She met his gaze calmly, but without enthusiasm. He thought she had gained a little weight in the few days since he had seen her, which was no bad thing.

'I'm looking for Mrs Wallace,' he said.

'She's in the laundry.'

He nodded his thanks and hurried down the basement stairs, anxious to give the Matron his news. He heard her voice before he saw her.

'No, my dear,' she spoke slowly and patiently, 'you fold it like so, with the outer corners tucked in.'

She looked up from the sheet as he arrived in the doorway. Kathleen Chalk also looked up, her mouth hanging open unattractively. She was their least intelligent resident, a borderline idiot, in his opinion. He regretted the impulse that had made him take her in, for he doubted she would ever be fit to emigrate.

'I wasn't expecting to see you here today, sir,' said Mrs Wallace. 'Is there something amiss?'

'No, not at all. On the contrary, in fact. Would you join me in the parlour for a moment?'

'Certainly.' She handed Kathleen the pillowcase. 'Keep practising, dear. I'll be back to see how you're getting on in a few minutes.'

She followed him up the stairs and into the parlour, where he waited until the door was safely closed before flourishing an envelope.

'Open it,' he said.

The Royal Academy and the Mayor of London invite Mr Charles Dickens to a Reception and Grand Gala, Tuesday 16th February

She looked at him, puzzled.

'Turn it over,' he instructed.

She read the handwritten note on the reverse.

Dearest Charles, I thought you might like to bring Mrs Wallace to this reception, together with one or two of our more presentable girls. I judge it to be time we showed to the world at large the value of the work we are doing at our Cottage.

It was signed by their patron, Angela Burdett-Coutts.

'A capital idea, don't you think?' said Dickens.

Mrs Wallace didn't look as pleased as he had expected.

'If you say so,' she muttered.

He chose to ignore her tone. 'We will have to select the girls carefully. They should be able to make at least a little conversation, and know how to behave in public. I saw Rebecca Wood just now in the hallway. I imagine she might do very well.'

'Actually,' Mrs Wallace hesitated, 'I wanted to speak to you about Rebecca. I doubt she's said more than ten words to me since she's been here. She seems terribly low-spirited.'

'Have patience. We have no idea of the trials she may have suffered before she came to us. It may take her a little while to adapt.'

Mrs Wallace nodded. 'There's another thing I would like to discuss with you. The Baroness has written to recommend a parson, to visit with the girls once a week.'

'A good thing, surely?'

'My friend Mrs Wexford, whose cousin attends his church in Spitalfields, tells me he's a notorious tub-thumper.'

'Ah.' He scratched his head. 'That's not so good, I must admit. Why, oh why, do charitable causes like ours always have to get tangled up with the Church? I don't want our girls bullied in that way. Perhaps Miss Coutts might be dissuaded from this particular parson? Would you like me to write to her?'

'If you wouldn't mind, sir.' Mrs Wallace looked happier.

'Consider it done. I'll accept the Gala invitation at the same time. Now, I have an hour to spare. Would you be so good as to fetch the account books and a pot of tea?'

When Mrs Wallace had left, Dickens smiled to himself. He was most gratified by Angela Burdett-Coutt's invitation to the Gala. With the Major and other worthies in attendance it was the perfect opportunity to publicise their cause. And then another thought occurred to him: perhaps two birds might be killed with a single stone? The more he thought on it, the more he liked it. It was a capital idea!

CHAPTER TEN

The sitting room was small, but cosily furnished. It had an armchair, a sofa, a fire in the grate, and a plentiful supply of coal in the bucket. Pilgrim sat on the sofa.

'I think you'll find it comfortable enough.' Mrs Charlotte Piper, Dolly's cousin, watched him anxiously.

Pilgrim nodded, resisting a powerful urge to cover the lower part of his face with his hand. It was a habit he had developed as an adolescent, and had never quite grown out of – whenever he was in the presence of an attractive woman his hand would creep up, as if by its own volition, to hide his pockmarks. And there was no doubt that Mrs Piper was attractive.

She had hair the colour of wheat, gathered into a sheaf at the nape of her neck, straight black brows, and eyes as wide and grey as a Norfolk horizon. Her black bombazine mourning gown set off her figure and fresh complexion. He guessed she was in her mid-twenties. Young for a widow. He wondered how her husband had died, and whether she had loved him.

'This room and the bedroom would be for your own personal use.' She cut through his speculations. 'There's a bathhouse just across the road. I'm afraid I can't offer cooking facilities, but I can serve a hot meal in the dining room every evening, at a time to suit.' She gave a smile that slammed into Pilgrim like a fist. 'All for just nine shillings a week.'

He turned away as if to review the room, but really to give himself time to regain his wits. He liked the lodgings, but didn't need, or want, complications in his life.

'I'll have to think about it,' he said. The words came out more harshly than he had intended.

'Oh.' It was obviously not the answer she was expecting. She frowned around the room, as if to find the cause of his displeasure. He looked away, shamed by her confusion, and looked back just in time to catch her in the act of sticking her tongue out at him.

She reddened, bit her lip, and turned away to hide her embarrassment.

A bolt of pure joy flashed through him. Surprising and inexplicable. He registered the sensation, and then squashed it. He really didn't need complications.

'No, I don't think so.'

She followed him back down to the front door, two red patches branded on her cheekbones.

'Good day, madam.' He tipped his hat to her.

'Is it the lack of bathing facilities?' she blurted. 'Or the ... ?'

'There's nothing wrong with the rooms.'

She recoiled, as if he'd slapped her. His emphasis on the word rooms had been unintentional. Unintentional and unfortunate: there really was only one way she could interpret it. He opened his mouth to try to repair the damage, but she held up a hand to stop him.

'You really are the most objectionable man.' She drew herself up to her full height, and glared at him. 'I suppose you think your disfigurement excuses your rudeness?'

'My disfig ... ?'

'I wouldn't rent the rooms to you now even if you begged me, begged me on your ruddy knees.'

And she slammed the door in his face.

Disfigurement? He stared at the door in disbelief. Had she really said that? His disfigurement? He didn't know whether to laugh or break the door down. In the end he did neither, but retreated down the steps like a whipped dog.

Charley Field's head appeared around the office door as Pilgrim took off his overcoat.

'You're back, Harry. Are you free next Friday evening?'

'I think so.'

'Do you want to check your diary?'

'I am free. Why?'

'How about you, Tanner?'

'Yes, sir, I'm free.'

'Why?' asked Pilgrim again.

'Mr Dickens has invited us to a reception at the Royal Academy. Quite a few bigwigs are going to be there. The Mayor, for one.' He caught Pilgrim's expression.

'It's good for the force, Harry. We rely on the goodwill of the press and the upper classes to be able to do our job properly.'

Pilgrim picked up the boy's vest from Dolly's desk, and made a show of looking at it.

'Mr Dickens thinks very highly of you.' Field glanced around. 'Where's Adolphus?'

'He should be back soon.'

'Tell him about Friday, will you? Oh, there you are.' He stood back to let Dolly into the room.

'What's that about Friday, sir?' asked Dolly.

'A reception, hosted by the Mayor.'

'Good for public relations, eh, sir?'

'I'm glad someone can see the wider picture.' Field cast a glum look at Pilgrim and left.

'It's not my job to see the wider picture,' muttered Pilgrim. He was still smarting from his encounter with Charlotte Piper. His disfigurement? He turned to Dolly. 'Have we had any news yet from the laundries?'

'Not yet, sir. But we've only done fifteen so far. 'Fraid we've ran out of "F's" already. And I've just been to Euston Square Station, but no one can remember the trunk, much less who brought it in.'

Pilgrim squinted at the mark on the vest. 'Does that still look like an "F" to you?' he asked Dolly.

'Yes, sir.'

Pilgrim took the vest to the window to examine it more closely. The mark did look like an 'F,' but it was badly faded. The horizontal lines were not straight, but slanted. He returned to his desk and copied the mark onto a piece of paper. He considered at it for a moment, and then extended the top mark of the 'F' backwards. It looked much less like an 'F' now.

Dolly, meanwhile, was rummaging through Pilgrim's pile of fan mail.

'You still haven't looked at these, sir.' He picked up a couple, and sniffed one. 'This one's from a lady. And this one's foreign. It has a fancy stamp.'

Pilgrim looked up from the piece of paper. 'What did you say?'

'It has a fancy stamp.'

Pilgrim stared at the paper again, and then dashed to Tanner's desk. He found the valise he had opened for Tanner earlier, and dragged it out from under the desk.

'What the hell are you doing?' said Tanner.

Pilgrim ignored him, and knelt to examine the labels on the valise. One was for Shanghai, written in both English and Chinese. He stared at the Chinese characters and then compared them with the mark on his paper.

'It's not an "F" at all. Get your overcoat, Dolly.'

CHAPTER ELEVEN

Limehouse was a part of the city unfamiliar to Pilgrim. Behind the respectable houses fronting the shipyards on the North bank of the river lay a warren of warehouses and smaller streets, housing businesses that catered for the sailors landing at the West India docks. Part of this warren was Pennyfields, an area considered out of bounds by other East Enders, and by the police, who left the exotic residents largely to their own devices. But it was there that Pilgrim knew he would find what he was looking for.

They hadn't gone more than a hundred yards into the tenements, when he nudged Dolly, 'That'll do.' He nodded at a battered wooden door that stood at the mouth of the alley. It had Chinese symbols written on it in chalk and below them the words 'Laundry by hand'. He pushed open the door.

The warmth hit them immediately, and steam billowed out to escape into the frosty air. Dolly's eyes grew round as he followed Pilgrim into a vaulted, windowless room, lit by torches. Clouds of steam rose from vast tubs of boiling water, heated with fires beneath. Dripping sheets, nightgowns, long johns, and blankets were hung from a series of ropes and pulleys from the ceiling. A dozen Chinamen, all with pigtails, were hard at work, some carrying baskets filled with clothes, others sweating over the vats, stirring them with paddles.

The two detectives attracted stares. An old man, dressed in a calico tunic with wide sleeves, approached them through the steam. He was stooped and wrinkled, but his eyes were sharp. He bowed.

'May I help you, Uncles?'

Pilgrim took the vest from his pocket. 'Can you tell me whose mark this is?' As the old man looked at it, two of the younger Chinese men peered over his shoulder, squinting at the mark in the dim light. Suddenly one of the young men threw up his hands.

'Ha!' He seized the vest and threw it onto the floor. He was about to stamp on it when Dolly snatched it up again.

'What the devil are you doing? That's Her Majesty's evidence, that is.' He squared up to the young man, his face red. 'I should arrest you for that!'

The youth shouted something in Chinese and squared up to Dolly.

'Constable Williamson.' Pilgrim's rebuke was soft, but effective. Dolly backed off.

The old man spoke sharply in Chinese. Whatever he said had an immediate effect: both of the young men slunk away.

Pilgrim frowned. 'I don't understand. Is that your mark?'

'It is not. It is "cow under a roof".'

'Cow? Speak plainly!' Dolly's patience had worn thin. Pilgrim glared at him, and he blushed.

The old man didn't seem to be offended. 'Cow under a roof is the sign for prison, young sir. Millbank Prison. Since my old friend Ho Chi went to oversee the laundry there they have been running it as a commercial enterprise. We have lost much custom.'

Dolly snatched the vest and marched out.

'Thank you for your help, sir,' said Pilgrim. He made to follow Dolly, but the old man grabbed his wrist.

'A word with you, Uncle, before you go to remonstrate with your young colleague.'

Pilgrim tried to free his wrist, but couldn't. The old man was stronger than he looked.

'Something bad has passed close to you.' His expression was earnest. 'You saw it, but did not truly see. It will come again.'

Pilgrim succeeded in wrenching his arm away, and joined Dolly, who had been watching from the doorway.

'What did the yellow devil want with you, sir?'

'Nothing. And he's a man, Dolly.' He glanced back at the old man, who was still staring at him through the steam. 'Just a man.'

They didn't see a Hackney carriage until they were well outside of Pennyfields, at the west end of Poplar High Street. Pilgrim hailed it.

'Millbank Prison, via Holborn,' he called to the driver.

Inside the cab, both men sat in silence with their thoughts. Dolly was still red from his altercation in the laundry, and Pilgrim guessed he was embarrassed. Pilgrim, too, was more shaken than he cared to admit. What had the old man meant by his cryptic warning? *Something bad had passed close to him*? That was hardly surprising, in his line of work, and yet ... the experience had left him with a strangely disconnected feeling.

Charley Field accosted him as soon as he got back to Whitehall.

'Have you got a minute, Harry?'

'Is there a problem?'

'In a manner of speaking. Come into my office.'

Hector Fairweather was waiting for them. Pilgrim couldn't remember ever seeing the pathologist outside of St Bartholomew's, so he guessed that whatever news he brought must be serious.

'Tell him, Hector,' said Field.

Fairweather came straight to the point. 'Johannes Appler didn't kill himself. He was murdered.'

'How do you know?' asked Pilgrim.

'It wasn't obvious, at first. It seemed a pretty straightforward case, although suicide by that method is relatively rare. The cause of death was blood loss, caused by the severance of the carotid artery. The incision was consistent with self-infliction, more elevated on the left-hand side than on the right. The depth of the wound, however, was unexpected, as was the lack of hesitation marks. That made me curious. When I inspected the rest of the body, I found three more cuts, small but deep: one on the pad of the left thumb, and two more between the second and third knuckles on the right-hand middle finger and ring finger. Defensive wounds. They made me go back and look again at the fatal incision, but I couldn't see anything else to make me question my original conclusion.'

'Appler was left-handed,' said Pilgrim. 'I noticed it when he was signing the paperwork after his arrest.'

Field threw a look of triumph at Fairweather. 'I told you he'd have spotted it.' He looked back at Pilgrim. 'I noticed it myself when I was questioning him.'

The pathologist's expression was sombre. 'Of course, when Charley told me, it changed everything,' he said. 'If Appler had cut his own throat the incision would have been more elevated on the right hand side than on the left. Someone cut his throat from behind and it wasn't an easy kill. My guess is that Appler realized what was happening and grabbed at his assailant. He cut his hands on the razor in the struggle.'

'Someone got into Appler's cell and murdered him,' said Field. 'But why? And how?'

'The keys were missing,' said Pilgrim. 'Phelps opened the cell with his spare set. We should ask him whether he ever found the originals.'

'I don't want to reopen the case officially,' said Field, 'for obvious reasons.'

Pilgrim could certainly see why. It would not only raise questions about Appler's guilt, but also make a laughing stock of the police force. Whitehall was the very heart of law enforcement in the city. The fact that someone had broken into a cell, committed a murder, and then succeeded in getting out again without detection would cause outrage. Questions would be asked. Heads would roll. He could guess what was coming next, and didn't like it.

'I want you to look into it, Harry. I know I can trust you to do it discreetly.'

Dolly was waiting for him when he returned to the office.

'Good news from the Millbank laundry, sir. They recognize the vest and the neckerchief. They do a collection from that customer once a fortnight. She lives in Camberwell.' He handed Pilgrim a scrap of paper. 'Hard by the slums, sir, around St Giles. Do you know it?'

Pilgrim turned on his heel and walked back out of the room without answering. Dolly blinked after him. After a moment Pilgrim's face reappeared around the door.

'What are you waiting for?' he snapped.

CHAPTER TWELVE

Dolly knocked on the peeling front door of a house in the middle of the terrace. The houses were black with soot and many of the windows boarded up, or stuffed with rags. Inside the house he could hear children playing and the thin cry of a baby. After an interval where nothing seemed to be happening, a skinny girl of thirteen or so threw open the door. She gave Pilgrim and Dolly a look of frank curiosity, and then turned to shout back into the house.

'Ma! Couple of gents for you.' She vanished back into the passage, to be replaced by an older woman. Her mother had a worn, undernourished look, although her gown and apron were clean. A half-naked toddler clung to her skirts.

'Mrs Johnston?' enquired Dolly.

She nodded, her eyes flicking from Dolly to Pilgrim and back again.

Dolly continued. 'We're from the Metropolitan Police. We would appreciate your help.'

There was no change in Mrs Johnston's expression. In the absence of any acknowledgment or encouragement, Dolly ploughed on. 'Do you recognize this undervest?'

She barely glanced at the vest before shaking her head.

'How about this?' He showed her the spotted neckerchief that had been used to strangle the boy in the box.

'No.'

'Look at it more closely.' He pressed it into her hand.

She thrust it back at him as if it might burn her. 'Never seen it before.'

The boy clinging to her skirts gave a whimper of protest and squirmed away. There were fingermarks on his shoulder.

'That's very peculiar, Mrs Johnston,' started Dolly, 'for you see … '

'There's obviously been some mistake,' cut in Pilgrim. 'We beg your pardon.' He tipped his hat to the woman and led a baffled Dolly away. The door banged shut.

Pilgrim steered Dolly into the mouth of an alleyway at the end of the street.

'She's lying,' protested Dolly.

'Of course she is. But there's no point putting her on her guard. If she comes out before I get back, follow her.'

'You're going to leave me here? On my own?'

'You'll be fine. Just stay in the shadows, and watch the house.'

From the mouth of the alley they could clearly see Mrs Johnston's door. But Dolly wasn't happy. 'What if she goes out a back way?'

'These houses have no back entrance.'

Dolly looked sharply at him.

'I may be a while,' said Pilgrim. 'If you have to follow her, I'll see you at the barracks.' He walked off, into the gloom of the alley.

Dolly settled down unhappily to watch the house.

Pilgrim walked down Brushfield Street, busy with workers coming home from the brushworks and the blacking factory, and others who had already started their night's drinking or whoring. The fading daylight couldn't disguise the smoke-stained buildings and rubbish piled in the gutters. He passed an open doorway where a young boy sat naked and filthy among a litter of kittens. The boy stared at Pilgrim with vacant eyes and a mucus-smeared face, oblivious to voices raised in anger in the passage behind him.

Pilgrim walked on.

A woman hurried past on the pavement, dragging a young girl behind her, who struggled in her grip, protesting. Neither looked at Pilgrim as they passed. Directly behind them was a group of boys, who assessed him with ancient eyes, calculating the value of his clothes. He heard one of them jeer behind his back as he crossed the street, heading towards the alehouse on the corner. It used to be the Three Bells, but now a different sign hung outside, and all its windows were either boarded up or filthy. But it was still open for business. Three men stumbled from the doorway, straight into Pilgrim's path, forcing him to swerve to avoid them. He heard a splash as one relieved himself in the gutter, and shouts from the other two, who had started to brawl.

Pilgrim walked on, turning down another street, even narrower and darker than the first. The sign on the wall was peeling and barely legible, but Pilgrim didn't need to read it to know where he was. In the doorway of number six Providence Row two figures grappled together in the throes of a tuppenny upright. The girl blew Pilgrim a kiss over the man's shoulder.

He stopped at a house almost at the end of the street. The door was peeling, hanging off its hinges, and creaked as he pushed it open …

'Is that you, Harry?'

'Shhh. Go back to sleep.'

He closed the door behind him, and undressed by the light of the fire dying in the grate. He shrugged off his swallowtail greatcoat and, after taking his truncheon and rattle from the pockets, hung it carefully on the back of the door. Piece by piece he removed the uniform he was so proud of – the heavy leather top hat, wellington boots, and the belt with its massive brass buckle – and placed them on the table. He unbuckled his shirt collar and removed the stiff leather stock. Finally, he stepped out of his trousers and folded them neatly onto a chair. Dressed only in his shift and stockings he went to the range, used a small bellows to fan the fire, and put a shovelful of coal onto it. Then he went to the alcove and pushed the curtain aside.

'Move over, woman.'

Bess gave a gasp that turned into a cough. 'Keep your feet off. Did I hear you bank the fire?'

'A few coals won't beggar us. It's like death in here. Look.' He exhaled into the air, watched his breath curl into the darkness.

'Hush. You'll wake him.'

He leaned up on his elbow to look at his son, sleeping on the other side of the bed.

'He's been easier today,' said Bess. 'The doctor thinks he'll improve when the weather warms up a bit.'

'It isn't the weather that's the problem, it's these bloody lodgings!'

'Don't curse, Harry.' Bess burrowed further under the blankets.

He stared up at the ceiling. 'Now I'm earning proper money we might be able to put something by. We'll have a house of our own. And a daily if you want one. Give me two years, Bess, and I'll get us out of here.'

When she didn't respond he turned his head to look at her. She had fallen asleep again.

'Two years,' he whispered to himself …

The table and chairs were gone, and dust lay thick on the floor and on the mantelpiece. The grate was empty. He went to the corner of the room, where a tattered curtain hung from the rail over the alcove. He pushed the curtain aside. The bed was still there, its mattress ripped and stained. He took a shuddering breath and closed his eyes.

Dolly's eyelids drooped.

'Dolly!' He jerked awake again to find Pilgrim glaring at him. 'Is she still in the house?'

'Yes, sir. I'm certain of it. I only rested my eyes for a moment.' He rubbed them. 'Two women have been to collect little ones. I think she must take them in for money.'

'If you've missed her …'

'I haven't, sir. My word on it.'

They continued to watch the terrace from the mouth of the alley. Some of the houses took on a deceptively cheery air as lamps were lit inside. People came and went along the street: two drunken women leading a goat, a pack of dogs, a man on crutches. One woman knocked on Mrs Johnston's door, and collected a child from her. The shadows thickened. A coal cart rumbled down the street, jolting some of its load onto the road as its wheels hit a rut. No sooner had the coals hit the dirt, when an old man scurried out of one of the houses, shirtless, to scoop them up. A second woman knocked on Mrs Johnston's door and took a toddler from her, the one that had been clinging to her skirt. Five minutes later, Dolly put his hand on Pilgrim's sleeve.

'Here she is.'

A woman emerged from the house. Before she pulled a shawl over her head they recognized Mrs Johnston.

They followed her through the terraces of Clerkenwell onto the bustling thoroughfare of Oxford Street, where wooden ramps supported two lines of moving vehicles. Crested carriages driven by liveried coachmen jostled with drays and coal carts. In Oxford Circus an omnibus horse had slipped, tipping the vehicle over and bringing traffic to a standstill. A crowd of pedestrians and passengers shouted encouragement and curses at the driver, who was trying to free the struggling animal from the traces. Mrs Johnston ignored the commotion and hurried on.

Some of the shops were still open, while others were in the process of closing – well-dressed shop assistants polishing door furniture and pushing up the awnings with poles. They passed an organ grinder with a monkey, and a costermonger holding up a spaniel for a lady to inspect. A poodle and a terrier gazed mournfully at them through the bars of their cage.

Mrs Johnston stopped suddenly to look in a shop window. Pilgrim and Dolly were forced to stop too, and turned towards each

77

other, as if in conversation. After a second or two Mrs Johnston hurried on.

Pilgrim glanced at the shop that had caught her interest; a toy shop, displaying brightly painted hobby horses, Noah's arks, and doll's houses. Any one of the toys would cost more than she earned in a year. Finally, Mrs Johnston turned off into a residential street, and Pilgrim realized they were reaching the end of their journey.

Upper Harley Street was very different from the terraces of Clerkenwell. Imposing detached houses were protected by high walls, and the pavements were illuminated by gas lamps that spilled pools of light onto the cobbles. There were very few pedestrians, which meant that Pilgrim and Dolly were obliged to put a greater distance between themselves and Mrs Johnston, so that their pursuit didn't become obvious. She hurried down a back lane. The detectives followed, then watched from the street corner as she opened a garden gate and slipped inside. They went to the gate.

Mrs Johnston stood at the kitchen door of a large, brightly-lit house, where a man in livery had come to speak to her. Pilgrim and Dolly couldn't hear what was said, but in the light spilling from the door they saw her face grow increasingly anxious. The servant finally shrugged his shoulders and closed the door, leaving the woman standing in the darkness.

Slowly, she returned to the gate.

Pilgrim stepped into her path. Her expression of fright turned to recognition, then defiance.

'What do you two want?'

'To buy you a drink, if you'll let us.'

The Jolly Fiddler was almost empty. Two ruffians scraped a tune from a fiddle and a squeezebox for the entertainment of a single customer and his lurcher. Dolly put a glass of gin on the table in front of Mrs Johnston, and glanced at Pilgrim who had already received his ale. The woman stayed stubbornly silent.

Pilgrim laid the spotted neckerchief on the table. She stared at it.

'How long had you been looking after him?' he asked.

Another long pause prompted Pilgrim to take something else from his pocket and push it towards her: Stella Drake's photograph.

'When did she bring him to you?' he asked.

'He's dead, isn't he?'

Pilgrim met her gaze. Her eyes moistened and she blinked. She sighed.

'She turned up on my doorstep two years ago, when he was just a babe in arms. Said she needed to work. I agreed to board him at a reduced rate, she looked so desperate.' She lapsed into silence.

Dolly opened his mouth to speak, but Pilgrim gave a faint shake of his head.

Mrs Johnston continued. 'Everything went smoothly at first. The money arrived every month, just as she'd promised. Then, about five weeks ago, it stopped. I made some enquiries and found out that she'd lost her place. I decided to bide my time a little longer. I heard she'd found another position, so I waited for her to contact me, or send some money.'

'But she didn't,' said Pilgrim.

'No.' Mrs Johnston picked up the neckerchief and ran it through her fingers. 'I dressed Louis in his best clothes and took him where I'd heard she was working, in Upper Harley Street. She wasn't pleased to see us. She begged me to take him for another week, but I refused and handed him over. Then she fretted about what he would eat. I told her he would eat anything. He was a good boy like that.'

'You left him there?'

Mrs Johnston's face crumpled and she thumped her fist onto the table. 'What would you have me do? She was his mother. I can't afford to feed an extra mouth for nothing.' The fire died in her eyes, just as suddenly as it had flared. She sighed. 'I admit, too, that I don't like being played for a fool.'

'When was that?'

'Last Tuesday.'

'And that was the last time you saw him?'

'I went back on the Friday to see how she was getting on. She told me he was staying with a friend. I believed her. Why wouldn't I? I asked her to kiss him for me, and she said she would.' She drained her glass. 'I did my best.'

'Has she left Harley Street?'

'Without notice, so that cocky footman says.' She handed the neckerchief back to Pilgrim. 'I have to get home. My Ruth's a good girl, but I don't like to leave her too long with the little ones.' She rose and left without looking again at the detectives.

Pilgrim gazed down at his beer, still brimming on the table.

Dolly drained his own tankard cheerfully. 'I suppose we should get off home now, sir.'

Pilgrim searched the constable's face. There was no sign he had been at all perturbed or moved by Mrs Johnston's story. Dolly had many qualities, but the ability to put himself in someone else's shoes wasn't one of them. It was probably just as well. Empathy wasn't necessarily an asset in their line of work.

'I need to take these back to the office,' he said, folding the neckerchief and putting it into his pocket with the vest.

'Would you like me to take them for you, sir?'

'No. Go back to the barracks. Get some sleep.'

CHAPTER THIRTEEN

Having guessed he was facing another sleepless night – one of what Queen Bess dubbed her 'white nights' – Dickens decided that his best plan of action was to expend as much energy as possible before he went to bed. He set off from Devonshire Terrace as soon as he had dined at eight o'clock, and was still walking two hours later.

He put his watch back in his pocket and looked up to see he was less than two hundred yards from Whitehall. He wondered whether any of the detectives were still at work.

'Evening Mr Dickens, sir.' The Duty Sergeant recognized him immediately.

'Good evening, Sergeant Phelps.'

'May I say, sir, how much I admired your latest edition of *Household Words*, sir? I am particularly enjoying the "True Story of a Coal Fire".'

'Thank you.' Dickens felt a familiar glow of pleasure. No matter how far his fame had spread – and some had dubbed him 'the most famous man in England' – he was always gratified by words of praise.

'I was wondering if any of the detectives are still upstairs?' he asked.

'Sergeant Tanner came in not above five minutes ago. Go straight on up, sir, if you'd care to speak with him.'

Dickens nodded his thanks and climbed the staircase.

The detectives' office was empty, but there were signs of life: an oil lamp lit in the corner of the room, and the window open to the night air. Dickens wandered over to it and looked out at Scotland Yard below.

Tanner came into the room, rubbing his face with a towel. He didn't see Dickens until he stepped into the light.

'Bloody hell!' Tanner jumped as if he'd been scalded.

'Sorry if I startled you, Sergeant.'

'Startled me? You damn near did me in!' He made a belated attempt to master his shock.

'You're working late,' said Dickens.

'Someone has to. What are you doing here?' He amended his tone. 'Is there something I can do for you, sir?'

'I was wondering if you had had any luck with the glove cleaners?'

'Not much.' Tanner finished drying his face and dropped the wet towel onto the sofa. 'I've worked my way through that list you wrote, or most of it. They all agree the gloves have been cleaned, but no one can tell me who did the job. I still have two left to visit, on Bond Street.'

'I have an appointment with my tailor on Albemarle Street tomorrow afternoon. That's just round the corner. I can take the gloves with me, if you like.'

Tanner shrugged. He opened his desk drawer and pulled out the gloves. Dickens heard something hit the floor. He picked it up and held it to the light.

'A pretty thing.'

It was an earring, made of black enamel with a symbol etched in gold, which glinted in the light from the oil lamp.

Tanner scowled. 'From the girl in the cab. It was in one of her ears. The other ear had been cut off.' He ignored the look of horror from Dickens. 'An octopus is a ruddy peculiar thing to put on a piece of jewellery. Still, there's no accounting for a woman's taste.'

Dickens peered more closely at the design. 'I don't think it is an octopus. I believe it is a hamsa, or the Hand of Miriam.'

'Eh?'

'A sign to ward off the evil eye.'

'Didn't do her much good, did it?'

Dickens gave him a level look. 'I'd say your victim was probably Jewish.'

'A yid, eh?' Tanner flushed. His embarrassment was making him careless with his choice of words. He looked again at the earring, but without any real interest. 'Makes no difference now, the case is closed.'

'Closed?' Dickens frowned. 'I don't understand.'

'Appler killed himself yesterday.' Tanner tossed the earring back into the drawer. 'And good riddance to him.'

'What about the girl?' said Dickens. 'We still don't know who she was.'

Tanner shrugged.

Dickens took the gloves from him. 'I'll let you know how I get on in Bond Street tomorrow. Good night, Sergeant.'

He tucked the gloves into his coat pocket on his way down the stairs. He was unsettled, irritated. Detective Sergeant Tanner certainly didn't improve on further acquaintance. He nodded to Phelps on his way past, and bumped shoulders with someone coming in through the double doors.

'I beg your pardon.' He peered more closely at the other man. 'Sergeant Pilgrim!'

If the detective was surprised to see him he didn't show it. His expression was as impassive as ever.

'I have just been discussing the Grimwood case with Sergeant Tanner,' said Dickens. 'We touched on the Appler case too. Would you care to walk with me a while?'

Pilgrim hesitated, then nodded.

They fell into step together on the pavement. In spite of the hour the street was still bustling with people on foot and in carriages, returning home from their evening entertainment.

'Isn't it a little late to be promenading?' asked Pilgrim.

'I often take a stroll through the city at this time of night. Set me down on Waterloo Bridge at ten o'clock in the evening and there is no happier man on earth.' He paused. 'I heard about Johannes Appler.'

'Your "Hackney Cab Killer"? Yes. It's a pity.'

'A fait accompli if ever there was one. And yet,' Dickens was obliged to dodge around a chestnut seller before continuing, 'I believe there is more to the case than meets the eye.'

'Your article in the *Chronicle* didn't present it that way,' said Pilgrim. 'You were judge and jury, as far as I could see.'

Dickens glanced at him. 'In my defence, my readers appreciate a firm view on a subject.'

'And your editor too, I imagine.'

'Quite so.' Dickens nodded. 'Did you know I went to visit Mr Appler after his arrest? My intention was to sketch his character. It takes a most singular kind of person to kill another human being, not to mention dismembering one in such a fashion. Appler protested his innocence. Most convincingly, I have to say, and I flatter myself that I'm usually a fair judge of such things.'

Pilgrim said nothing. They walked on.

After a minute or two, Dickens spoke again. 'If Appler was innocent, then the note I received and passed on to you, the "tip-off" I think you call it, was a false trail, laid by someone with a vested interest. Perhaps even the real murderer. There was something about that note … do you still have it?'

'It's in my office.'

'You might consider sending it to a graphologist. I can recommend …'

Pilgrim halted, forcing Dickens to stop beside him.

'A man is dead.' Pilgrim's tone was cold. 'His throat is cut. We cannot mend it. And, with respect, you should leave police work to those better qualified to do it.'

Dickens looked into the other man's eyes, and after a moment, nodded. 'Inspector Field's opinion exactly. Of course, he has never actually said as much, but I am aware he has been instructed to indulge me.' Dickens paused. 'Have you taken any supper yet, Sergeant? The Lyceum Theatre is just across the way. We can enjoy a pie and a shilling's worth of entertainment, and I can highly recommend the restorative qualities of its punch.'

'I don't drink.'

'Nor do I. Not to excess. But bear me company, I beg you. I'm in a sociable mood.'

Pilgrim surrendered, and allowed Dickens to bear him off in the direction of the theatre.

'I've seen some passably good comic singers here, and the Mexican Boneless Wonder, an unremarkable-looking little man who performed the most unlikely contortions. It's just what you need to distract your thoughts from a day's sleuthing.'

The supper room of the Lyceum was crowded with a different class of audience than was generally found in the main theatre. That didn't concern Dickens at all. He was always on the lookout for stories and faces, and was happy to find them wherever he could. They found a place at a table at the side of the stage, and whispered their order to a waitress so as not to distract the female singer who was in the middle of her performance.

When the song was finished they applauded.

'Excellent,' said Dickens. 'Almost as good as Jenny Lind. I saw Miss Lind last year, you know, during my tour of America.'

Dickens couldn't tell whether Pilgrim was impressed or not; the Detective Sergeant's expression never changed. Pilgrim was a man not prone to smiles or laughter but, thought Dickens, he was by no means melancholic. The solemnity of his face was due rather to the concentration of his intellect on the problems that continually presented themselves for solution in his line of work. It gave him an unstudied air of superiority, of perfect confidence in his own abilities. Very useful for a detective.

A plump baritone took the stage, and, after a certain amount of throat clearing and shuffling, nodded to the pianist and began.

Dickens recognized the song with a jolt of pleasure, although he couldn't remember the author. It had been inspired by one of his characters. The lyrics were moving in the extreme.

What are the wild waves saying,
Sister, the whole day long,
That ever amid our playing
I hear but their low, lone song.
What are the wild waves saying?

Yes! but there's something greater
That speaks to the heart alone:
'Tis the voice of the great Creator
Dwells in the mighty tone.
What are the wild waves saying?

When the song was finished and the applause had died away, Dickens leaned towards Pilgrim, and spoke over the chatter of the crowd.

'Are you familiar with my "Dombey", Sergeant?'

'Dombey?'

'My novel, *Dombey and Son*?'

'I don't have much time for reading.'

'That song was inspired by one of my characters, little Paul Dombey. Only six years old, and the apple of his father's eye. His death scene still has the power to move me to tears.'

Pilgrim said nothing.

Dickens was prevented from any further elaboration on Dombey by the arrival of their mutton and kidney puddings. A savoury steam rose from the plates, encouraging consumption, rather than conversation for several minutes.

'How is the Grimwood investigation going?' asked Pilgrim at last, around a mouthful of pastry.

'Slowly, I'm afraid. Extremely slowly. It is the nature of the lady's profession, I fear, that makes it difficult to find reliable witnesses.'

Pilgrim nodded.

'It's a pity so many women have to resort to it.' Dickens leaned forward, glad of the opportunity to pursue one of his favourite topics. 'Have you heard about Urania Cottage, my refuge for fallen women in Shepherd's Bush?'

'No.'

'It is a cherished project of mine; a place where these poor women have a chance to rise out of their sad lives and regain their sense of worth.'

The detective put down his fork. 'Charity has its place. But women shouldn't have to bow and scrape to put food in their mouths.'

'Is that less preferable than doing it on their backs?' Dickens frowned. 'I don't believe our demands are unreasonable, above asking the girls to show a willingness to behave well, and to change their ways. Our aim, ultimately, is to help them emigrate.'

'A harsh condition.'

Dickens lifted his eyebrows. 'Not at all. They see it as a blessing, an opportunity to make a fresh start in a new world.'

'Are you sure of that?' Pilgrim's expression was still neutral. 'Even prostitutes have families and friends. And what happens if they change their minds?'

'Then they simply go back to their old life. No one forces them to do anything they do not wish to.'

'You send them on their way with a purse? New clothes? References?'

Dickens swallowed a piece of gristle, and said nothing.

CHAPTER FOURTEEN

'Rise and shine, sir.'

Dolly prodded Pilgrim until he opened his eyes. 'I saw you hadn't come back to the barracks so I've brought you a bite of breakfast.' Dolly pointed to a greasy package on Pilgrim's desk. He swung his legs off the sofa and rubbed his face. Dolly frowned at him. 'I never thought to bring you a razor, though,' he said.

'What time is it?'

'Five thirty.'

Pilgrim opened the package on his desk. He took a bite of the pie, and put it down again with a grunt of disgust. It dripped gravy onto the pile of letters.

'Enjoy a glass or two last night, did you, sir?'

Pilgrim shook his head. 'I was with Mr Dickens. I've never known a man sit so long over one glass of punch. Or talk so much about nothing in particular. We stayed so late I thought it was easier just to come here, rather than go back to Holborn.' He brushed out his crumpled clothes. 'What are you doing up so early?'

'I thought I'd write down what Mrs Johnston told us last night, while it was fresh in my mind.'

'Good idea.' Pilgrim shrugged on his overcoat.

'Are you off somewhere, sir?'

'I'm going back to Upper Harley Street, to talk to the servants about Stella Drake.'

'Are you going directly there?' Dolly peered anxiously at Pilgrim's stubble.

Pilgrim grinned. 'Don't worry, I'll drop into the barracks on the way and have a shave.'

'Sir … !' He had almost reached the door, when Dolly called him back.

'Yes?'

'I was wondering … whether you'd had the chance to call on cousin Charlotte yet?'

'Cousin Charlotte?' Pilgrim knew perfectly well who he was talking about, but was playing for time.

'Mrs Piper. With the rooms. At Holborn?'

'Yes. I decided not to take them. They were too expensive.'

'Oh.' Dolly looked crestfallen.

'And there was a bad smell on the landing.'

'A bad smell? But I thought … ?' Dolly caught the look in Pilgrim's eye and he pursed his lips. 'I see.'

No, thought Pilgrim, I seriously doubt that you do.

Pilgrim tried to look in mirrors as little as possible, but it was something he could hardly avoid while shaving. He lathered the coal tar soap in the dish, using hot water from the ewer, luxuriating in the fact that the barracks was unusually, blessedly, silent. He hadn't often been in the dormitory at that time of the morning, in the curtained alcove he called home. He applied the lather with the badger brush, enjoying the feel of it on his cheeks and chin, and slid the razor from its case. He had to take more care shaving than most men, because of his scars. The cratered skin caught the blade in unpredictable ways, making it very easy to cut himself. He tried to concentrate, but found his attention wandering. The sight of the blade pressing into his throat inevitably made him think of Appler's death. What had been going through the Dutchman's mind in those last desperate moments?

He rinsed the blade thoughtfully. Appler's killer had somehow got into the locked cell, and out again. He must have taken the keys from under Phelps' desk. Pilgrim frowned. Why hadn't Appler called out? Surely, if he had seen the man who had asked him to move the packages, he would have had time to alert his gaolers. Pilgrim lifted the blade to his chin again, and paused, leaving it in mid-air. There was something else nagging him, in the back of his memory. Something that didn't quite fit, but that remained stubbornly out of reach. Was it something he'd heard? Something he'd seen? He shrugged. He knew from experience that it wouldn't come if he tried to force it. It would occur to him eventually, but in the meantime, he had to make himself respectable to visit Upper Harley Street. He finished with the razor and rinsed his face, then dried it with the towel.

He hoped that the servants at the big house would be able to tell him something useful about Stella Drake. It was astonishing how the phrase 'detective police' would loosen the tongues of innocent people. Of course, it usually had the opposite effect on anyone with something to hide. Well, he would see.

The household in Upper Harley Street was up and about its usual business when the footman opened the door to him.

'The master and mistress are out,' he said, when he had read Pilgrim's card. 'I don't know when they'll be back.' It was the same footman who had spoken to Mrs Johnston at the back door the night before. 'Cocky' she'd called him, and Pilgrim reckoned she was right.

'I'll wait,' said Pilgrim.

The young man looked him up and down with the air of a horse trader considering a purchase.

'As long as you ain't after doin' it in the parlour,' he said, lapsing into his natural diction.

'The kitchen will do.' Pilgrim wasn't in the least bothered. He could never tell how he was going to be received in people's homes, being neither trade nor gentry, and was happy to take whatever came. He followed the footman to the kitchen and took a seat at the table, where the young man was in the middle of polishing silver. The footman put on his apron again and applied himself to a candlestick.

'There you go, sir.' A kitchen maid thrust a mug of tea at Pilgrim and returned to her place beside the cook. The cook muttered something to the maid, and darted him a resentful glance. He ignored it and turned his attention back to the footman.

'I'm looking for Stella Drake,' he said.

'Oh?' The youth gave him a sideways look.

'She used to have a position here.'

'If you say so.'

'When did you last see her?'

'I don't rightly remember.'

Pilgrim gave him a cool look.

The footman reconsidered his strategy. 'Friday night,' he said. 'She banked the upstairs fires, as usual, and then went up to her room as I locked up. On Saturday morning she was gone.'

'She had a room of her own?'

'As housekeeper she was entitled.'

'Housekeeper? That's a responsible position for a girl her age.'

The footman snorted. 'She was twenty goin' on two hundred, that one. The mistress took to her, on account of her bein' so well spoke.'

'Before she disappeared, did you notice anything out of the ordinary? Did she have any visitors?'

'The lad, you mean?' He grinned at Pilgrim's expression, and rubbed hard at the candlestick. 'Oh yes, I saw him. We all did. A woman turned up out of the blue and dumped him on her. That set some tongues wagging.' He sent the cook a poisonous glare. 'Old besom,' he muttered.

The cook flounced into the pantry and slammed the door.

'What happened to the boy?' asked Pilgrim.

'Drake took him somewhere. Must have been somewhere close, 'cause she was back in half an hour, actin' like it had never happened.'

'Is it possible she took him upstairs?'

'Smuggled him in, you mean?' The other man considered the question. ''Suppose it's possible.'

'Can I see her room?'

The footman glanced at the pantry door. 'As long as the Guv'nor don't get to know.'

The room Stella Drake had occupied was in the attic. It was furnished with a bedstead, a chest of drawers, and a washstand with a ewer and basin. A knotted rag rug was the only nod to comfort. Pilgrim knelt to inspect the floorboards, but they had been swept clean, even under the bed.

'What are you looking for, exactly?' asked the footman. 'She took everything with her.'

Pilgrim got to his feet, still looking at the floor. His eyes were caught by two deep scuff marks, about three feet apart.

'What about her trunk?' he asked.

The footman looked at him. 'Don't know what you mean.'

'A big one. About,' he measured the width between the two scuff marks with his hands, and then held them up, 'so wide. Too heavy for her to carry herself.'

The footman shrugged.

'No matter,' said Pilgrim. 'I'll call back later and ask your master about it. I imagine he'll be home for dinner?'

The footman bit his lip. 'I'd rather not bother him.'

'I need to know what happened to the trunk. If you can't tell me … '

'I took it to the station for her. She must have packed everything in there. God knows it was heavy enough.' He fidgeted with his apron. 'Don't tell the Guv'nor. If he found out I'd known she was going to do a runner … '

'Which station?'

'Euston Square. I left it with the stationmaster, like she asked me to.'

'You often did her favours?'

'We were … friendly, like. A couple of times a week.'

'Where did you send the trunk?'

'By the time I got the ruddy thing down the stairs and into a cab I wasn't fit to notice the label. I do remember how much it cost, though: three shillings and sixpence she paid me for it after.' He flushed. 'Why are you asking so many ruddy questions, anyway? What's Drake done?'

Pilgrim said nothing, but watched the play of emotions on the other man's face as belligerence melted into confusion, and was replaced a second or two later by horror.

'Christ Almighty.' The footman sat heavily on the bed. 'We did it right here, with that ruddy trunk not three foot away.' He jumped up again, away from the bed, and shuddered.

'You really have no idea where she is now?' asked Pilgrim.

'She didn't say, and I didn't ask. I imagine there's a bloke involved, or she's gone to family somewhere. Otherwise … '

'Otherwise?'

'She has no references. A girl like that there's only one way she's goin' to earn a living, ain't there?'

CHAPTER FIFTEEN

The beast market at Smithfield was one of the oldest in London, with a tradition of selling and slaughtering animals stretching back to the twelfth century. On market days it was a sight to behold, the pens in the five acre field crammed with every type of domestic animal, a heaving sea of wool, hide, horns, and feathers. The noise was unimaginable – grunting, bleating, and stricken squealing – as animals were slaughtered to satisfy the demands of the customers. Above it all, the traders could be heard, competing for the attention of the managers of the pie shops, chophouses, prisons, workhouses, and the great households of the city:

'Buy, buy, buy, buy, bu-u-uy!'

Pilgrim was deaf to it all. He wasn't there to buy. He stepped over a gutter puddled with piss and blood, thankful yet again that he had no sense of smell. The market wasn't quite as busy as it had been. Already sitting low in the sky, the sun was falling lower still, and a few of the traders had begun to herd what was left of their livestock away from their pens through the streets. A small boy, grasping three or four onions in his hands, crept among the crowd, wriggling through gaps, asking for custom in whining tones.

'Scallions, Mister? Fresh scallions.'

Pilgrim shook his head, weary to the marrow of his bones. He had spent the whole afternoon visiting the taverns and alehouses in the streets around the market – the aptly-named Cow Cross Street, Pheasant Court, Goose Alley, and Cock Lane – showing customers his photograph of Stella Drake. Smithfield was a flesh market in more ways than one. On market days prostitutes would flock from all over the city to satisfy the appetites of the butchers, porters, and wholesalers. He'd shown the photograph to women of all sizes, shapes, and colours, thinking that one of them might recognize Stella Drake.

There was a lot of sense in what the footman at Harley Street had said. Stella had no references, little money, and nowhere to call home. It was unlikely she'd be able to find respectable work. Even though Pilgrim had spent hours looking for her, it was too early to judge if that assumption was wrong, for the city was huge, and a woman could easily disappear into it if she had a mind to. As he knew all too well.

His belly grumbled, reminding him that he had eaten nothing since his single bite of pie at breakfast. He made for the food stalls set up on the edge of the market, and stopped to examine the wares: pigs' trotters set in jelly, fried fish, blood puddings, oatmeal puddings in bladders, and the ubiquitous pies that he could guess consisted only of lard shoved into a crust, sent to the oven and 'done brown.'

He decided he wasn't hungry after all.

'Pork pie, Mister? I can do one cheap.' The boy behind the stall looked at him with the desperation of one who knew he was running out of time to clear his stock. Pilgrim shook his head. The boy hawked and spat, narrowly missing Pilgrim's boot.

Looking up, Pilgrim recognized the medieval crenellations of St John's Gate that marked the boundary between the market and Clerkenwell, and headed towards it. He ducked into the doorway of Gay's Tavern, set in the shadow of the arched gateway. He needed a little time to rest, and to decide what to do next.

The cramped interior of the tavern was smoky, with little light penetrating the leaded windows. It was noisy too, crowded with men with bloodstains on their sleeves and women with harsh voices and cheap clothes. From their raucous laughter it was obvious they had already had a fair amount to drink.

He elbowed his way to the bar.

'Afternoon, my lovely, what can I get you?' The barmaid, a flat-chested woman with yellow hair, grinned at him, revealing a surprisingly good set of teeth.

'Just ale.'

'We have faggots, fresh made today?'

Pilgrim eyed a passing plate. He liked faggots, as a rule, but the greasy objects on the plate didn't look like any he'd seen before. 'Just ale.'

The barmaid shrugged. 'Suit yerself.'

She plonked a tankard in front of him with an injured air.

He stared into it, with no intention of drinking. He needed to think. If he put himself in Stella Drake's shoes, where might he go? The obvious place was a doss house. But there were hundreds of doss houses in Clerkenwell and Whitechapel alone, and they didn't allow anyone in until eleven o'clock. He slipped the photograph of Stella Drake into his pocket beside Wainwright's sketch of Martha Drewitt. Guilt prodded him: he could have shown Martha's picture to the women at the same time as he had showed them Stella's, but he had promised Charley he wouldn't get involved. More to the point, he had promised himself he wouldn't.

He scanned the taproom over the rim of his tankard. He recognized Happy Billy Brandon, the bookies' runner, moving from table to table with his leather pouch. Happy Billy had a scar that ran from the top of his skull to his chin, a souvenir from a tanner's hook, which had torn away one of his eyes and a goodly portion of his upper lip. The result was his perpetual and hideous grin. Pilgrim knew he should arrest him – it was illegal to make a wager anywhere except a racecourse – but he didn't see the point. There would always be another runner to take Billy's place. As far as Pilgrim was aware there was no horse racing that day, but that didn't signify. If the gentry weren't racing horses, they were setting their animals to fight each other, whether it was dogs, fowl, or footmen.

'Sixpence on the Gypsy to win.' A fat woman brandished a coin at Billy. He bit it, and then pushed it into his already bulging pouch.

A fist fight, then. And a big one, by the look of it.

His thoughts were broken by a crash. One of the men behind him had tipped his stool over by accident. Pilgrim turned to watch, as, with much laughing and jeering, the man's friends helped him off the floor. Then his eye was caught by a bright gleam of russet, and he saw a woman going out of the door. She was tall, supple backed, with a green gown and fox-coloured hair pinned on top of her head. Blood pounded in his ears.

He shoved his way through the bar, but by the time he made it out onto the street the woman had vanished. He cast around, desperate. The narrow thoroughfare was still thronged with people: she could have gone in any direction. He jumped onto a nearby bollard to get a better view. There! The russet head was less than forty yards away, making for the market. He leapt down and followed it, dodging through the crowd.

'Watch it!' shouted a butcher carrying a pig's carcase dripping with blood.

Pilgrim dodged around him without apology, skidding on the gore. 'Arsehole!' He pushed through the crowd, but by the time he reached the market proper he had lost sight of the woman again. He cast around, saw a cart of cabbage stalks and jumped up onto it. From his new vantage point he could see almost to the far end of the square. This time he saw the slender figure clearly, turning down an alley less than twenty yards away. He jumped off the cart, scattering greenery, and ran after her. She had only gone a few yards down it when he caught up with her.

'Bess!' He clutched her arm and spun her around. Disappointment slammed into him. 'I beg your pardon,' he said. 'I thought you were someone else.'

The woman was a similar build, with the same hair colour, but that was where the resemblance ended. Bess was fine boned, but the woman in front of him was thicker featured, with brown eyes rather than blue. She smiled and his heart lurched. He turned away.

'Don't go, darlin',' the woman caught at his sleeve. 'I can see you're hurtin'. I can be your Bess, if you'd like me to be.' Her voice was low-pitched. Not dissimilar. Pilgrim turned back to face her. She gave a knowing smile, took his hand and placed it on her breast.

'There now, ain't that nice?'

Need sluiced through him, washing away his natural reserve, common sense, and even thought. He clutched her to him as a drowning man might clutch at a raft, and groaned. He buried his fingers in her hair, shaking it loose, scattering pins, his lips seeking hers.

'Steady on, darlin'. She laughed, low and throaty, surprised by his ardour. 'There's no need to be in such a hurry. I have a nice little place just around the corner, where we can take our time.'

CHAPTER SIXTEEN

Dickens emerged, frowning, from the establishment of Messrs Bolt and Son in Blenheim Street. He was discovering the life of a detective to be decidedly unglamorous, consisting more of the wearing out of shoe leather than anything else. His tailor had given him the names of two more glove cleaners in the area, in addition to the names Tanner had given him in Bond Street. He was now down to the final one, having discovered nothing but disappointment at the others. He looked at the second name his tailor had written on the receipt. Thankfully it was no more than a five minute walk away.

In the front parlour of G. Witton and Sons, a respectable looking house on Gilbert Street, he found an old man in a white apron. There were no sons in evidence, but plenty of daughters, all rubbing away at dozens upon dozens of pairs of gloves. It was a strange sight, and one that Dickens found oddly disconcerting. One pair of gloves, so unremarkable in the singular, seemed absurd and even sinister when encountered in such numbers. Dickens took Eliza Grimwood's gloves from his pocket.

'I'm sorry to disturb you,' he said, 'but I was wondering if you could tell me who is responsible for cleaning this pair of gloves?'

'Is there a problem with them?' asked the old man.

'Good heavens, no,' said Dickens, hurrying to disabuse him of the notion. 'It's a strange story. I was dining over at Lambeth the other day, at a chophouse with some friends, when a gentleman left these behind. One of my friends laid a wager of a sovereign that I wouldn't be able to find out who they belonged to. I've spent seven shillings already, trying to discover, but if you could help me I'd gladly give you another seven. Look, there's an "R" and a "T" inside.'

The old man took the gloves and squinted at the initials. 'I should say I should know 'em, seeing as it was me what cleaned 'em. Or one of my girls, at any rate. They belong to Mr Trinkle, the upholsterer in Cheapside.'

Elation surged through Dickens. 'Could you give me the address?'

It took a moment or two for the old man to find a pen and paper and to write his directions down. Dickens thanked him and put his hat back on. 'Beg pardon for mentioning it, sir,' said the glove cleaner, 'but you said something about remuneration?'

'Indeed I did.' He counted out the promised seven shillings, exchanged them for the address, and left the old man in Gilbert Street surrounded by a knot of girls, all clamouring for ribbons and confectionery.

He paused on the pavement outside, wondering what to do next. It was probably unwise to beard Trinkle, a possible murderer, in his den, so the best thing to do would be to go to Whitehall, to inform Sergeant Tanner of his discovery. He had intended to call at Urania Cottage to see how Mrs Wallace's preparations for the Lord Mayor's Gala were progressing, but the banners of Justice had to be flown, and, at that particular moment, there was no one but him to fly them.

CHAPTER SEVENTEEN

The sky was washed with broad bands of purple and pink, the bellies of the clouds limned with gold. Staring at it through the grimy glass, Pilgrim saw its beauty and felt soiled, desperate, and damned. He thought of the Reverend Bonwell, so sure of his own goodness, so sure of salvation, and, for a moment, envied the man his certainty. But only for a moment. Whatever redemption Bonwell had earned through public piety he had surely forfeited in private, if the bruises on his wife were anything to go by. Pilgrim pushed himself up on the grubby sheet, and reached for his shirt.

The woman – he still didn't know her name – was almost fully dressed again, and was fastening her garters, her hair hanging down her back. Her hair was her best feature: thick and wavy, with highlights of burnished copper. She went to the mirror that hung over the mantel next to a print of the Virgin and Child, and pinned up her hair. She caught his eye in the glass and smiled at him. He just stared back. He had no words. He stood up, tucked in his shirttails, and looked around for his jacket that was hanging on the back of a chair.

'That's a shillin', darlin'.' She turned from the mirror. 'And cheap at twice the price.'

He reached into his pocket for his pocketbook. As he pulled it out, something else fell onto the floor. The woman reached for it.

'This your Bess, is it? Pity you, if it is. She's got more front than Brighton, this one. Nabbed a cully off me last week.'

To his surprise he saw that it wasn't Stella Drake's photograph she was looking at, but Wainwright's sketch of Martha Drewitt.

'Are you sure it was her?'

'Sure as you're standin' here.'

'Where? Where did you see her?'

'She took him to rooms in Drover's Yard. Sported her diddies right there in the street. What chance did I have after that?'

He pushed the coins into her hand, and strode from the room.

'The name's Clara, since you ask.' The woman called after him, her smile still in place, but her tone bitter. 'Be sure to tell your friends about me.'

Drover's Yard in Paternoster Row, Spitalfields, had once been the site of a coaching inn. The inn had long since gone, taken over by landlords with an eye for packing as many families as possible into the looming tenements. The courtyard where wagons and horses had once jostled for space was now thick with mud and rubbish, the buildings strung with soot-speckled washing. Even before Pilgrim entered the yard he could hear voices raised in excitement. He pushed his way through the crowd that had gathered around one of the doorways. The passageway beyond was narrow, crammed with people. A fat man dressed only in an undervest and trousers was standing, arms braced, blocking the door to one of the rooms. A woman tried in vain to dislodge him.

'Let us past, you old sot.'

'The gennleman paid me a month in advance.'

'I don't care if he paid a king's ransom, we won't put up with it a minute longer.'

Many of the other people standing in the passage way had their hands over their noses. They muttered and cursed their mood ugly.

The woman nodded to a big man wearing a leather apron. 'Smash it, Jem. And smash his bleedin' head if you have to.'

'What's going on?' demanded Pilgrim, elbowing his way to the front.

'What's it to you?' asked the woman.

'Metropolitan Police.'

The crowd muttered. The woman eyed his clothes. Quite a few of the people at the back of the crush melted away into the shadows.

Pilgrim turned to the man in the doorway. 'Who are you?'

The man blinked at him over red-veined cheeks.

'He's the landlord,' said the woman. 'There's something in that room stinkin' worse than a gully hole, but this old fool won't let us in. It ain't sanitary.'

'Do you have a key?' Pilgrim addressed the landlord again, but the man didn't seem capable of processing the question, let alone providing an answer. Pilgrim pulled him out of the way, and nodded at the meaty man in the apron. The man lifted a boot and kicked in the door, filling the air with the sound of splintering wood. The room beyond was dark. As the crash died away, the people at the front of the crowd took a step back, clutching their noses with horrified expressions. The mouth of the doorway gaped black.

'I need light,' said Pilgrim.

'Jest a minute.' The meaty man crashed away, and, after a few seconds, crashed back again with a tinderbox and a candle. The woman lit the candle and thrust it into Pilgrim's hand. He advanced into the room, while the others hung back in the doorway.

At first it was difficult to see anything, but, gradually, his eyes adjusted.

'Mother of God!' The woman crossed herself.

Behind her the landlord craned his neck to see. 'What is it?'

Candlelight washed over the body of a woman lying on the bed. She was naked, her hands carefully folded over her chest, eyes wide and staring. There was a clotted cavity where her abdomen had been, and blood had soaked through the mattress to pool onto the floor, where it had congealed, black as treacle.

The landlord vomited.

CHAPTER EIGHTEEN

'Give him a night in the cells. We'll see if he can tell us anything when he's sober.'

'As you say, Sergeant Pilgrim, sir.' Sergeant Phelps eyed the fat landlord stoically. 'As long as he don't mind gettin' cosy with other prisoners. We're havin' a busy night tonight.'

'I hear you've found another dead drab,' said Tanner as Pilgrim entered the office. 'Is it mine? Was the throat cut?'

'No.'

'Where is it now?'

'"It" is at St Bartholomew's.'

Tanner ignored Pilgrim's irony and pushed roughly past him, out of the door.

Charley Field shrugged. 'He brought in a suspect tonight, for the Grimwood case. I've a notion he's barking up the wrong tree, though, and I think he knows it too. Who's your victim?'

'Martha Drewitt.' Pilgrim ran a hand through his hair. 'She was a friend of Frances.' He paused. 'At least, I think it is. She's been dead for a while.'

'You said you weren't going to get involved.'

'I didn't intend to.'

Field turned to Dolly. 'Be a good boy, Adolphus, and fetch the Sergeant a cup of tea, would you?'

'Of course, sir. Right away, sir.' Dolly hurried out.

'Do you have a suspect?' Field asked Pilgrim.

'A man paid the landlord for the room in advance. But we have no description. And I doubt we'll get one.'

'And what about our child killer? Any progress with that?'

'We're looking for the boy's mother. It's just a matter of time.'

'The newspapers haven't got wind of it yet. You notice I say "yet". I'd like to have someone in custody by the time anyone starts asking questions.' Field paused. 'And, speaking of questions … are you ready for tomorrow night?' He saw Pilgrim's blank look. 'The Royal Academy Gala?'

Pilgrim set his lips into a stubborn line.

Field narrowed his eyes and he stepped closer. 'I will see you there, Harry. Everyone wants to meet the famous Sergeant Pilchem.' He fingered Pilgrim's ragged jacket. 'And do try to brush up a bit, eh?'

When Field had gone, Pilgrim sat heavily at his desk. He reached into his pocket and took out a locket that he had found on the body at Drover's Yard. Apart from the long dark hair there had been nothing else to identify the body. He knew he was going to have to show the locket to Frances, but there was no hurry: it would wait until the morning.

'Here you go, sir, the cup that cheers.' Dolly reappeared, bearing a brimming teacup. 'That body you found was a ripe one, I hear. Where do you want this?'

Pilgrim cleared a space on the desk. As he pushed the pile of unopened mail to one side, something caught his eye, something he hadn't noticed before. He picked up a small package, addressed to 'Sergeant Pilgrim, Whitehall'. Two things attracted his attention: the first was the fact that it was addressed to him using his proper name, not his alias at *Household Words*, the second was the use of red ink. He opened a drawer in his desk and rummaged in it until he found what he was looking for: a buff envelope, also written in red ink, addressed to 'Mr Charles Dickens' at *Household Words*:

the tip-off note he had received about Appler. The red ink and the handwriting were identical to the unopened package in his hand. He frowned, and opened it.

It contained a small parcel, neatly wrapped in canvas and secured with string. There was a note, too.

Dear Sergeant Pilchem, or can I call you Harry?
For I feel I know you. We have a lot in common, you see. We
both love our work, ha, ha. By now I'm sure you'll have
found my bit of business at Drover's Yard. I know you
appreciate all the trouble I've taken to keep you and your
boys busy, so I thought I'd send you a little souvenir, just for
jolly. Hope you like it. Must get on – you know what they
say, practice makes perfect.

It wasn't signed. Pilgrim looked at the neat little parcel.

'Don't let your tea go cold.' Dolly nodded at the still-brimming cup.

'No.' There was a tight sensation behind his eyes.

'What have you got there, sir? A present from an admirer?' Dolly came over to stand beside Pilgrim's desk, and ogle the parcel. 'Aren't you going to open it?'

Pilgrim picked up his teacup. 'You're right. This is cold. Get me a fresh one.'

'But I only made it two minutes ago.'

'It's cold.' He thrust the cup at him. He scowled and bore it away. Pilgrim waited until his footsteps had faded down the corridor, and then took out his pocket knife to cut the string from the parcel. The canvas unfurled. Taken out of its usual context, the object inside was as pale and innocent as a seashell, holed and worn smooth by the waves. It was pierced by an earring – a black enamelled drop, etched with a symbol in gold.

*

The five men gathered in Charley Field's office waited in silence for the Inspector to speak. He clasped his hands behind his back and puffed out his chest.

'Last night, as you all know, we had several significant developments.' He raised an index finger. 'One, another female victim, discovered by Sergeant Pilgrim, at Drover's Yard. Two,' he lifted a second finger, 'a possible suspect for the Grimwood case – a Mr Trinkle, upholsterer of Cheapside, arrested by Sergeant Tanner with the assistance of Mr Dickens.' He nodded at the writer to acknowledge the part he had played, and then raised a third finger. 'And, last, a note and a pretty "souvenir" from our Hackney Cab Killer. We know it's him, because the earring is a companion to the one we found with the decapitated head. We've all been investigating our own cases, but the question we now have to ask ourselves is this: are some of these cases linked? Could we be looking at the same killer for the Hackney Cab victim, Eliza Grimwood, and the girl at Drover's Yard?' He paused for dramatic effect. 'Three murders, one murderer? Tanner, what do you think?'

Tanner flinched. 'I wouldn't like to say, sir. Some of the murders are similar, to be sure … but they're different too.'

Everyone waited, expecting more. Tanner clamped his lips shut again.

Field blinked. 'Thank you for that most … penetrating observation.'

Tanner flushed scarlet.

'He's right,' said Pilgrim. 'The Countess had her throat cut. We haven't had the post-mortem report yet on Martha Drewitt, but there was no incision on her neck. There was a bruise on the back of her head that looked as if she'd taken a blow.' He took a breath, unused to speechifying. 'The fact that the body in the Hackney Cab was cut into pieces made it difficult to pinpoint the exact cause of death, but Hector Fairweather thinks she was likely smothered. Which means we have three different murder methods?'

Dolly cut in. 'If it wasn't for the note there would be no reason to think that any of them were linked.'

Field wouldn't meet Pilgrim's eye. What neither he nor Pilgrim could say, was that Appler's murder made a possible connection between Grimwood and the Hackney murder – both killers were handy with a razor. Field had forbidden Pilgrim to say anything about it, for he wanted to keep the news that the Dutchman was murdered under wraps until after the Royal Academy Gala.

Field rubbed his nose. 'We can assume from the post-mortem on the Hackney Cab victim that she was killed first. But we don't know which of the others came next. Dolly, I want you to go to see Hector Fairweather as soon as we've finished here. He'll be doing the autopsy on Martha Drewitt some time today. Ask him to make time of death a priority, if you please.' He spun on his heel. 'It's also possible that there are still victims we know nothing about. Wainwright ... did you do as I asked and find out what else we've had lately in the way of cadavers?'

Wainwright flushed and read out from a piece of paper. 'Two self-murders, both male, one drowned, one hanged. Two fatalities from domestic incidents, both females. One male, found beaten to death in the Vauxhall Gardens. One foetus, discovered in a privy. A sailor what died from his injuries after a fight. And a foot, sir.'

'A foot?'

'A woman's foot. Found in the river by Hungerford Stairs.'

'That's another possible victim, I suppose.' Field furrowed his brow. 'Unless one of our Hackney victim's feet wasn't accounted for?'

'No, sir,' said Dolly. 'They were both there.'

Charles Dickens sat forward in his chair. 'Something puzzles me, Chief Inspector. Why are we even considering that the Hackney Cab murder is connected? I thought Appler was the guilty party there.'

Field gave him a quelling look. 'Because Appler is dead, there is no way of knowing that for certain. He can hardly confess to it now, can he? That being so, I believe we should keep an open mind.'

Dolly raised his hand, like a schoolboy at lessons. 'If Appler wasn't guilty, sir, why did the real murderer set him up? He could have disposed of the woman's body himself. Or simply left it to be found, like the other two. Why didn't he do that?'

'Perhaps the killer knew the first victim?' suggested Pilgrim. 'The Countess and the woman I found last night were prostitutes. But, according to Mr Dickens, the first victim was a Jewess. Not a race known for promiscuity.'

'If you ask me,' burst out Wainwright, 'there's more bleedin' questions than what there are answers!'

'Couldn't have put it better myself,' muttered Field. 'I think for the time being we should work on the hypothesis that all three women – our Jewess, The Countess, and the woman in Drover's Yard – have been killed by the same man. Tell me more about your Mr Trinkle, Tanner.'

'There's nothing to link him to any of the victims, other than the gloves under Grimwood's pillow. But I have hopes, sir, high hopes.'

'Interview him this morning.' Field turned to Pilgrim. 'Harry, I'd like you to pursue the Jewish line of enquiry. We need to find out who the lady was.' He turned. 'Mr Dickens. I don't want you to think me ungrateful for your help in finding Trinkle, but it freezes my blood to think you might have been in danger. As an observer, observe. Observe as much as you like. But I beg you: do not enquire, interrogate or – God forbid – detect.' His jocular tone didn't quite hide the flint in his eyes.

Dickens flushed. 'As you wish, Chief Inspector. I would hate to obstruct. I have links with the Jewish community that Sergeant Pilgrim might find useful.'

Pilgrim nodded, feeling oddly embarrassed for the writer. 'Can I speak to you later about it? There's something I have to do first.'

Dickens looked about. He caught Tanner's reluctant eye. 'In that case, Sergeant Tanner, may I sit in on your interview with Mr Trinkle?'

'A capital idea,' agreed Field, ignoring Tanner's scowl. 'And I will, of course, see you all at the reception this evening.' He turned to the others. 'I'll send a cab to pick you up at seven.'

A bespectacled clerk with a harassed air poked his head around the door. 'Inspector Field, sir?'

'What is it? Can't you see we're busy here?'

The clerk ran inky fingers through his hair. 'Joint Commissioner Mayne would like to see yourself and Sergeant Pilgrim, sir.'

A subtle current ran through the room. Backbones stiffened, eyebrows raised, and glances were exchanged. Dickens looked from man to man and back again, obviously baffled by it. Pilgrim caught Charley Field's eye. He had only seen Mayne half a dozen times, from a safe distance, but never been introduced to him. He would have preferred it to remain that way. Field shrugged, and straightened.

'Come on, Harry, we'd better see what he wants.'

CHAPTER NINETEEN

They followed the clerk out of the station and into the building next door. Number Four Whitehall Place had at one time been a private residence, but was now occupied by the administrative offices of the Metropolitan Police. John May, the Superintendent of A Division, and his senior officers occupied the ground floor. The junior clerks worked on the first floor, while the Chief Clerk shared the second floor with the Receiver and his staff. Joint Commissioner Sir Richard Mayne had the third floor all to himself.

They climbed the winding staircase to the third floor, where the clerk tapped on a set of double doors. Pilgrim glanced at Charley Field, who was smoothing his hair and checking his waistcoat in the manner of a schoolboy about to enter the headmaster's study. Field caught his eye.

'Let me do the talking,' he said sotto voce.

Pilgrim wasn't going to argue. He had no intention of bringing himself to Mayne's attention, if he could help it.

There was no answer from inside the room. The clerk was obliged to knock a second time. This time there was a terse response.

'Come.'

The clerk ushered them into a large oak panelled room, and backed out again, closing the doors behind him.

Pilgrim looked about. Winter light flooded the room through three windows that overlooked Whitehall Place. One of the windows was open, but did nothing to disperse the banner of cigar smoke that hung beneath the ceiling. The room was silent except for the distant rattle and clop of traffic, and the rustle of newspaper.

Sir Richard Mayne sat behind his desk, reading the *Evening Chronicle*. He looked older than his fifty-four years, with thinning grey hair, mutton chop whiskers, and features that could have been carved from a memorial stone. When he finally put the newspaper down and deigned to look at the detectives, his eyes were hooded and utterly humourless. Pilgrim noticed that the article he was reading was the one Dickens had written about the 'Hackney Cab Killer'.

'I suppose it's too much to ask, Field, that you refrain from turning police work into a circus performance?' His voice held no trace of an Irish accent, although Pilgrim knew he had been born in Dublin.

Field wisely kept quiet.

'When the Home Secretary asked us to cooperate with Mr Dickens,' continued Mayne, 'I'm sure he didn't intend you to use it as an opportunity for self-glorification.'

There was a long silence. Mayne pointed to the newspaper. 'And it surely goes without saying that I do not relish hearing about this gaudy business second-hand?'

Pilgrim groaned inwardly. With everything that had happened since the chase through the sewers he still hadn't written up his report on Appler's arrest, even though Field had asked him for it several times.

'We have been extremely busy, sir.' Field stepped in and took the bullet.

'Busy?' Mayne nodded. 'Yes, I imagine you have. Too busy, certainly, to inform me of Mr Appler's suicide in the cells.' He skewered Field with a cold stare. 'And much, much too busy to inform me that the suicide was, in fact, murder.'

112

Field flinched. Mayne continued to stare at him. 'At what point, precisely, were you planning to enlighten me with that information?'

'We had to be certain, sir,' said Field, 'before we disturbed you with it.'

'How could you allow such a thing to happen,' Mayne's voice rose, 'in the very heart of Whitehall?'

Pilgrim shifted from one foot to the other. It was bad form for Mayne to give Field a dressing-down in front of a subordinate, but he had the air of a man only just getting into his stride. Pilgrim realized he had probably only been included in the summons so that Mayne might have that pleasure.

'Can I remind you that this is not some insignificant East End Police Station?' Mayne continued, spitting out the words 'East End' as if they were dirt in his mouth. 'This is the seat of government, the very heart of power in this country. The fact that a murderer has been allowed to stroll in and stroll back out again is a matter of national concern.' He touched the Order of the Bath pinned to his jacket: a subconscious gesture. 'Something that you appear to hold lightly, Chief Inspector.'

Field flushed brick red and lifted his chin. 'With respect, sir, the security of A Division's custodial facility is Superintendent May's responsibility, not mine. It was one of his uniformed officers who left the razor in Appler's cell, and another that was careless with the keys. If he … '

'With respect,' Mayne's tone was glacial, 'you are here only on the sufferance of Superintendent May and I. You are a whim. An experiment. Make no mistake, if it was up to me, you would be put somewhere well away from here, where you would cost less and not be such an inconvenience.'

Field opened his mouth to speak, but the Commissioner was in no mood for interruption.

'I should, by rights, inform the Home Secretary about your bungling. But if I do, he might decide to scrap the Detective Force altogether, which would be a pity.'

Pilgrim smothered a snort. It was no secret that the Commissioner considered the Detective Force a waste of energy and resources. In his, often stated, opinion, the primary objective of an efficient police force was the prevention of crime, and to have to resort to detection after the fact was an admission of defeat. But Pilgrim also thought that he was bluffing. Like it or not, the Detective Force was under Mayne's jurisdiction, and he wouldn't want to lose face by having it disbanded through ineptitude.

The bluff was confirmed by his next words. 'I have decided not to inform the Home Office about Appler, but I will still have to tell Sir Charles.'

Again, Pilgrim thought it unlikely. Sir Charles Rowan was the other Joint Commissioner, several years senior to Mayne. He had been suffering from a debilitative stomach complaint for months, provoking rumours of his retirement. That would leave Sir Richard Mayne in sole control – unless Sir Charles was to recommend the appointment of another Joint Commissioner to take his place. Mayne couldn't afford to have his abilities questioned, not if he wanted to hold the reins of power on his own.

'How close are you to catching the killer?' he demanded.

Pilgrim noted the 'you', as opposed to a 'we', and glanced at Field. In spite of Charley's earlier exhortation to let him 'do the talking' he clearly wasn't enjoying the experience. Pilgrim took pity on him.

'We believe he's murdered others, sir,' he said. 'Not only the girl in the cab, but two other women. We're following several promising leads, particularly with regards to … '

Mayne cut him off with a wave of his hand. 'I'm not interested in the details.' He turned back to Field. 'I want to know if we can expect an arrest.'

'Yes, sir.'

'An imminent arrest.'

'Yes, sir.' Field hesitated. 'Reasonably imminent.'

Sir Richard nodded, picked up his paper, and opened it again. He read a few lines, then looked up and frowned, as if surprised to see them still there. 'You may go.'

When they were back outside, and the doors safely shut behind them, Field blew out his cheeks and gave Pilgrim a weak smile. 'We'd better catch this bastard quickly. I don't know about you, Harry, but I'd rather have an Irish Stand Down with Big Bill Thompson than go through that again.'

CHAPTER TWENTY

A group of bare-chested boys pushed past Pilgrim as he climbed the stairs of the tenement in Gloucester Street, almost knocking him back down. A mongrel dog scrabbled behind the boys, barking and nipping at their heels. Their shrieks of fear and delight made it almost impossible for Pilgrim to think properly. And he really did need to think. Wainwright was right: there were more questions than answers about the murders. The Hackney killer had lured Pilgrim into the sewer, laying a trail that led to Appler's house, knowing that Appler had promised to deliver his parcels for him. But why then kill Appler? If it was to protect his own identity, why go to the trouble of setting up Appler in the first place? The timing was also a puzzle. Surely it was too much of a coincidence that the package with the ear had turned up as soon as Pilgrim had discovered Martha Drewitt's body at Drover's Yard? It hadn't come with the mail from *Household Words*, but had been addressed to him directly. Yet it definitely hadn't been on his desk early that morning with the rest of his post. So it had to have been put there at some point after he had discovered the body. But how? How had the killer known when the body had been discovered? And how had he got into his office? The same way, presumably, that he had been able to get into Appler's cell and out again without being seen. Was the killer invisible? Obviously not. But there was one thing for certain: he liked to play games. The thought was unsettling, for it meant that the usual rules of logic couldn't be applied.

And, at the back of Pilgrim's mind, ever present, was a small boy in a spotted neckerchief. He liked to think that Stella Drake would turn up eventually, but knew, from hard experience, that she might not. She had vanished into the city like a stone into a pond, leaving barely a ripple on the surface.

The noise of the children and their dog had faded by the time he reached the top of the stairs. He paused outside Frances' room, where he could hear the sound of sobbing coming through the chipped and split door. He knocked. The sobbing stopped. Footsteps, and then the door opened a couple of inches. A bright blue eye peered at him.

'What's your business?' it said.

'Tell Frances it's her uncle to see her.'

Frances' voice came from inside the room. 'Let him in, Ida.'

The door opened, and the owner of the eye was revealed as a girl of about twelve, with a profusion of frizzy, carrot-coloured hair and a striped waistcoat. She glared at him, as if he might produce a knife at any moment.

''E looks well dodgy to me,' she proclaimed, as if he wasn't right in front of her.

Frances met his eyes. 'You're right, he does. But he's all right.' She was sitting on the bed clutching a handkerchief her face blotched with tears. 'Be a love and buy us a twist of tobacco.' She pressed a couple of copper coins into the girl's hand.

'Are you sure?' Ida gave Pilgrim a glare in which suspicion warred with defiance. 'I don't like to leave you.'

Frances shook her head. 'It's family business.'

Ida went to the door. 'I'll leave this open just a smidge,' she said, 'to be on the safe side. If 'e gives you any trouble, just shout out. Fat Nellie's downstairs, I just seen 'er puttin' out washin'.'

'I'll be fine.'

Ida left.

Frances read the curiosity in Pilgrim's eyes. 'Her father's long gone, and her mother died last year, God bless her. She's a good girl, but she'll probably end up on her back, like the rest of us. If you've come to tell me about Martha you're too late,' she said. 'All the girls are buzzing with the news.'

Pilgrim pulled the locket from his overcoat. 'Is this hers?'

Frances bit her lip as she took it.

'If it's any comfort,' he continued, 'she was dead before you came to me. Probably the first night she went missing.'

'Did you even look for her?'

'I found her.'

'Duty done, then.' She offered the necklace back. 'Congratulations.'

'I daresay she'd have wanted you to keep it.' He glanced around the room. The grate was empty, and several bottles lay on the floor.

'Do you need anything?' he asked.

She stared at him for a moment, and then gave an incredulous laugh. 'A hot meal. A bucket of coal. This week's rent. A punter who doesn't put his fist in my belly instead of paying me what I've earned.' She paused before continuing. 'Why is it a man will always resort to fists, in the end?'

He blinked. She stared back, defiant.

'She told you,' he said.

'She told Ma, just before she took off.' She pushed herself off the bed and pulled her shawl around her shoulders. 'Don't worry, I'm the last one to judge anyone else's domestic affairs.' She stooped to pick up the bottles.

He hesitated, then took out his pocketbook and opened it. As he pulled out a banknote he saw the photograph of Stella Drake tucked behind it. He hesitated, and then took it out. What was there to lose?

'Have you ever seen this girl?' He showed the photograph to Frances.

She barely glanced at it. 'Why bother looking?' She wiped her face and took the money from him. 'She's just another whore, like me.'

'You know her?'

'She's a greengown. Used to work out of the Bluebird Tavern at Charing Cross, but I haven't seen her in a while.' She turned away to put the bottles into a basket.

'Greengown?'

'New to the game. Some of the other girls were giving her a rough time for stealing their regulars. Saw her off, I reckon.'

'Frannie,' he began. But he didn't know what to say.

'Just go.' She refused to look at him. 'And don't call me Frannie. Little Frannie's long gone.'

CHAPTER TWENTY-ONE

'You say you lost these gloves?'

'Indeed I did, sir. Just last week.' Angus Trinkle, the upholsterer, grinned up at Sergeant Tanner. He was a redhead, with a peppering of freckles over skin so pale it was almost bloodless. 'I daresay I left 'em somewhere. Always doing that. Spend a fortune at the haberdashers on account of my carelessness. However did you come by them?'

'Have you ever heard of a woman by the name of Grimwood?'

'Grimwood? No.'

'You know the Waterloo Road?'

'Of course.'

'Do you happen to have heard of a young woman who was murdered there?' Sergeant Tanner stepped closer to the tradesman, his eyes glittering.

'Indeed I have. I read it in the papers. Dreadful business.'

'The fact is, Mr Trinkle, that I found these very gloves, your gloves, under her pillow the morning after she was murdered.'

The young man dropped the gloves back onto the table. 'That … that ain't possible.'

Tanner glared at him.

'Upon my oath I was never there, sir. I never so much as saw any woman called Grimwood, to my knowledge, in all my life.' Trinkle, already pale, went whiter still, until Dickens thought he was going to expire on the spot. Dickens decided to intervene. He sat down beside Trinkle, disregarding all Inspector Field's earlier exhortations not to involve himself in the investigation.

'My colleague is anxious to apprehend the murderer, as I'm sure you will appreciate.'

'You must believe me … '

'I do.' He interrupted smoothly. 'It's clear to me that you are innocent of the matter.' That earned him a glare from Tanner. 'But we need to discover how your gloves came to be in the murdered woman's bedroom. You say you lost them? Can you think where?'

Trinkle's forehead furrowed in frantic thought, and then his brow cleared. 'Anna Summerson!' he shouted, then dropped his voice. 'The lady is, um, an … acquaintance of mine. I was at her house the morning I discovered my gloves missing. I woke up there, if you understand my meaning.'

Dickens passed him a notebook and pencil. 'Would you be so kind as to make a note of the lady's name and address?'

'Of course … of course.' As Trinkle wrote with a shaking hand, Dickens risked a glance at Sergeant Tanner. It was what he feared; the detective was beet-faced and fuming.

'Here you go, sir.' Trinkle passed it back.

'Covent Garden: we should be able to make it there and back in time for the Gala, don't you think Sergeant Tanner?'

Tanner turned on his heel and marched from the cell. He spoke not a word to Dickens all the way in the carriage to Covent Garden, not even when the driver stopped to ask directions to Maiden Lane. He said nothing to anyone, in fact, until both men were standing in Anna Summerson's sitting room, before the lady herself.

'Do you know Eliza Grimwood?' he snapped.

'I'm her cousin, sir, but it's not something I would readily own to, what with her being no better than she ought to be.'

'Dead, you mean?' said Tanner. The detective ran a sceptical eye around the room, and over Anna Summerson herself. She was a fey looking creature, bedecked with yellowing lace and feathers.

'No,' the girl flushed, 'that wasn't precisely …'

'We understand your meaning, my dear,' soothed Dickens.

'Do you recognize these?' demanded Tanner, slapping the gloves onto the table. Miss Summerson raised plucked eyebrows.

'Why yes, they belong to Mr Trinkle, a great friend of mine. He left them there, upon that very table, when he came to call on me.'

'So how come you don't still have them?' asked Tanner.

'There's no mystery to it.' Miss Summerson gave a flirtatious laugh. 'Who should come in here, shortly after Mr Trinkle left, but my cousin Eliza? "Whose gloves are these?" she says, taking 'em up. "Those are Mr Trinkle's gloves", says I. "Oh", says she, "they are of no use to him I'm sure. I shall take 'em away for my girl to clean the stoves with." And she put 'em in her pocket. I did think it very presumptuous, but she always was a pert piece.' She gasped. 'Oh my Lord! Trinkle don't think I stole 'em, do he?'

Dickens opened his mouth to speak, but Tanner forestalled him.

'You're missing the point,' he snapped. 'I found the gloves under your cousin's pillow.'

'Her girl must have used 'em to clean the stoves with, and I have no doubt she left 'em lying on the bedroom mantelpiece, or on the drawers, or somewhere, and our Eliza, looking around to see that her room was tidy for her gentleman caller, must have caught 'em up and put 'em under the pillow.'

Dickens gave her an encouraging smile. 'When did Eliza take the gloves, Miss Summerson?'

'The very same day she was killed. If I'd known she was going to meet her maker that day, I'd never have let her leave this house. "Eliza" I'd have said to her, "You mustn't go, not for any amount of …"'

'You mentioned a gentleman caller,' Dickens interrupted gently. 'Did she tell you she was expecting someone that evening?'

The girl nodded and wiped her nose with a questionable-looking handkerchief. 'That's why she paid me a visit. It wasn't in our Eliza's nature to pay a social call for no reason. I knew she wanted something the very moment I clapped eyes on her, and I was right. "Anna" says she, "you have to lend me that jet parure Gran'ma left you. I want to look my very best tonight". She always was vain, our Eliza, and never happy that Gran'ma had left me the choker and earbobs in her will. She'd always coveted them. Even contested the will, she did. Got herself a lawyer … a nasty, shifty sort. Not that it got her anywhere, 'cept lighter in the pocket. But I'm not one to hold a grudge, so I lent them to her. I suppose I may have the parure back now she's dead, but it's a dreadful way to get it back, sir, a dreadful way.'

'Did she tell you who the man was?' A vein pulsed visibly in Tanner's forehead.

'All she said was that he was a gentleman and that she'd met him at the theatre in Covent Garden.' The girl frowned. 'I will get the choker back, sir, won't I? Only it was my Gran'ma's, and I wouldn't want Eliza to be buried in it.'

Tanner smiled horribly. 'The victim wasn't wearing any necklace when she had her throat slashed, as far as I could see for all the blood. And I didn't find one in her room. I dare say the murderer will have given it to his own girl by now.'

'I'm not sure that was the most tactful thing to say.' Dickens looked sideways at Tanner as they rode back to the barracks. 'I thought the poor child was going to faint.'

Tanner ignored him.

'I suppose you will release Mr Trinkle now?'

Tanner continued to ignore him.

'Sergeant?'

'I'll let him go when I see fit.'

Dickens dropped Tanner at the barracks, and headed home to Devonshire Terrace to change for the Gala. But he hadn't even had the chance to take his overcoat off, when his housekeeper handed him a note.

*

Please come to the Cottage as soon as you may. Something dreadful has happened.
Elizabeth Wallace

'When did this arrive, Mrs Herring?'

The housekeeper gave him an anxious look. 'About an hour since. I had no idea where you were, sir, or I would have fetched you.'

'That's quite all right. Kindly pack a bag with my evening clothes, and tell Mrs Dickens I have had to go out again.'

Dickens was worried. It wasn't like Mrs Wallace to make a mountain out of a molehill, and it was a symptom of her agitation that she had signed the note using her Christian name. What might the 'dreadful' occurrence be? Trouble with one of the girls, most likely, but which? In a flash of premonition he saw Rebecca Wood's face, smooth and sullen, in his mind's eye. Was she the culprit? He would have to wait until he got to the Cottage to find out.

CHAPTER TWENTY-TWO

Kathleen Chalk answered the door, her mouth drooping open as usual, and one of her apron straps hanging loose on her bosom. The Cottage was quiet. Unnaturally so. Dickens swallowed his irritation. He knew there was no point asking Kathleen what was happening. He gave her his bag, his overcoat, and his scarf.

'Missus is in parlour,' she muttered.

He headed for the parlour, but before he could reach the door, it was opened by Mrs Wallace herself. When she saw him, her handsome features flooded with relief.

'Mr Dickens, sir! Thank the Lord.' She stepped out of the room and closed the door behind her.

'Whatever has happened, my dear?'

'Prepare yourself for a shock.' She glanced up the stairs to make sure they weren't being overheard, and lowered her voice. 'Rebecca Wood has stabbed the parson.'

Dickens gaped.

'Fortunately, it's only a flesh wound,' continued the Matron, 'but you can imagine ... '

'Which parson?' he demanded.

'The new one recommended by Miss Coutts.'

He frowned: in all the excitement of the Gala and tracking down murderers he had quite forgotten to ask the Baroness to cancel her tub-thumper. 'When you say "flesh wound", how bad is it, precisely?'

'You'd better come in and see for yourself.'

He followed Mrs Wallace into the parlour.

A man sat in one of the armchairs by the fire. He rose to greet Dickens, and as he did so, Dickens saw he had a towel pressed against his cheek. There was a fair amount of blood on the towel, as well as spattered on the front of his stock.

'My dear sir,' said Dickens. 'Whatever has happened?'

'The devil, sir! These women have the very devil in them!' The parson had prominent eyes, and lips like molluscs prised from their shell.

'Sit down, sit down, sir, and tell me all.'

The clergyman took his seat again, with a martyred air. 'I was explaining to some of your girls the workings of the Lord, when, completely unprovoked, one struck me on the cheek with a pair of sewing scissors!'

Dickens glanced at Mrs Wallace, who nodded faintly.

'You doubt my word, sir?' The parson glared at Dickens.

'Not at all, not at all.'

'I should fetch a magistrate.' He jumped up. 'I would have done so already if your,' he flapped a hand at Mrs Wallace, 'brothel-madam here … hadn't prevented me from leaving.'

Dickens glanced at the Matron, but she didn't appear to have taken offence. 'I beg you, sir, not to be precipitous.' He hurried to press the man back into his chair. The involvement of the law was to be avoided at all costs. Angela Burdett-Coutts had an abhorrence of adverse publicity, and it might very well make her withdraw her patronage from the Cottage.

'Give me one good reason why I should not fetch a magistrate, or even the police, this very minute?'

'Does not the Lord himself say: "do not resist an evil person. If anyone slaps you on the right cheek, turn to them the other cheek also" ?' The words were out of his mouth before he had time to think. He was dazzled by his own effrontery.

The parson purpled. 'I hardly think a slap can equate to what has happened here. I was slashed, sir, assaulted, and slashed!' He took the towel from his face and pointed to his wound. It was about two inches in length and appeared to be quite deep, but the flow of blood had slowed to a sullen ooze.

'Pour a glass of brandy, Mrs Wallace,' said Dickens.

'I don't take liquor, sir!'

'For medicinal purposes. Even the most rigorous of abstainers could hardly object. Why, my own physician prescribes it regularly, as a remedy for the shock, and you couldn't wish to meet a more sober or pious gentleman.'

Dickens silently urged Mrs Wallace to hurry as she fumbled with the lock on the tantalus and poured a generous measure of brandy from one of the decanters. She put the glass into the parson's hands. He took a cautious sip.

'There, sir, is that not better?' soothed Dickens.

The parson sipped again, less half-heartedly. Some of the high colour ebbed from his cheeks. A trickle of blood ran onto his chin.

Dickens took the seat opposite. 'You can't begin to imagine the trials I face with these girls on a daily basis but I shall persevere, sir, I shall persevere. For I am a good Christian, and I believe the Lord would have it so. Did not our Saviour himself allow his feet to be washed by the penitent Mary Magdalene?'

The parson grunted, unimpressed by his knowledge of the scriptures. But, for the time being at least, he seemed to have abandoned thoughts of escape.

Dickens continued. 'I persevere, my good sir, as I am sure you yourself would. For did our Lord himself not say: "He which converteth the sinner from the error of his way shall save a soul from death"?' He paused to see whether his words were having any effect, but the parson's face was hidden in his glass. He plunged on. 'I am always on the lookout for a lost soul to save ... or a good cause to support. Haven't I heard that your own church is in need of funds?' He had heard nothing of the sort, of course, but was prepared to gamble that he wouldn't be contradicted.

The parson nodded. 'Yes, indeed. Those old buildings, you know … riddled with vermin and foul humours … they are in constant need of repair.'

'Perhaps you would accept a small donation?'

'A … that would be most generous.' The parson blinked into his empty glass.

Dickens helped him to his feet, and took the glass. 'Do you have a card?' he asked. 'I shall send you a banker's draft first thing in the morning. Shall we say, for a hundred pounds? Mrs Wallace will see you out.'

The parson stopped half way across the room. 'I'm prepared to forget this outrage, in the light of your generosity, on condition that the girl is dismissed.' His eyes were bright with brandy and malice. 'Immediately.'

Dickens nodded.

Mrs Wallace steered the parson outside, and Dickens went to the decanter to pour another two glasses of brandy. He was careful to lock the tantalus again afterwards, knowing it would be empty by morning otherwise. When Mrs Wallace returned she sank into one of the armchairs. He offered her a glass, but she shook her head.

'What happened?' he asked.

She sighed and shrugged. 'The wretched man arrived unannounced, and I had no choice but to invite him in. Rebecca and Julia were already in here, darning stockings, as peaceful as you like. He sat down beside them and started to go on in the usual way, talking about repentance and suchlike. Kathleen came in with the tea tray, I turned to take it from her, and the next thing I knew there was an almighty shout, and there was blood pouring down the Reverend's face. Rebecca dropped her scissors and ran from the room. There was quite a lot of blood, as you can see, and Kathleen and Julia were screaming fit to bring the house down. It took me a while to get them upstairs and to clean him up. He was all for going to the magistrate there and then, but I persuaded him to wait for you.'

'You did well.' He patted her hand. 'Very well. Did Julia see what happened?'

'I haven't had the chance to ask her.' She bit her lip. 'I suppose we will have to dismiss Rebecca?'

He sighed. 'I fear we have no choice.'

Julia Albright was one of their older charges, as thin as a spear, with a sharp tongue to match. She stood in front of Dickens and Mrs Wallace, bubbling over with self-importance and malicious joy.

'Did you see what happened, between Rebecca and the Reverend?' asked Dickens.

'Nothing, sir, as far as I could see. She just leapt on 'im. Like a tigress, she was.'

'Did he do anything? Say anything to her?'

'Not that I know of, unless 'e was playin' pat-a-cake with 'er under the table.'

'I think we may rule that out,' said Dickens. 'Where is she now? Has she said anything to anyone?'

'She's locked 'erself in the bedroom. I could have told you she was a bad un, sir, from the minute she got here.'

'I'm sure you could. Would you please ask her to join us?'

Julia hadn't reached the door when it opened and Rebecca entered. He was surprised to see she was dressed in the clothes she had arrived in: the grey gown cleaned of mud, but the shawl as gaudy as ever.

'You're for it now,' hissed the skinny girl.

'Thank you, Julia,' said Mrs Wallace. 'You may go.'

She slammed out of the room.

Rebecca Wood looked at them, her chin held high.

'Well,' said Dickens. 'Have you anything to say to us?'

'Is there any point?'

'You're fortunate not to have been arrested.'

'I am aware of that. Thank you.'

The three stared one to the other, and when it seemed that no one could find anything else to say, Rebecca Wood turned on her heel and headed back to the door. Mrs Wallace looked entreatingly at Dickens. Pilgrim's words chimed in his head. *You send them on their way with a purse? New clothes? References?*

'Do you have any money?' he called after her. 'Somewhere to sleep?'

The girl replied without looking back. 'I'll manage.'

And then she was gone.

Dickens crossed to the window and parted the curtains, shading his eyes with his hand so that he could see into the garden beyond. He watched as Rebecca Wood pulled the shawl over her head and made her way slowly down the path. He forced himself to harden his heart. She had brought her misfortune on herself, and had almost brought it down on everyone in Urania Cottage. Rebecca Wood wasn't the first girl he had had to turn out into the night, and she wouldn't be the last.

But he couldn't help wonder what would become of her.

CHAPTER TWENTY-THREE

'Pregnant?'

'Yes, sir,' said Dolly. 'About seven months, in Dr Fairweather's opinion. But there was no sign of the baby. I hope we don't get it in a parcel.'

Pilgrim scanned the autopsy report:

The stomach contained little food … no alcohol … evidence of malnutrition. Approximate time of death, evening of 6th February. Minor injuries, including bruising to the right hip, and a sizeable contusion on the back of the skull, consistent with a blow from a blunt instrument. Cause of death: the intestines had been severed from their mesenteric attachments, whilst from the pelvis, the uterus and its appendages with the upper portion of the vagina, and the posterior two thirds of the bladder had been entirely removed. No trace of these parts could be found and the incisions were cleanly cut, avoiding the rectum, and dividing the vagina low enough to avoid injury to the cervix uteri … also evidence of thickening of mucous membranes and significant development of alveoli in the breasts.

He sighed and put the report on the cabinet next to the photograph of Stella Drake. 'You'd better hurry up and finish dressing, Dolly. The cab's due in ten minutes.' He frowned. 'Am I right in thinking that Wainwright's list of bodies included a foetus? We should look into that in the morning.'

Dolly vanished back through the curtain, leaving Pilgrim alone with his thoughts as he shrugged on his tailcoat, and adjusted his collar. The voices of Dolly and Tanner drifted to him through the curtain, filling him with a terrible despondency. He didn't want to be there. He didn't want to be dressing in rented finery, and he didn't want to be living in the barracks at his age. He had to find a new lodging. The thought conjured a figure in black bombazine, with wheat-coloured hair. He blinked it away.

He sighed and reached for the clothes brush on his bunk, disturbing Thomas the cat, sleeping there. The cat spat at him and leapt off the bed. He ignored it and brushed the sleeves of his coat. Field had made it clear he was expected to attend the Gala. But why? To promote the new Detective Force? To be patronized by the other gentlemen present, who thought themselves masters of the Empire? What were they, any of them, but cocks crowing on a dungheap?

He gave himself one final, reluctant inspection in the mirror. As he turned away again, his eyes met those of Stella Drake. He took up her photograph. What could drive a woman to kill her own son? And where had she gone? Tomorrow he would follow up Frances' lead about the Bluebird Tavern, but, for the time being, he had no choice but to give his full attention to the Royal Academy and the Lord Mayor of London. He pushed though the curtain.

'Ready?'

Tanner was already waiting at the door, but Dolly lingered at his mirror.

'One minute sir. For the life of me, I can't get this cravat straight.'

'Come here.' Pilgrim fastened the cravat with a few twists of his fingers. 'We'd better hurry; we have to collect Wainwright on the way.'

The interior of the cab was shabby, the leather seats cracked and worn with use.

'It smells of piss in here,' muttered Tanner. He glowered at the other two men. 'And we look like trained monkeys in these suits; sent to entertain the lords and ladies.'

Pilgrim stared out of the window into the passing streets. Tanner had echoed his own thoughts exactly. As detectives they were in a no man's land between the classes, neither one thing nor another: a source of curiosity to the middle and upper classes, perhaps, or even of sympathy, but never fellow feeling. Dickens no doubt meant well in his attempt to champion the new Detective Force, but it was a lost cause. The profession was destined to a life in the shadows. Pilgrim was glad of it: he had no desire for the limelight.

Tanner tugged viciously on his starched collar and glared at Pilgrim. 'Has Dolly told you about the autopsy on Martha Drewitt?' he demanded.

Pilgrim nodded.

'Wainwright mentioned a foetus on that list of his,' said Tanner. 'I wonder where it was found.'

'In a privy,' cut in Dolly. 'But he didn't say where. Here's his lodging now, we can ask him.'

The Hackney drew up in front of a large detached house, where Wainwright was waiting on the pavement. He climbed up into the cab.

'Not a bad sort of place, for a Peeler,' said Tanner. The men were thrown back onto their seats as the cab lurched forward again.

'It's cheap, sir,' said Wainwright. 'Landlady's a hundred if she's a day. She's deaf as a bloomin' post, and there's more holes in her roof than what's in her clothes, and that's sayin' something. There're mice too. Big uns that would fright a lady into 'asteriks to see.'

'No rats, though,' said Pilgrim with a smile, remembering Wainwright's reluctance to go down into the sewers.

The constable shuddered. 'No. Old Nick himself couldn't drag me in there if there was.'

'We were talking about the murders,' snapped Tanner. 'Wasn't there a foetus on that list of corpses of yours?'

'Yes, sir. What of it?'

Pilgrim answered his question. 'Martha Drewitt was pregnant, but the baby gone.'

Wainwright turned to him with eyes as round as cheeses. 'No!'

'Can you remember where it was found?'

'Not right off. But I'll look it up in the morning.'

'What's that?' Pilgrim pointed to a red smear on Wainwright's sleeve.

Wainwright rubbed at the mark. 'Oil paint, sir. I hadn't noticed it there. But it should come out with a drop of naphtha, right as ninepence.'

'Don't suppose you have any naphtha on you?' asked Pilgrim. He saw the consternation on Wainwright's face. 'It doesn't matter,' he said.

Wainwright's expression became eager again. 'I've been lookin' forward to this.'

Pilgrim and Tanner sent him a look.

'No, truthfully … they have some capital drawin's by Mister Hogarth, and there's Titians too. I go whenever I get the chance.'

'If you're so keen on art,' said Dolly, 'what made you become a policeman?'

'I would've gone to art school, but Ma couldn't afford the fees. I applied for one of them scholarships, but never stood a chance of gettin' one, not really. People like me, from the Rookery, we don't get nothin' for free.'

'You look very cheerful about it,' said Tanner.

'What's the point of complaining?' Wainwright shrugged. 'I got myself a job at a printer's, and managed to get onto the Force from there. There're not many so lucky.'

The four men alighted onto the pavement in Trafalgar Square, in front of the Royal Academy. The windows were aglow, and music and the murmur of voices spilled down the steps under the monumental portico. Dickens was greeting guests at the top of the steps, together with a woman, and a man with a chain of office around his neck.

A spot of rain fell onto Pilgrim's cheek. He lifted his face to the sky. He didn't want to go inside.

'Just in time, boys.' Field dashed down the steps to join them, at the same time as another carriage arrived at the pavement. The footmen hurried to help the passengers alight. Field nodded at them as they passed.

'Sir Harold. Lady Maud.'

The woman smiled and went eagerly up the steps. Sir Harold glared at the group of detectives before following his wife.

Field's smile vanished. 'Let's have a look at you.'

He surveyed them critically: Pilgrim, with his pock-pitted face and bruised eye; Tanner, with his jaw rubbed raw from his over-starched collar; Dolly, whose hair was sticking up resolutely, despite lavish amounts of hair oil; and Wainwright, who had paint on his sleeve and under his fingernails.

'God help us,' muttered Field. 'Come on, we'd better go up.' He nodded for them to climb the steps ahead of him. Pilgrim tried to hang back, but Field pushed him ahead.

The Lord Mayor, as host, was waiting to shake their hands first. He stared at their cheap evening suits, with obviously no idea of who they were.

'These are our new detectives, Your Honour,' Dickens announced, over his shoulder. 'May I introduce Constable Williamson, Sergeant Tanner, Constable Wainwright, and Sergeant Pilgrim? And, of course, you know Chief Inspector Field.'

'Of course. Of course. A pleasure, sirs.' The Lord Mayor pumped their hands in turn. 'Come along to keep an eye on the silver, eh?'

Dickens caught Pilgrim's eye and smiled.

'This is our Chief Patron of the Royal Academy, Baroness Burdett-Coutts. She is also a great friend of mine. Angela, these are the gentlemen I've told you so much about.'

A slender woman in a fox fur wrap turned to greet them. With her stern features and severely parted hair, she seemed an unlikely friend to Dickens. But she shook Pilgrim's hand warmly enough.

'Angela is also patron of Urania Cottage, the refuge I was telling you about, Sergeant. We had hoped to bring some of our girls along tonight, but,' Dickens tailed off and glanced at the Baroness, 'they were indisposed.' He smiled. 'Do go on in. Not you, Chief Inspector. There are some people I would like you to meet.'

They made their way inside, and followed the flow of guests through the impressive reception hall into one of the main exhibition galleries, where the Gala was being held. They paused on the threshold to take in the scene.

The gallery was a soaring space, topped by arched clerestory windows that, by day, would provide the daylight necessary to view the hundreds of paintings hanging on the walls. For the Gala, however, the gallery was illuminated with dozens of candelabra, and dotted with extravagant planting displays. Footmen darted between the guests and the plants, bearing trays filled with glasses. The chatter of refined voices competed with the sawing of a chamber orchestra in the corner.

The detectives moved further into the room. They collected glasses from a footman.

'I've never been to a shindig like this before,' said Wainwright. 'It's grand, ain't it?'

The nearest group of guests turned to stare. Wainwright slurped his champagne and grinned.

Pilgrim slipped away from the others and headed to the edge of the room. He hated feeling so conspicuous. It made him itch, made him want to crawl out of his skin and leave it there. In an attempt to distract himself he looked up at the paintings. He didn't pretend to know anything about art, but as he wandered around the circumference of the gallery even he could see there was little consistency in period, skill, or subject matter. Seascapes, landscapes, and portraits hung hugger-mugger on the walls.

He almost bumped into a round-shouldered youth staring upwards through a pair of opera glasses at the pictures on the topmost row. He looked up to see what had caught his attention:

a wanton Venus, her flesh spilling onto the cushions of a sumptuous divan. She was surrounded by a jumble of nymphs, satyrs, gods, and goddesses, all in an equal state of nudity. Scattered here and there among the profane paintings were a few sacred ones – a naked Mary Magdalene, a pale and writhing St Sebastian – but even they appeared to be painted with the same desire to titillate. Pilgrim's gaze was drawn by a dark Salome, dressed in red, bearing the Head of John the Baptist on a platter. The saint's eyes were half closed, his mouth gasping in coital ecstasy.

Just under Salome, a second Venus was seated, looking at her reflection in a mirror. She reminded Pilgrim of Mrs Piper. Charlotte Piper, of the swaying hips and wheat-coloured hair. *I suppose you think your disfigurement excuses your rudeness?* He gave an exclamation of annoyance, loud enough to make the youth put down his opera glasses to stare at him. Pilgrim left him to his pleasure, and headed back to find his colleagues.

Field was in a group surrounding Mr Dickens. The writer had his audience enthralled with some tale or other that seemed to require much nodding and gesticulation. Under their attention he seemed even larger, even more colourful, even more ... Dickens than usual. Pilgrim smiled to himself and went to find Tanner, Wainwright, and Dolly.

They were exactly where he had left them, but had been surrounded by a group of ladies, all eager to find out more about the detective police, and anxious to put them at their ease. Unfortunately, they seemed to be having the opposite effect. Tanner's expression was pained to the point of tortured, and Wainwright was blushing so hard he looked as if he might burst a blood vessel at any moment. Only Dolly seemed to be enjoying himself, flirting with a pretty girl in ringlets. The little group was being observed, Pilgrim saw, by a line of gentlemen standing with their backs to him. He moved closer, until he could hear what was being said.

'Just look at them. Ruffians and upstarts, to a man.' Pilgrim recognized the man as the person whom Field had greeted as Sir

Harold on the steps. The commentator puffed out his cheeks. 'I blame Charles Dickens, filling their heads with prattle about deduction and justice for all. It will come to nothing, mark my words.'

'I can't imagine what the Academy was thinking.'

Sir Harold snorted. 'They're not likely to gainsay the Baroness. Her money's too useful. They forget, of course, that she's only a generation away from trade herself.'

Pilgrim gave his glass to a passing footman and headed for the door.

CHAPTER TWENTY-FOUR

The Bluebird Tavern was a cut above most of its neighbours in Charing Cross. Bank clerks, tourists, and shop girls sat in the walnut-panelled bar to flirt and discuss the day's business. Pilgrim found a seat in the corner, and positioned himself to watch the door. His smart evening clothes set him apart from the other customers, but his expression invited neither comment nor conversation. He sat, perfectly motionless, as time passed. The tavern filled and emptied, then filled again. Bottles were drained. Clothes loosened. Faces reddened. The noise gradually increased. Candles burned down.

Two hours later, Pilgrim was still sitting exactly as he was.

'Something the matter with that ale, is there?' The landlord nodded at Pilgrim's tankard.

When Pilgrim didn't answer, the landlord threw him a disgruntled look, and strode back to the bar, muttering. Pilgrim ignored him, his attention pulled to the door, where a man and a girl had entered. The man was tall, dressed in blue, with the air of a soldier. The girl was just as tall, and wore a grey gown and a gaudy shawl. She had her arm threaded through her companion's, and, although she was laughing at something he'd just said, her face was strained. Her whole body was tense, like a bowstring on the verge of snapping. Pilgrim stared. He didn't need the photograph to know he was looking at Stella Drake.

She laughed again, but her eyes didn't register her mirth. They scanned the bar, moved over Pilgrim, and then returned to him. Perhaps she had sensed his interest. Or perhaps her attention had been caught by his evening clothes. Their eyes locked … and held. Something passed between them. Her face drained of animation. Without a word to her companion, she turned and walked out of the door.

''Ere, where are you off to?' The soldier called after her. When she didn't answer he shrugged and joined the crowd at the bar.

Pilgrim shook off his trance, and hurried out.

The street was deserted. Clouds raced across the sky driven by a wet wind. A high moon, bright as a sixpence, shone on pavements still gleaming from the earlier rain. At first he couldn't see Stella Drake, but then a movement caught his eye. A pale flash – her face turned towards him – as she ducked into an alleyway. He heard the echo of her heels as she ran. He raced to the mouth of the alley and plunged after her. The tunnel was black, and he had to stretch out his hands to prevent himself from careering into them. His breath came loud in his ears, and his footsteps ricocheted off the brickwork. He was glad when he spotted a blur of light. He ran out into a yard, lit fitfully by moonlight. Stella Drake was gone.

He stopped, chest heaving, and looked about. The yard was large, empty apart from a stack of crates and several piles of gravel. As his breath steadied he heard a noise – a scattering of shale – from the other side of the yard, by a wooden fence. He ran to it, splashing through puddles. The ground fell away steeply on the other side to a railway line. Stella Drake was at the bottom of the embankment. Her frightened face flashed up at him, and then she took off again, along the railway line, towards the mouth of a train tunnel.

'Bollocks.'

He jumped the fence. The embankment was steep, and he had to slow his descent by sliding down it on his backside, and using his heels and hands. By the time he reached the bottom his palms were bloody, and Stella was already halfway to the tunnel. He put on a burst of speed, desperate to catch her before she reached it. He was still forty yards away, however, when she arrived at the tunnel mouth. Rather than run into the darkness, she started to scramble up the embankment to one side. He propelled himself up after her, close enough now to hear her ragged breathing, ducking to avoid the stones and mud she dislodged down on him as they climbed. When he reached the top, he heaved himself to his feet, and slithered to a halt.

Stella Drake was climbing onto the girder that served as a parapet halfway along the bridge. She wobbled, and then stood upright. It was a deadly drop to the railway line below.

Pilgrim bent over, gasping for breath, not daring to take his eyes off her. A distant train whistled on the track. Her foot slipped on the wet metal. He darted forward. 'No! Stay there.' She regained her balance, and shuffled around on the narrow girder to face him. 'Stella, please.'

'How do you know my name?'

'I've met your sister, Alice. In Great Barrow.'

She clenched her fists.

'Did she get ... ?' Her face crumpled, and she swayed.

Pilgrim flung up his hand as if to stop her from falling. But again, she managed to steady herself.

'Yes,' he said, 'she did.'

'Did Horace bury him properly?'

Pilgrim stared at her, lost for words.

'Did he?'

'Yes.'

'That's something, at least.' She paused before speaking again. 'You think me a monster.'

'No.' He shook his head, wanting to distract her from the fact that he was inching closer.

'It wasn't the way you think,' she said. 'I tried to do it gently. I waited until he was asleep but I couldn't ... I wasn't strong enough … ' She broke off with a wail. 'What else was I supposed to do? We'd have ended up in the workhouse. And what would have become of him then? Do you have any idea how they treat children in there? Like animals. Worse than animals.' She paused, dashed her tears away with the heel of her hand. 'It was a kindness, what I did. You wouldn't understand.'

'I know you don't need a neckerchief to kill a child,' he said. 'Poverty will do it just as well.'

'Poverty?' She looked scornfully at his mud-spattered evening clothes. 'What would you know about poverty?'

'I lost my boy that way.'

The train whistled again, coming closer on the track below. The bridge started to vibrate.

'Come down.' Pilgrim held out his hand, steady as steel. 'Let me tell you about him.'

The train rumbled closer, the vibration increased. Her feet skittered involuntarily on the wet metal.

'His name was Jonathan,' he continued, 'he died of pneumonia because I couldn't afford to keep him warm. When he died … ,' he broke off. 'I woke up one morning, and my wife had gone too.' All the time, he was edging closer to the bridge. 'Come down, Stella. You don't have to do this.'

She smiled at him. 'Doesn't it say in the bible that the wages of sin is death?' She lifted her chin. 'No one escapes His punishment, and I'm tired, so tired of trying.' She sniffed. 'He'll punish Horace too.'

'Horace?' Pilgrim's mind whirled.

Stella stared at him. There was defiance in her eyes, and something else too: a mute appeal. For what? Absolution? Understanding? Pilgrim caught his breath. 'Bonwell,' he muttered. 'The bastard!'

The train was almost under the bridge. He was out of time. On impulse, he dropped onto his knees. 'Come down.' He had to shout to be heard above the noise.

'I can't. Don't you see? It's a mercy.' Her expression smoothed.

He ran towards her. There was an ear-splitting whistle as she stepped backwards off the bridge into a cloud of steam. He coughed, blinded by the vapour, his ears ringing, his lungs scalded. Gradually, however, sight and sound were restored to him. Stella had gone.

He groaned and bent over. The rumble of the train gradually faded into nothing, and, as it did, it was replaced by another sound. A woman's sobs. He dashed to the girder and hoisted himself up to look over it. Two white hands clung to the other side.

'I couldn't do it.' Her face twisted with fear and pain as she looked up at him. 'May God forgive me!'

He reached out to grasp her wrists and felt her bones move under his fingers. The girder was pressing into his stomach and the weight of her body meant that he couldn't get a secure grip on her hands. The parapet was so high he was forced to stretch on his toes. There was nothing he could brace his legs against to get the purchase necessary to pull her up.

Another whistle blew. A second train was coming, this time from behind him. The bridge began to vibrate again. He looked about. There was no living thing in sight.

'I'm going to get help.'

'No!' she shrieked. 'Don't leave me!'

The vibration increased. It juddered through his bones and made the flesh on his face shiver.

'I'm slipping!'

'No!' He knew that if she lost her grip on the metal he wouldn't be able to hold on to her wrists without her weight dragging them both over the parapet.

The train thundered towards them, relentless. Her eyes stared up, two holes carved into her face, but he couldn't look down into them. He watched her fingers instead, noting with horrible fascination how white they were as they slid slowly, inexorably, off the metal. There was nothing he could do. The engine burst out of the tunnel. Steam swept over them. As it cleared, Stella Drake finally lost her grip on the girder.

For a few seconds he took all of her weight, until he felt himself being pulled over the parapet with her. Then he let go of her wrists.

He wanted to close his eyes, but couldn't. He saw her twist in the air as she fell. She landed on the edge of a speeding coal truck and bounced off it, spinning into the next truck, her legs and arms flung out at improbable angles. She bounced again and landed. He saw her for a moment, lying broken on the coal, before the train sped her away from him.

CHAPTER TWENTY-FIVE

'Well done, sir,' said Phelps. 'I hear the baby killer came to a bad end, but it was no more than she deserved.'

Pilgrim's expression gave nothing away. He had only spent an hour at the mortuary, yet the news had beaten him to Whitehall.

'What time is it?' he asked.

'Nigh on two o'clock, sir. Inspector Field was in here just before midnight, in his fancy duds, asking if I'd seen you. He didn't look pleased.'

The Gala. He imagined that Charley might forgive his truancy in the light of Stella Drake's ... what? Her capture? Her just reward? If he'd succeeded in saving her she would have either been hanged, or sent to the Bedlam hospital. Perhaps her death had been a kindness, in comparison.

He was too tired to think straight. He went upstairs to the office, and, not bothering to turn on the lamp, went to the window and looked out.

The sky above the rooftops was vast, unfathomable. It made him anxious, as if he was nothing but a speck of soot that might rise up and float off at any moment. He pushed away from the window and lay down on the sofa in the light from the corridor. The upholstery sagged in the middle so that his backside was almost on the floor. But he was beyond caring. He pulled his overcoat over his head and slept.

He woke a little while later, unsure what had disturbed him. His heart was pounding, and sweat cooled on his face in the breeze from the open window. The light in the corridor had gone out, leaving only moonlight spilling across the floor and silvering the edges of the furniture. For once, there was no noise, from neither the cells below nor the street. The air was filled with that supernatural hush that comes in the hour before dawn. So why was his heart pumping so? He must have had a bad dream. Gradually, his panic ebbed away, leaving only a residue of guilt. He pushed away the thought of Stella Drake, and tugged the coat back up to his chin. The wool was soft against his skin. Comforting. He fell asleep again.

'Get up. Get up, sir. There's another of them horrible packages for you!'

Wainwright's voice, close to Pilgrim's ear, dragged him back to consciousness. He groaned and sat up.

'Where?'

'Right here, sir. It was on your desk in plain view when I came in.'

He pushed himself up and went to the desk to see what Wainwright was gabbling about. It was larger than the last package, but wrapped in identical canvas, addressed in red ink to 'Sergeant Pilgrim'.

There was no one else in the office, apart from Wainwright, and the sky outside the window was still dark. Outside the open window. Hadn't the window been closed when he had fallen sleep? Was that what had woken him in the night? He strode to the window and looked out. The office was one floor up, but a drain-pipe ran less than a foot from the frame; an easy scramble from Great Scotland Yard. Pilgrim heaved the window shut.

'What time is it?' he asked.

'About half six, sir.'

'Your shift doesn't start till seven, does it?'

'No, sir. But I promised Dr Fairweather I'd do some drawings for him this morning, and I'd left my charcoals here.'

They both looked at the package.

'I hope it's not that ruddy baby.' The young constable voiced what they were both thinking.

'You're spending a lot of time at St Bartholomew's, lately,' said Pilgrim, in an attempt to distract him.

'Inspector Field says we should cooperate with the hospital. Pathology, he says, is the way forward for detection.' Wainwright's attention hadn't strayed from the package.

'On you go, then,' said Pilgrim.

'Beg pardon, sir?'

'To St Bartholomew's.'

'Don't you want me to hang about, like, while you open it?'

'If it's what we both think it is, you'll see it soon enough.'

'As you say, sir. I'll be off then.' Wainwright found his charcoals and went reluctantly out of the door.

Pilgrim took a deep breath and examined the parcel more closely. The canvas was definitely the same as both the last package and the one used to wrap the woman in the Hackney carriage. It was distinctive, more coarsely woven than usual. Perhaps that was a possible line of enquiry? The string was sturdy, unremarkable, and tied securely around the package.

He took out his pocket knife and carefully sliced the string from the parcel, and then unwrapped the canvas. Inside there was a sturdy carton, packed with straw. He put his hand into it. At first he could feel nothing, but he searched around in the straw and his fingers closed on something hard. He pulled it out. Another box. A cigar box this time, of plain wood, stamped with the words 'Vincente Martinez Ybor'. He let go of the breath he hadn't realized he'd been holding. The cigar box was too small to contain a foetus. It was wrapped with string that had a piece of paper tucked underneath. He pulled it out and unfolded it.

ha ha. Were you expecting something else, Harry? I do like to keep you on your toes. I took this special for you, thinking

*you might like to give it to your wife, but that's not likely, is
it? Give it to a sweetheart then, or maybe one of them
whores you like so much.*

The paper shook in his hand. He put it down and leaned on the
desk. Rage sluiced through him, white-hot, and strangely cleansing.
When it had passed, he opened the cigar box. Inside, packed in
more straw, was a necklace. He lifted it out. It was constructed of
black oval links with a black pendant the size of a penny, carved
into the shape of a rosebud.

'Where the buggering bloody hell did you get to last night?'
Charley Field crashed into the room and stopped. 'What's that?'
His gaze had dropped to the cigar box, straw, and canvas.

Pilgrim laid the necklace back in the box. 'Another present
from our killer,' he said.

Field joined him. 'Another note?' He picked it up. He read the
message and his eyes flew back to Pilgrim. He opened his mouth
to speak, but Pilgrim forestalled him.

'Did you hear I solved the Bonwell case last night?' he said. His
anger swelled. 'That's where the buggering bloody hell I got to,
instead of fawning around at your Lord Mayor's Gala.'

Field narrowed his eyes. 'Don't start on me, Harry. I'm not your
whipping boy.' He flicked the note with his index finger. 'This
fellow seems to know an awful lot about you.'

Pilgrim shrugged.

'If I was playing by the rule book, I'd take you off the case.'

Pilgrim glared at him.

'Fortunately for you, I'm not a great one for rules.' Field blew
out his cheeks. 'Is the Bonwell killer in the cells, then? Was it
the mother?'

'She's in the mortuary. She fell under a train.'

Field raised his eyebrows. 'An accident?'

'What else would it be?'

'I thought she might have killed herself,' Field said, matter-of-fact.

He picked up the note again and frowned at it. 'I hope you're being careful, Harry.'

Pilgrim decided to change the subject. 'We need someone to come down from Great Barrow to identify Stella Drake. Can you arrange it with Chief Inspector Moxton?'

Field nodded. 'I'll send a telegram. I'll be glad to get the old bastard off my back.'

Dolly and Tanner arrived within seconds of each other. They both spotted the package on Pilgrim's desk and came to examine the necklace.

'What's it made of?' asked Dolly.

Tanner picked it up and weighed it in his hand. 'It's too heavy for Bog Oak or Whitby jet. I'd say it was French jet. Heavier, but cheaper.'

Pilgrim raised an eyebrow. Tanner scowled.

'My father had a pawnshop,' he muttered, by way of explanation, and stomped to his own desk.

'Wainwright is at St Bartholomew's,' Pilgrim told Dolly. 'Can you follow up on that foetus? Where it was found, and how many months old? Where it is now? I have to go. Mr Dickens has arranged for me to meet one of his Jewish acquaintances.' He turned to Tanner. 'Do you still have that hamsa earring?'

Tanner opened his desk drawer. 'I have them both.' He tossed one to Pilgrim. 'Rather you than me. Yids make my skin crawl.'

Isaac Simmons was a wealthy businessman in Whitechapel, owning, amongst other businesses, the Black Lion Inn, a grocery on St Giles High Street, and a hatter's shop on Middlesex Street. He was a privileged member of the Great Synagogue, and a leading light of the League of Commerce. He had agreed to speak to the police, as long as the detectives would visit him at his office on Middlesex Street, and his friend Charles Dickens was present.

The office was expensively furnished with mahogany panelling and a massive partner's desk. Simmons himself was equally substantial, with a barrel chest, a full beard, and a shrewd, self-deprecating air.

'We're trying to discover the identity of a young woman,' Pilgrim told him. 'We think she might be a member of your community. Are you aware of anyone who may be missing a daughter, a wife, or a sister? She's about eighteen years of age. Long dark hair. Blue eyes.'

'There are more than forty thousand of our people in the city,' said Simmons. 'I fear that your description fits many of them. Can you not be more specific?'

Pilgrim frowned. He hadn't thought to ask Wainwright whether he had made a sketch of the girl's head.

'This young woman,' continued Simmons, 'this child … I take it she's dead?'

'Sadly, yes.'

'What makes you believe she is Jewish?'

Pilgrim reached into his pocket for the earring and gave it to Simmons.

Simmons frowned. 'I hate to disappoint you, Sergeant, but the hamsa is a Mussulman talisman as well as a Jewish one.' He handed the earring back. 'However, I will make some enquiries.'

'We would be very grateful, Isaac,' said Dickens.

Simmons tilted his head to consider Dickens. 'How is it that you are involved in this matter, my friend?'

'I had wanted to write about one particular investigation, but the business turned out rather more complicated than expected. I imagine I shall write about it in due course.'

'I look forward to reading it.'

'In the meantime, if you have any news, Isaac, you know how to reach me.'

The two men shook Simmons' hand and took their leave.

When they were back in the cab, Dickens sighed. 'I apologize, Sergeant. I understood that the hamsa was purely a Hebrew symbol. It seems I've led you down another blind alley.'

Pilgrim shrugged. 'Our murderer is playing games.' He hesitated. 'I received another parcel from him this morning. Not a body part this time, thankfully, but a woman's necklace.'

150

Dickens looked interested. 'Made of jet, by any chance?'

Anna Summerson clapped her hands. 'Gran'ma's necklace! Have you got the earbobs too? I'm only asking for the sake of having the complete set. It wouldn't do to wear both at once. My Gran'ma, she said, "Anna", she said, "you've got to be careful with jewellery, on account of it's possible to over-egg the pudding. Wear a necklace, or earbobs, but never both together else you'll look no better than a wreath done up for Christmas". She put out her hand for the jet choker.

'I'm sorry,' said Pilgrim, 'but I need to keep this.'

The girl flushed. 'What do you mean? That's mine, that is.'

Dickens stepped in. 'You will get it back, my dear, just as soon as the investigation into your cousin's murder is complete.'

'You've not got 'im yet, then? Seems an awful long time to be investigatin' a murder.'

'We haven't caught him yet,' said Pilgrim. 'But we will.'

He and Dickens excused themselves and made their way back down the stairs of the lodging house. Pilgrim's face was set.

Dickens glanced at him. 'Perhaps Sergeant Tanner hadn't made the connection between the necklace in the package and Eliza Davis' missing choker?' he suggested.

Pilgrim said nothing. Dick Tanner had many faults, but he wasn't dim-witted.

'Can I drop you somewhere?' he asked Dickens. 'I have to get back to Whitehall.'

'And I'm telling you, it's no way to run an investigation, Charley.'

Pilgrim slammed his hand down on the desk, making the other men jump. In the time he had spent in the carriage he had worked himself into a rare temper. It was a measure of how far he had forgotten himself that he had called Field by his first name in front of Tanner. 'Not only do I have to put up with Charles Dickens poking his nose in at every opportunity, but now I find out that he,' he pointed at Tanner, 'has deliberately been keeping information from me.'

'I did not!'

'"This case".' Field interrupted his tone cold. 'You said "this case". You're sure, then, that we're looking at one killer?'

'I'm certain of it now. Whoever sent Eliza Grimwood's necklace and the package with the ear knew that I was expecting to see Martha Drewitt's baby when I opened that last box. He knew it, and he mocked me for it!'

'Sit down, Harry.'

Pilgrim stayed on his feet.

'I said sit down!' boomed Field.

Pilgrim did as he was commanded, but he refused to stay silent. 'There are too many of us working on this investigation. We're pulling in too many different directions.'

Field nodded. 'My sentiments exactly. And that is why I'm taking you off the case.'

CHAPTER TWENTY-SIX

Pilgrim waited until Field had shown a gloating Tanner out of the door.

'You can't mean it.'

Field crossed to the dresser to pour himself a glass of port.

'I'm afraid I do.' He sat and stared at Pilgrim. 'Take a look at yourself.'

Pilgrim swallowed the sour taste in his mouth. He was unshaven, exhausted, and still wearing his dinner suit from the night before.

'I think the Bonwell case has affected you more than you care to admit,' said Field. 'The boy. The way his mother died last night. It all takes a toll. And it's not only that ... this Hackney killer is writing to you. He is trying to make it personal, to gain some kind of upper hand.'

'Do you think I'd let ... ?'

Field held up his hand. 'It's already affecting your behaviour. Your judgement. I know you, Harry. I know what makes you tick. Bess has been gone for years, and you're a red-blooded man. One with appetites.'

Pilgrim's blood pounded in his temples. 'You think ... ?'

But Field cut across him again. 'It's not so much what you've done, as the fact you've been careless about it. The killer knows you visit whores. I'm taking you off this investigation because I care for you. You think this is humiliating? It's nothing compared to what could happen if I let you get more involved.'

Pilgrim stood up. He could find no words.

'Come back to work in a week, Harry. I guarantee I'll have another case for you to sink your teeth into.' Field leaned forward. 'You do see, don't you, that I have your best interests at heart?'

Pilgrim couldn't bring himself to answer. He strode to the door and slammed out of it without looking back.

He lay on his cot and stared at the ceiling, trying to ignore the snores of the nightshift constables on the other side of the curtain. There was no way he could stay in the barracks. At seven o'clock Dolly and Tanner would be returning from their shift, and he didn't think he could bear either Dolly's sympathy or Tanner's triumph. He had to get away. But where could he go?

An idea came to him. He swung his legs off the bunk and packed his things into his carpetbag.

Pilgrim rang the bell and waited on the step. After a few moments, he heard a tread on the other side of the door, and it opened.

He took off his hat. Charlotte Piper stared at him as if she'd never seen him before. She had obviously been baking: there were traces of flour on her hands, and her face was flushed from the oven.

'If you haven't let the rooms yet,' he said. 'I'd like to take them.'

She blinked, and pressed her lips together.

'These are for you.' He offered her the bunch of unseasonal – and very expensive – chrysanthemums he had bought from the flower market.

She blinked, and put her floury hands firmly behind her. 'If you think, for one minute … '

'I know I was rude,' he said. 'I'm sorry. Sometimes I'm not good with words. Not … accurate.'

She flushed to the roots of her hair. He guessed she was remembering her own, all-too-accurate, words. Her mouth opened, and then closed again.

154

'What do you think, Mrs Piper?' he prompted. 'Can we start again?'

She lifted her chin. 'I don't know. I'll have to think about it.'

He nodded, and placed his hat and the flowers carefully on the step. He knelt down.

'What in God's name are you doing?' she asked.

'What do you think?' He gazed up at her, knowing the conclusion she had jumped to, and relishing it. Her eyes were round with horror. He stretched the moment deliberately before he spoke again. 'I'm begging for the rooms on my ruddy knees.' He watched as at first recognition and then amusement flickered on her face. She snorted.

'Get up, you fool. And come inside, people are watching.'

CHAPTER TWENTY-SEVEN

Charles Dickens looked down onto the street through the rain-spattered window of his study in Devonshire Terrace, watching pedestrians jostle with their umbrellas and slip around on the muddy pavements. It had been raining since the night before – not a clean, hard rain, but the sort that couched itself in bad-tempered fog, confounding the daylight so that it was impossible to tell whether it was dusk or dawn. In fact, it was almost noon. All the horses were splashed to the blinkers in filth, and the dogs that threaded through the crowd were so slimed in mud as to be almost unidentifiable. But Dickens was content. He could feel words welling up inside him, the old familiar quickening that signalled he was ready, at last, to begin his next novel.

Anna Summerson's witless chatter about wills and disreputable lawyers had set him thinking about his own time as a clerk in Chancery, and the interminable meanderings of legal procedure. Looking out at the weather, a pleasing metaphor had just occurred to him, one that, if he was lucky, might sustain him throughout the course of a story.

He strode to his desk and took up his pen. Started to write.

London. Michaelmas Term lately over, and the Lord Chancellor sitting in Lincoln's Inn Hall. Implacable November weather. As

*much mud in the streets, as if the waters had but newly retired
from the face of the earth, and it would not be wonderful to meet
a Megalosaurus, forty feet long or so, waddling like an elephantine
lizard up Holborn Hill ...*

He didn't lift his head again until his pocket watch chimed two
o'clock, its silvery notes echoed by the bass thumps of the clock
on the mantel. He shook himself and put down his pen. He would
have to order his carriage if he wasn't to be late for his appointment with Inspector Field. The Inspector had asked him to call
at Whitehall as a matter of urgency. Dickens had a fair idea what
he wished to talk to him about and guessed he should gird his
loins, ready for battle. He was right.

'Is there nothing I can say to convince you to abandon your interest
in the Grimwood case?' Having settled Dickens in a comfortable
chair and furnished him with an excellent glass of port, Charley
Field favoured him with his most disarming smile.

But the writer shook his head. 'Once I have determined on a
course of action, I always see it through, Inspector. Perseverance
is one of my particular character traits – any of my friends will
tell you so.'

Field gave him a look that was close to despair. 'I must be honest
with you; the case is in danger of turning into a circus. Surely you
don't wish to make us a laughing stock?'

'Nothing could be further from my intention. You know I have
always championed your detectives. I may decide, in the end, not
to write about the investigation at all, but I would like to reserve
the right to make that decision until the affair is concluded.'

'So you'll not write anything until afterwards?' Field's face
betrayed his relief.

'You have my word on it.' Dickens took a sip of his port. It really
was very good. 'But surely, Inspector, things are not as desperate
as that? Sergeant Pilgrim has everything in hand.'

Field rubbed his nose and looked away.

'Inspector!' They were interrupted by Sergeant Tanner who entered Field's office red-faced and without knocking. 'We've just received a note from Dr Fairweather. He thinks he might have another victim at the hospital.'

'Another one?' Field took the paper from Tanner's hand and went into the main office to read it. Dickens followed and watched with Dolly, Wainwright, and Tanner, as Field's face grew darker.

'Bugger it,' he said. 'I suppose someone better get over to St Bartholomew's and take a look.'

Tanner headed for the door. 'Get your coat, Williamson.'

'Can I come too, sir?' asked Wainwright. 'Only I'm supposed to be a detective and I ain't done much detectin' of late. I've been drawin' mostly, which ain't really what I'm paid for.'

Tanner sighed. 'If you must.'

'I'd like to go too,' said Dickens. 'With your permission, Inspector?'

Field blew out his lips, and nodded.

Tanner scowled. 'We'll need a bloody omnibus to fit everyone in.'

'Not at all,' said Dickens. 'I'm sure we can all manage in my Brougham.'

Luckily the carriage had two foldaway seats in the front corners of the cabin, but it was still something of a squeeze. When they were all settled Dolly turned to Sergeant Tanner.

'I found out about that foetus, sir,' he said.

'Oh?'

'It was left in a privy at the back of Temple Lane. It's shared by fourteen brick-maker's cottages. The mother might live in any one of them, or none. Apparently that kind of thing happens all the time. The mortuary often doesn't bother logging them before sending them to the common pit at St Brides.'

'How many months gone was it?'

'According to the officer that fetched it, it was no bigger than a kitten.'

'Not Martha Drewitt's, then.'

'No, sir.'

'Another goose chase.'

When they arrived at St Bartholomew's, it wasn't the Coroner who met them, but Townsend, the Coroner's assistant. The young American led the three detectives and the writer to the mortuary storeroom.

'Where's Dr Fairweather?' asked Tanner.

'In court.' Townsend blinked at them through his spectacles.

Dolly glanced at Dickens, and tugged at Tanner's sleeve. 'Perhaps Mr Dickens might like to wait for us outside, sir.'

Tanner turned to Dickens and said, with false jocularity, 'You don't want to wait outside, do you?' He turned back to Dolly. 'Of course he doesn't. He wouldn't want to miss finding out what police work is really all about.' His face lit with a savage glee.

The room was long and narrow, lined on both sides with tables that bore shapes covered in grey sheets. Townsend stopped two-thirds of the way along, and turned down one of the sheets. Although Dickens thought he had prepared himself for the sight he still couldn't stifle a gasp of dismay. A woman lay naked on the gurney, her body white, hip bones jutting out. Her hair was stringy and clotted with blood, and a crudely stitched incision ran from her throat to disappear under the sheet at her groin.

'She was found on Tuesday.' Townsend's breath smoked in the air. 'They thought it was natural causes.'

'What made them change their minds?' asked Tanner.

Townsend leaned over, caught hold of the woman's arm, and raised it up. It ended in a stump, the flesh severed cleanly around a white jut of bone.

'The hand's been sliced off post-mortem,' said Townsend, 'just for jolly.'

Dolly flashed the youth a startled look, and frowned. Dickens swallowed, hard. He saw with a certain amount of relief that he wasn't the only one struggling to master his revulsion: Wainwright looked distinctly green.

'Hard to miss, surely?' snorted Tanner.

Townsend snorted back. 'They'd already issued a death certificate for pneumonia when one of the assistants spotted it.'

'So what is the cause of death?' asked Dolly. His usually rosy cheeks were pale, and he was regarding the young medical assistant with more than a trace of disapproval.

'Prussic acid,' said Townsend. 'Not common, but easy enough to diagnose. The gastric fluids have a distinctive odour.'

'Do we know who she is? Where was she found?' asked Tanner.

Townsend shrugged. 'It'll be in the paperwork upstairs.'

'If Sergeant Pilgrim ain't on the case no more,' said Wainwright. 'Who's the killer going to send the hand to?'

Dickens flashed him a look. *Pilgrim not on the case?*

'Me, I suppose,' said Tanner. 'That's something to look forward to.' He stomped out.

Wainwright stared down at the woman on the gurney, the tip of his nose red with cold.

'Why?' he asked. 'Why make such a ruddy mess of them?'

Dickens was at a loss. 'Who knows what goes through the mind of such a man?'

Wainwright turned to him, his eyes glittering. 'I wasn't talking about the killer.' He glared at Townsend. 'I was talking about him and Dr Fairweather.' He followed Tanner out.

Dickens caught at Dolly's sleeve as they followed the others. 'Is it true that Sergeant Pilgrim has been taken off the case?'

Dolly nodded.

'That's a pity.'

'A pity?' Dolly's look was ironic. 'A tragedy, more like.'

'The tart's name was Clara Donald,' said Tanner, reading through the paperwork in the mortuary admission office. He had stopped modifying his language for Dickens's benefit, and seemed to have decided to ignore the writer altogether. 'She was found in a lodging house at 16 Worship Street. Top floor.' He nodded at Dolly. 'Take Wainwright and have a look at the room. See if you can discover how he gave her the poison. Question the neighbours. Ask if they saw or heard anything. I'll get back to Whitehall and tell the Inspector we definitely have another victim.'

'What should I do, Sergeant?' asked Dickens.

Tanner shrugged. 'Please yourself.'

Wainwright, Dolly, and Dickens were out of breath by the time they climbed the five flights of stairs at Worship Street. There were two doors on the attic landing. They could hear children and the pounding of feet on floorboards coming from the nearest one. Dolly knocked.

'Come on in, whoever you are,' called a voice. 'The more the merrier!'

The garret was poky, and strewn with wriggling bodies. In the light filtering through the skylight they could see children of all ages, playing on the floor, romping on the bed, and running from one side of the room to the other, giggling and shrieking. In the middle of it all sat a massive woman, giving suck to one babe, while another, barely walking, tried to climb up onto her lap. A portrait of the Virgin and Child smiled serenely down on the chaos from over the mantelpiece.

The woman adjusted the baby's position on her breast, releasing her spittle-glossed nipple and then pushing it back into the baby's mouth. She looked at them expectantly.

'Sorry to intrude,' said Dolly with a blush, 'we thought Miss Donald lived here?'

'She moved out.'

'When?'

Dickens glanced around the riotous, heaving room. Whatever traces there had been of the poisoner or his victim were surely undetectable now?

'You'd have to ask the neighbours that,' said the woman. 'Or the landlady. We've just got here.'

'Did she leave anything behind?' asked Dickens. 'Bottles or liquids of any description?' He watched, aghast, as a toddler grappled with a stone bottle and took a swig of the contents.

'No,' said the woman. 'There was nothing here when I moved in.'

A look of relief passed between the men. Dolly nodded and beat a retreat; pushing Wainwright and Dickens back out onto the landing ahead of him.

'That's that, then,' said Wainwright.

'Pssst!'

They spun around. A red-rimmed eye peered at them from the other door on the landing. The crack opened wider to reveal an old man in a flannel gown.

''Ave you 'eard that racket in there?' he demanded. 'It's like livin' in a bloody farmyard. Widow Kelly moved that lot in this morning, with the other girl not cold in her grave. It ain't decent.'

'What happened to her things?' asked Dolly.

'The widow has 'em. You'll find 'er at the bottom of the stairs. Tell 'er I want my ruddy rent reducin'!' The door slammed shut again.

The three men went back down the stairs. They had to pick their way through a group of men smoking at the bottom to reach the door. A middle-aged woman dressed in black answered their knock.

'Metropolitan Police,' Dolly announced.

'Come in … come in, for gawd's sake.' She pulled Dolly, Wainwright, and Dickens into the hallway, and slammed the door behind them. 'I don't want that idle lot knowing my business.' She ushered them into a sitting room that was crammed with furniture and knick-knacks, and stifling hot from the fire that blazed up the chimney. The room smelled of tobacco and grease. The widow Kelly sat in an armchair, took a clay pipe from her apron, and appraised the writer's Persian lamb overcoat.

'You don't look like no Peeler.'

Dolly took charge of the situation. 'We're detectives. We'd like to know who found Clara Donald.'

'Me, the day before yesterday.' She tapped out her pipe in the hearth, and then took a tin of tobacco from her pocket. 'She was dead in bed. Fitting, I suppose. She spent most of her life there.'

The three men exchanged a look.

'We wanted to examine her room,' said Dolly. 'But you've let it already.'

'The dead don't pay their rent, officer. And the girl owed me three weeks.' She pushed tobacco into the bowl of the pipe. 'Don't suppose I'll be gettin' it now.'

'There was no money in the room?'

'Couldn't say for sure. Half the building were in and out after I found her. Who's to say what might or mightn't have been there?' She met their eyes directly, defying them to challenge her. 'Everything that was left is in that there box.' She waved her pipe at a tin box in the corner, of the kind used to store dry goods.

Wainwright picked it up.

'Do you know if she had any gentlemen callers the night she died?' asked Dickens.

'Gentlemen callers?' The widow hooted with laughter. 'That's one word for 'em!'

'But no one in particular?' pressed Dolly.

'How should I know? If Clara Donald had a sweetheart, she'd have kept it to herself. Love ain't good for business in the whoring trade.'

CHAPTER TWENTY-EIGHT

Fog clung to the cobbled streets, turning them grey and greasy underfoot. The illumination of the streetlamps was confined to haloes, and did little to guide the few chilled pedestrians who were up and about. Shadows moved in the gloom, only resolving into human form as they passed Pilgrim who pulled his scarf up to his nose and picked his way over gutters clogged with ice and rubbish. Although he had slept well in his new lodgings, he had woken before dawn, disturbed by the knowledge of a duty yet to be done. As soon as he had shaved and dressed he set off for St Martin-in-the-Fields.

It was a good half an hour's walk from Holborn, but Covent Garden was behind him now, the rattle of its carts muffled and flattened by the fog. The chimes of St Martin-in-the-Fields struck nine o'clock, sounding as if the great bell was wrapped in a blanket. He hurried on and came at last to a miserable covered walkway, with a single lamp burning over a gate. The rusted metal gave with a groan and he plunged into the walkway that led towards the burial ground.

He stopped when he reached the end, aware he was sinking into ooze. The burial ground was overlooked by houses, their walls splotched and blackened with mould. In that sodden space, less than 200 feet square, was buried more than 80,000 former inhabitants of the city.   He saw he was too late. In a far corner of the ground half a dozen black-clad figures stood among the piles of mud and heaps of broken stones. They were gathered around a pit, no more than a couple of feet deep, in which a bundle was plainly visible. All the figures held kerchiefs to their noses, including the priest, who was coming to the end of his service.

The gravediggers stooped to shovel mud into the hole. The women moved away, and picked their way towards him over boards laid on the slimy ground. As they got closer he saw they were all red-eyed with weeping. The tallest among them lifted her chin.

'I didn't think to see you here,' said Frances. She had her arm around the smallest figure. He recognized Ida by the carrot hair frizzing out from under her bonnet, jewelled with droplets of mist. The two women stopped beside him, allowing the others to pass on either side.

'I heard you were burying Martha this morning,' said Pilgrim.

'We scraped some money together. Not enough for a coffin, but at least she's not in the common pit.'

'Why didn't you tell me she was pregnant?'

'Would you have found her any faster?' Frances shook her head, making her black earrings swing against her cheeks. 'At least she and the babe are at rest now. God have mercy on them both.'

Pilgrim pursed his lips. What would she say if she knew the baby wasn't with its mother?

'Frannie … ' He paused, corrected himself. 'Frances … '

She interrupted him. 'Come on, Ida, let's get you home.' She moved away without looking at Pilgrim.

'I'll call on you at Gloucester Street,' he said.

'No.' She did look at him now, but her expression was blank. 'Please don't.'

He watched them pass down the walkway and out through the iron gate into the street. Another figure appeared by the gate, carrying a pole and a stepladder. He waited for Pilgrim make his way out of the tunnel too, before climbing the ladder to snuff out

165

the lamp. Pilgrim nodded his thanks and hesitated. What should he do now? His feet itched to head to Whitehall, no more than five minutes walk away, but he knew he wouldn't be welcome there. And he didn't want to go back to his new lodgings. He turned instead towards Trafalgar Square.

The Square was so wide and featureless in the fog that he could have been standing on the edge of a field. He set off across it anyway. After a few paces, the equestrian statue of Henry IV loomed up in front of him. A little further on, the newly-finished monument to Admiral Nelson appeared, the top of the column vanishing into the air like a fakir's rope.

'Violets! Two bunches a penny.'

A flower seller sat by the railings at the base. She wore a thin cotton gown and carpet slippers instead of shoes. A sodden basket lay at her feet. He guessed she was no more than eight years old. Pilgrim swore under his breath. He and the girl might have been the only people left in the city. He stiffened his resolve and walked faster.

'Violets, sir,' she said again. 'For your lady-love.' She sniffed. The sniff sounded in danger of turning into a sob.

He sighed and stopped. He tossed her a penny, but declined the bedraggled bunch of flowers she offered him. When he met her eyes he saw no gratitude there, only resentment, raw and burning. He didn't take it personally. He knew how it felt to have every scrap you were given begrudged by those with more. He walked on, his wet overcoat dragging on his shoulders. He was cold to the bone. What he needed was something to warm him up.

'News, guv'nor?' A vendor popped out of the fog and thrust a paper at him as he reached the other side of the Square. 'Sixpence a sheet.'

He bought one and took it into a coffee house. As he settled himself in an armchair and ordered a hot chocolate he wondered whether this was how gentlemen of leisure filled their time. It felt strange to the point of absurdity to have nothing to do at that time of the morning. He had nowhere to go, and no one to see. He picked up the newspaper, the *Illustrated London News*, and opened it. Towards the middle of the paper, past the foreign news and the reports from the Royal Court, between an article about a boiler explosion on Lilly Lane and an account of the Gala at the Royal Academy, was a smaller article.

DEATH OF A CHILD MURDERER

The horrid slaughter of an unknown child and his unnatural conveyance to the dwelling of the Reverend Horace Bonwell in the hamlet of Great Barrow, near Chelmsford, on the morning of Saturday week has been mentioned previously in this Journal. The child was but four years old, his tender life passing from babyhood into boyhood, when he fell into the pitiless hands of an assailant who choked the breath from his lungs, and then submitted his unshriven body to be delivered by parcel.

We can now reveal the assailant as none other than the boy's own mother – Stella Agnes Drake. There is no need here to dwell upon the abhorrence that such a vile and unnatural act will provoke in every Christian breast. We may be consoled, however, that the culprit has already been brought to justice, for while being pursued by a member of our own Detective Police in the early hours of Tuesday morning, Stella Drake fell beneath the wheels of a steam engine and died there. And so, by attempting to evade earthly justice, she met headlong the implacable will of that great Protector of Children, the Almighty Himself.

A post-mortem was performed and Death Certificate issued by H. R. Fairweather MRCS.

Beneath the article was another that Pilgrim found interesting:

*

DROVER'S YARD MURDER – DETECTIVES BAFFLED?
We reported last week the discovery of the body of another young woman at the notorious slum Drover's Yard, the third such unnatural female death in as many weeks. One would imagine that this latest grim discovery would inspire our Detective Police to redouble their efforts to unmask the person or persons responsible.

But an inexplicable hush has fallen on Whitehall. Questions are being whispered in those illustrious corridors, questions that this humble journalist will not dare to repeat, for danger of undermining the public confidence. However, we question the wisdom of our own Detective Chief Inspector, who, with these recent murders yet unresolved, has nevertheless permitted his most successful and celebrated detective to take leave of absence. We can only hope that the Chief Inspector may revoke this decision, and rally his troops to prove himself equal to the challenges presented by these grave and dreadful times.

Pilgrim snorted, causing several of the other coffee shop customers to glance at him. What would Charley say when he read all that?

CHAPTER TWENTY-NINE

'What do you mean he isn't at the buggering barracks?'

Dickens could hear Charley Field before he reached the top of the staircase. Not wanting to see the Inspector at that particular moment, he veered away, and ducked into a doorway to listen.

'He just ... ain't there, sir,' replied Wainwright. 'We ain't seen him since the morning he caught the baby killer. The morning you ... well, you know.'

'That was three days ago. Did no one think to mention it to me? What about his things?'

'Gone, sir.'

'Gone?' There was a beat of silence as Field cast around for someone else to vent his displeasure on. 'Do you know where he is, Adolphus?'

'No, sir.'

'Where's Tanner?' demanded Field.

'He said something about talking to Dr Fairweather again, sir,' said Wainwright. 'About the poison what killed Clara Donald.'

'Damn it all! If Mr Dickens turns up, be so good as to show him the door, or you might very well have another murder on your hands.' Field strode out of the office.

Dickens turned hastily away so the Inspector wouldn't spot him, and waited until his footsteps had faded down the stairs before heading into the office.

'Good morning, gentlemen!'

Dolly and Wainwright both turned to look at him, their eyes round.

'Mr Dickens, sir!' said Dolly. 'The Inspector's out at present, and I ... um ... wouldn't wait around for him, if I were you.'

Dickens pulled a face. 'It wasn't me, you know, who spoke to the *News*.'

'If you say so, sir. I haven't seen the article.'

'I need to talk to Sergeant Pilgrim, most urgently. I've been to Holborn, but they tell me he's not staying at the barracks. Do you know where I might find him?'

'No idea, sir,' Dolly's eyes slid away from the writer.

He narrowed his gaze. He had seen the constable attempt to lie before; the boy had no facility for it. 'It's almost luncheon,' he said, conversationally, 'do you have plans, Adolphus?'

'No. Yes.' Dolly gazed around. 'I'm ... um ... going for a walk.'

They both looked out of the window, where the fog had surrendered to a hard rain that pounded the glass. Dickens raised an eyebrow. Dolly sighed, took his elbow, and steered him out of the room, away from Wainwright.

'I'm not sure I do know the Sergeant's whereabouts, sir, not exactly,' he said. 'But I have a suspicion where he might be. I need to speak to him myself. If you can stand the cost of a cab, we could look for him together.'

There was no need to summon a cab, for Dickens had his carriage waiting in Great Scotland Yard.

Within minutes they were standing on the steps of a lodging house in Holborn. It was better kept than the neighbouring houses, with fresh paint and a scrubbed step. Dolly lifted the gleaming brass knocker, and after a little while they heard a commotion on the other side of the door.

'I'm coming. Why don't you use your bloomin'...' A handsome young woman, dressed in black, blinked at the two men. 'Oh, it's you, Dolly. What a surprise.'

'This is Mr Charles Dickens,' said Dolly.

'Mr Dickens? What, *the* Mr Dickens?' Dickens was gratified by her confusion, and utterly charmed by the blush that rose in her cheeks. 'Come in, sir,' she said, 'come in out of the rain, for goodness sake.'

'This is Mrs Piper,' said Dolly to Dickens. 'She's my cousin. We're looking for the Sergeant, Lotte. Is he here?'

'He went out first thing.'

Dolly's face registered his relief.

Mrs Piper looked from one man to the other. 'I don't know when he'll be back,' she continued. 'Would you care for some tea?'

'No wonder the Inspector's in such a temper.' Dolly put down Mrs Piper's copy of the *Illustrated London News,* and helped himself to a slice of Madeira cake. Dickens did the same, but regretted it almost as soon as he took a bite: it had the texture of porridge.

'I wonder who spoke to them?' Dolly asked.

'I may … um … have mentioned it, in passing, to an acquaintance who's a correspondent on their foreign pages.' Dickens spoke around a clinging mouthful of cake. 'Discretion's never been a strength of mine … not out of any wish to cause mischief, you understand. I daresay it will get me into trouble one of these days.'

Mrs Piper took the paper and scrutinized the article about Pilgrim's dismissal. 'So many murders,' she sighed. 'Dolly's mother worries about him, Mr Dickens. We all do.'

The tips of Dolly's ears turned red.

'We live in hard times, Mrs Piper,' said Dickens. The statement had a pleasing ring to it.

'More tea?' She proffered the teapot, utterly self-possessed now that she had recovered from their unexpected appearance on her doorstep.

'That would be splendid.'

'More cake?'

Dickens eyed the cake. 'No, thank you. I've had a sufficiency.'

Dolly gave a start as the clock on the mantelpiece chimed one. 'I can't wait any longer,' he said. 'I have to get back to the station. Sergeant Tanner will have returned from the hospital by now.' He stood up. 'You'll be sure to tell Sergeant Pilgrim I need to speak to him, Lotte? And that it's urgent? I'll come back as soon as I've finished my shift.'

'You can leave a message, if you like,' suggested Mrs Piper.

Dolly shook his head, his expression grave. 'It's something I really need to speak to him about, face to face. Please do tell him that it's … '

'Urgent. I know.'

CHAPTER THIRTY

Pilgrim shook the water from his overcoat and wiped his boots on the mat. Another man's coat hung on the hooks in the vestibule. It was obviously expensive, dyed midnight blue, with a pink silk lining. He was surprised, at first, that Mrs Piper would know anyone who owned a coat of such flamboyance. Then he recognized the walking cane and hat.

He could hear familiar rich tones coming from the other side of Mrs Piper's parlour door. He knocked and opened it. Mrs Piper and Dickens both looked up.

'You have a visitor, Sergeant,' said Charlotte.

He didn't reply.

'There's tea in the pot.' She rose and pushed past him to leave the room. 'I'll give you some privacy.'

He wiped the rain from his face with his sleeve. Rather than take a chair, however, he remained standing.

'I can't think what you might have to say to me, Mr Dickens. I'm no longer working on the investigation.'

'So I understand.' Dickens nodded. 'A grave mistake on the Inspector's part, in my opinion.'

Pilgrim relaxed slightly. 'You wrote the article in the *News*?'

'No.'

He lifted an eyebrow.

'I merely … ' Dickens hesitated, '… planted the seed.'

He poured himself a cup of tea. 'What can I do for you?'

'I have received a note from Isaac Simmons. He thinks he may have found our missing Jewess.'

'Sergeant Tanner will be delighted to hear it.'

Dickens gave a snort of impatience. 'Simmons is my friend. His people have to be handled with patience and sensitivity.' He hesitated, and pulled at his earlobe.

'How well do you know Sergeant Tanner?'

Pilgrim frowned. 'We were on the beat together for years, in H Division, but we're not friends. Why?'

'There's something … brutal about the man.'

'That's true enough. But he's a good detective.'

Dickens nodded, and pulled a piece of paper from his pocket. 'The girl is called Mena Levy. Her brother reported her missing to the Great Synagogue a week ago.'

'Why didn't he go to the police?'

'He believes she has eloped. With a Gentile. So you see the need for a delicate touch in this matter? Tanner would be a disaster.'

Pilgrim put down his cup. He could see his point. He knew he shouldn't get involved, but he had already had quite enough of sitting in coffee shops.

'Very well. I'll look into it,' he said. 'On one condition.'

'What's that?'

'I do it on my own.'

The houses in Artillery Lane, in the heart of Spitalfields, were so close together that anyone leaning from the upper floors might shake hands with his neighbour opposite. Daylight struggled to reach the pavement, and the shop windows were illuminated with oil lamps even though it was the middle of the day. Two men stepped around him, both sporting beards and side locks, and he felt the weight of their attention. It was not entirely benign.

He turned, thankfully, out of the narrow thoroughfare into a broader one, the aptly named Widegate Street, where he stopped an elderly man who was wearing the large, flat crowned hat so distinctive of his brethren.

'I'm looking for the Levy bakery,' said Pilgrim.

The man grunted and pointed to a large building on the corner. Pilgrim wondered how he had missed it. The window was stacked with loaves and the frieze above was carved with figures of men occupied with the various stages of the trade: heaving sacks of flour, mixing dough, carrying trays of rolls.

Rather than going into the shop, Pilgrim found the alley that led around the side of the building to a gated yard. The gates were open, and several men were busy filling a waggon with covered trays. A handsome young man, red cheeked with the cold, supervised the others, checking off the trays from a list, as they were loaded. Pilgrim approached him.

'I didn't expect to see you open this late in the day,' he said.

The youth stuck his pencil behind his ear and grinned. 'Normally we wouldn't be, but it's only eight weeks to Passover. This delivery of Matzo bread has to sail tonight if it's to make it to Cape Town in time.' He gave Pilgrim a speculative look. 'Is there something I can help you with?'

'I'm looking for Aaron Levy.'

'I'm Woolf Levy, his cousin.'

'I'm here to talk about Mena.'

The youth's grin evaporated. 'You'd better come inside.' He thrust the list at one of the other men. 'Here, Raphael, keep tally.'

Pilgrim followed him into the building through a passageway that opened out into a massive, double-height room. Warmth hit him, and noise too, from a massive hopper that stood in the centre of the floor, its cog wheels grinding, spinning a massive canvas belt onto more cogs set on beams running across the ceiling. A bank of ovens flanked one end of the room, the upper ones accessed by stairs and a narrow walkway. More than a dozen men, stripped to their shirtsleeves, hurried to and from the ovens, carrying baking sheets of dough, or trays steaming with pliable discs of unleavened bread. Pilgrim's mouth watered at the sight. He realized that he hadn't eaten anything that day, except a slice of Charlotte Piper's questionable Madeira cake.

On the opposite side of the room to the ovens there was mezzanine; a glazed office accessed only by stairs with open treads, little more than a ladder. He scrambled up it after Woolf Levy.

A man looked up from a ledger as Woolf knocked on the office door and opened it.

'This man has come about Mena.'

'I am a detective,' said Pilgrim, 'from the Metropolitan Police.'

Aaron Levy was considerably older than his cousin, and much heavier. He wore his long hair tied back, apart from two side locks that framed his ursine features. He nodded at Pilgrim, but did not invite him to sit.

'Thank you, Woolf. I will call if I need you,'

Woolf hesitated, and pushed black curls out of his eyes. 'If it's about Mena I want to know.'

'Do you think I would keep any news from you? I said I will call you afterwards.'

Pilgrim waited until the young baker had clattered back down the ladder, before addressing his cousin.

'I understand your sister is missing.'

'She is lost, yes.'

When the other man didn't expand on the statement, Pilgrim had to prompt him. 'When did she go missing?'

'Two weeks ago.' Aaron Levy closed the ledger and stood to replace it on the shelf behind him.

'Why didn't you report it to the police?' asked Pilgrim.

'What business is it of yours, or of any other goyim? You think badly enough of us, without our women running around like whores.'

'You think she's with a man?'

'A man has been following her around. Writing her letters.'

'Letters?'

'I found them after she left. Burned them. My sister is dead to us now.'

Pilgrim closed his eyes. After a moment he opened them again and took something from his pocket.

Aaron Levy grasped the earring and stared at it. His heavy features flickered with some emotion.

'You know it?' asked Pilgrim.

'It was my Mother's.'

A few minutes later, on his way out through the yard, Pilgrim caught the sleeve of Woolf Levy who was watching the loaded waggon clatter out of the gates.

'Did Mena have a friend?' he asked. 'Someone she confided in?'

'Amalia Cohen. Her father is a tailor on Artillery Lane.' The young man stopped Pilgrim as he was about to walk away. 'You said, "did". You said, "did Mena have a friend?"'

Pilgrim swore silently. 'You had better go in to your cousin.'

He retraced his steps to Artillery Lane, and found a shop with bolts of fabric and ribbons on display in the window. The sign said Cohen and Sons. A bell rang as he entered.

A young woman emerged from a back room behind a curtain, and considered him from under heavy brows. 'Papa is out just now. If you're here for a fitting I'm sure he will only be a few minutes.'

'I'm not here for a fitting. Your name is Amalia?' Pilgrim watched her carefully. 'I'm a police detective. I would like to ask you about Mena Levy.'

She turned to a bolt of cloth that lay unravelled on the counter, lifting the heavy roll with ease. She wound the cloth back onto it, and slammed it down again. She was angry, he realized. About what?

'You should come back when Papa is here,' she snapped.

'Did Mena tell you she was going to run away?'

Amalia snorted, but said nothing.

'Her brother Aaron thinks she eloped with someone,' he pressed. 'A man who sent her letters.'

'So much he knows. That big bear.'

'You don't think she did?'

She snorted again.

'Aaron found the letters after she left,' he said. 'Burned them.'

Some of the tension seemed to go from her body.

'Did you know about them?' he asked.

'Yes.' She took a breath. 'Local people bring in pies and bread to put in the bakery ovens. One day a man came in while Mena and I were there, and was staring at Mena. After that we'd often see him hanging around the bakery, in the street, and even outside the synagogue. He never tried to talk to her. Just stared, like a fool. We used to laugh at him. Then he started sending the letters.'

'Do you know what they said?'

'Oh, the usual: that her eyes were like stars, her hair like midnight … No imagination.'

'Did he sign them? Put an address on them?' A thought occurred to him. 'Were they written in red ink?'

She looked at him as if he was mad, and shook her head.

'Was he young? Old? Tall? Short? Dark? Fair?'

The girl shrugged. 'All goyim look the same. Except for you.'

He realized she was alluding to his scars, and almost laughed. Was she as rude to everyone?

'Is that all?' she asked. 'I have to shut up the shop. Find Papa. Aaron and Woolf will need him.'

Pilgrim frowned. After his slip with Woolf Levy, he had been very careful not to imply that Mena was dead.

Amalia gave him a scornful look. 'You say you are a detective? You know nothing of a woman's heart. What woman would elope with a man and leave his letters behind?'

Pilgrim thought about her words as he walked back to Holborn. She was right, of course. When Mena Levy had left home, it hadn't been to elope with her mysterious admirer. So where had she gone? There was another thing puzzling him: why was Amalia Cohen so angry? Her whole body had been vibrating with rage. Towards whom? Aaron Levy? Mena Levy? Herself? It was possible, of course, that she was one of those people perpetually dissatisfied with life. Like Dick Tanner.

He let himself into the house with his key, and took off his overcoat. The clatter of kitchen utensils echoed up from the basement stairs.

'Is that you, Sergeant?' Charlotte Piper called up. 'Supper's ready in half an hour. And there's a package just arrived for you. It's on the parlour table.'

He went into the parlour. The table still had tea things on it, a tin of biscuits, and a sewing basket. There was also a package, wrapped in canvas, with a label written in red ink. He picked it up. It was addressed to 'Sergeant Pilgrim, care of Mrs C Piper, 27 Greville Street, Holborn'.

'Something nice, I hope?'

Pilgrim spun around. Charlotte Piper stood in the doorway, wiping her hands on her apron.

'I beg your pardon,' she said. 'I didn't mean to make you jump.'

'You didn't.' He resisted the urge to hide the package behind his back.

'Aren't you going to open it?'

'Later.' He pushed past her. 'I'll open it later.'

CHAPTER THIRTY-ONE

'You have to put me back on the investigation, Charley.'

'I'm on my way home.' Field buttoned his overcoat. His eyes looked sore, as if he had been rubbing them.

'You have to see this first,' said Pilgrim.

Field scowled at the cigar box. 'What is it this time? A hand?'

'A finger.' Pilgrim frowned. 'How did you know?'

'Walk with me.' Field nodded at the box. 'Leave that abomination here.'

They walked for a long time. Field volunteered no conversation, a fact that was startling in itself, without the glowering expression he wore as he strode along. They took the path along the embankment, keeping pace with the river running black and silent beside them. Pilgrim avoided looking at it. He had never learned to swim and the Thames always filled him with a deep unease. Particularly at night. The thought of so much water rushing through the city – a primitive force, heedless of the life that clung to its banks – disturbed him. To distract himself he noted the changes that had taken place on the embankment. It had been some time since he had been there after dark, and the transformation astonished him. What was once broken ground, scarred with ditches, was freshly paved and lined with lamp posts, as bright as any city thoroughfare.

Eventually he spoke.

'I take it we have another victim?'

Field nodded. 'Poison this time. Prussic acid. Not so easy to get hold of as arsenic. According to Tanner, it's only used by chemists, jewellers, and photographers. And miners. But we don't get many of those in the city. Why did you move out of the barracks, Harry?'

Pilgrim was thrown by the change of subject. 'I needed some distance.'

Field nodded. 'Probably for the best. Did you find good lodgings?'

'Good enough.' He was impatient with small talk. 'Put me back on the investigation.'

'You're making this personal.'

'I'm not. The killer is. He sent this last package to my new lodging. What if my landlady had opened it? What if … ?' He blinked back the image of Charlotte Piper, lying naked on a blood-soaked mattress. 'You have to let me fight this man, and I can't do it if I'm not on the case.'

Field strode on. 'You're putting me in an impossible situation.'

'I realize that.' Pilgrim kept pace with his old friend, not wanting to press him too hard. Charley Field had never responded well to direct pressure.

'Here we are.' Field stopped. Without Pilgrim realising it, they had arrived at the yellow-brick house that Field called home. It sat in the middle of a terrace, in the shadow of the grim walls and fairytale turrets of Millbank Prison.

'You'll stay for dinner?' asked Field. 'Alice and Mother Molly would be glad to see you.'

Pilgrim didn't feel at all sociable, but he wanted his answer. He nodded and followed Field into the house.

'Harry!' As soon as he stepped into the hall, he was enveloped in the embrace of Alice Field, a bird-like woman with a substantial bosom. She stood back to look at him.

'Mother,' she called, 'you'll never guess who's here to see us.'

181

'You have the voice of a costermonger. I heard you from here.'
Another voice, querulous with age, came from within the house. 'Harry
Pilgrim, is it? Come through to the parlour, boy, and let me see you.'

The parlour was brightly lit. An old woman sat in the rocking
chair beside a blazing fire, so close that her stockings were in
danger of scorching.

'Mother Molly,' said Pilgrim.

She embraced him, then held him at arm's length.

'Merciful heavens,' she said, 'but you need feeding up.'

He smiled. Molly Mulligan was over eighty, but looked much
the same as she had thirty years before. Her currant eyes fixed on
him, black and unnerving.

'Do you still have your token?' she asked, as she always did.
'Let me see it.'

He fished beneath his shirt for the cockleshell he wore on a
thong around his neck. It was the size of a sixpence, made of silver,
of the type awarded to the pilgrims at Santiago. His father had
left it with him at the Foundling Hospital: the token by which he
could identify and retrieve him. Not that he ever had.

'Never forget where you come from,' said Mother Molly. 'It
stops you getting above yourself.' She looked pointedly at her
son-in-law, who ignored her. In police records Charley Field was
officially noted as the son of a publican from Chelsea. In fact, he
had been found on the steps of St Martin-in-the-Fields. Hence his
name. Molly Mulligan, mother to all the orphans at the Foundling
Hospital, had a literal turn of mind.

'It's mutton broth tonight,' said Alice. 'Your favourite, Harry.
I'm just about to dish up. Come through to the dining room.'

Pilgrim gave his arm to Mother Molly and helped her to totter
through to the other room.

'Sit here next to me,' she said, 'and tell me what you've been
doing with yourself.' She waited until he had settled her in her chair
before firing one of her famous cannonballs into the conversation.
'Aren't you an Inspector yet?'

Field and Pilgrim exchanged a glance.

'Why haven't you made him Inspector yet?' she jabbed Charley with a bony finger. 'And don't tell me he ain't good enough. I've been reading about him in Mr Dickens's journal.'

'You better ask Harry.' Field helped himself to buttered potatoes.

'Leave it, Mother.' Alice spooned the broth into bowls. 'It's none of our business.'

'None of my business? My boys are always my business.' Molly jabbed at Pilgrim just as he was about to take his first spoonful of broth. 'What does he mean, "I'd better ask you that?"'

Pilgrim lowered his spoon, and was about to answer, when Field spared him the trouble.

'I wanted to promote him before Christmas, but he wouldn't have it.'

'He wouldn't have it?' Molly turned her incredulous gaze on Pilgrim. 'Why ever not?'

'He doesn't want the responsibility.' Field answered for him again, his bitterness only thinly veiled. 'He doesn't want to have "underlings", isn't that right, Harry?'

Pilgrim lifted his spoon again.

Molly looked from one to the other. 'Boys!' she snorted. 'I should just knock your heads together, the way I used to do.'

'Charley tells me you've moved out of the barracks,' said Alice. 'Are you still convenient for the station?' She steered them into less contentious waters. Alice had always been a diplomat, even as a skinny six year old. It was something she'd been obliged to cultivate, being Molly's daughter. Her tact made her an asset to any man of ambition, as had soon become obvious to the young Charley Field.

'I'm at Holborn,' said Pilgrim. 'So I'm close to Whitehall. Too close, in truth.'

Charley and Alice exchanged a smile, and Pilgrim felt his isolation yawn, cavernous, around him. He glanced at Mother Molly and noted that she was watching him. If anyone could penetrate his careful facade, it was Molly. She pursed her lips.

183

*

'Got yourself a sweetheart yet, Harry?'

Charley almost choked on his broth.

'I'm married,' said Pilgrim, eyes narrowing. 'As you know very well.'

Alice jumped to her feet. 'There's treacle pudding, if anyone wants it.'

The broth bowls were cleared away, and the pudding dispensed, complete with custard and walnuts. It proved too much for Pilgrim – he couldn't remember the last time he'd eaten so much.

'I'll have that,' said Molly, 'if you're finished with it.' She pulled his bowl towards her and emptied it in three spoonfuls, smacking her gums with relish. Pilgrim watched Charley devour his own gigantic portion. It was easy to see how his friend had acquired his impressive physical presence. When they were finished Alice collected the dishes.

'Come on, Mother, let's leave the boys to their port. They'll have things to discuss.'

Pilgrim was subjected to a hug from Alice and a whiskery kiss from Molly, and then left alone with Field. He sighed and leaned back against the cushions.

'They're glad to see you,' said Field. 'It's been too long.'

'You're right. It has.'

They fell into silence again. Field rubbed his nose and stared into the fire. When he finally spoke, his tone was grave. 'This one could bring us down, Harry. Theft and burglary we can handle. Murder even, in the common way. But this killer … he's making fools of us. If we don't catch him soon, the Home Secretary could be forced to disband the detective division.'

'You think that's a possibility?'

'More than a possibility. Sir Richard has tabled a motion to the Law and Order Committee.' Field rubbed his hand over his face. 'The thing is no one wants us. The upper classes don't. The politicians don't. And ordinary folk think that detection should be a part of every policeman's job.' He gave a bitter laugh. 'That's when they think at all.'

'How much time do we have?'

Field shrugged. 'Another week? After that we'll be considered a failed experiment, and Sir Richard, George Moxton, and their ilk will rub their hands together and crow "We told you so". It could be years before anyone tries again. The pity of it, Harry, is that this city may not want a Detective Force, but it needs one. It bloody needs one.' He subsided into silence.

Pilgrim stared into the fire. What would he do if he could no longer be a detective? He couldn't imagine returning to the beat. The alternative was to push paper around at Whitehall, and he couldn't imagine doing that, either. He glanced at Field, who was also staring into the fire, his bluff face illuminated by the flames. His friend seemed to be more concerned for the population of the city than for himself, but Pilgrim was worried on his behalf. What would become of the flamboyant Chief Inspector Field if he were deprived of his position? It didn't bear thinking about. If ever there was a man born to the job it was Charley Field.

'I think the key to the murderer's identity could lie with Mena Levy,' he said.

'Who?' Field's head whipped round.

'The woman in the Hackney carriage. I found out who she was today.'

'I distinctly remember taking you off the case.' But there was no heat in the words.

'We wondered why he hadn't left her body to be discovered, like the others. I think he didn't want to risk anyone finding out who she was, because she wasn't a random victim. She was being followed by a young man who wrote letters to her.'

'Letters … ?'

'Don't get your hopes up. Her brother burned them. But her friend, Amalia, saw the man.'

'Can she describe him?'

'No.'

'What, nothing at all? Hair colour? Height?'

'Nothing.'

'A pity.' Field tapped his chin with his index finger. 'So … our boy murders this Jewish girl, and then … what? Two things bother me. Why go to the trouble of setting up Johannes Appler for the girl's death, if he intended to kill him rather than letting him take the blame? And why then go on this bloody spree?'

'I think he chose Appler for a reason. I think he's choosing them all for a reason. I just haven't worked out what it is yet.' Pilgrim paused. 'You need me on the case.'

Field sighed. 'Would you like to sleep here tonight? I'll ask Alice to make up a bed.'

'What about putting me back on the case?'

'I'll think about it.'

CHAPTER THIRTY-TWO

'Good to see you back, Sergeant Pilgrim.' Phelps turned to Field. 'The Reverend Bonwell's here to see you, sir. He's been waiting above an hour. I've put him in the waiting room.'

'Damnation.' Field pulled a face. 'I'd forgotten he was coming this morning.'

'He's here to identify Stella Drake?' asked Pilgrim.

Field nodded. His gaze flashed speculatively to Pilgrim. 'I have a meeting this morning. I don't suppose … ?'

'Do I have a choice?'

Field grinned and made his escape up the staircase.

The station waiting room was emptier than usual, with only four occupants on the wooden benches. Pilgrim recognized the first one.

'How are you, Blackey?'

'Jolly, sa!' The bundle of rags gaped up at him, his single remaining tooth white in his mud-smeared face.

'What are you doing so far from the river?' Blackey was a mudlark who earned his living on the banks of the Thames at low tide, searching for anything he might sell: rags, scraps of bone, iron, or copper nails.

'I found this. I thought I'd come and see if you Peelers might give me a bob or two for it.' He held up a police rattle, the wood splotched and blackened from contact with the water. He saw the cigar box under Pilgrim's arm. 'You brought me a cigar, sa?'

Pilgrim shook his head and patted the man's shoulder.

A little further along the bench from the beggar sat an elderly, soberly dressed couple. A pall of sadness hung over them. Pilgrim was going to pass them by, but something made him stop.

'Can I help you?'

'We are waiting for a release form. For our boy's body. We were told it would only be a little while.' The man read the question in Pilgrim's eyes. 'We are Hindrik and Gertrude Appler.'

'Detective Sergeant Harry Pilgrim.' He held his hand out to the man. 'I'm in charge of the investigation into your son's death.'

'God bless you, sir.' The man pumped his hand. 'We know Johannes would never take his own life.'

The woman also got to her feet, her eyes raw with weeping. She clutched at his sleeve.

'Wanneer zult u de moordenaar van mijn zoon vinden?'

Hindrik Appler blushed. 'I beg you to excuse my wife, she has no English.'

'What did she say?'

'She asked when you are going to find Johannes' killer.'

'Soon. Tell her it will be soon.' He moved away as the man relayed the words to his wife, wishing he had something other than platitudes to give them.

The last occupant of the waiting room sat as far away as possible from the other three, his body taut with outrage.

'Reverend Bonwell.' Pilgrim greeted him coldly.

'About time! Dragging me all the way down here for no reason.'

'Someone has to identify your sister-in-law's body. Perhaps you would rather we ask your wife?'

'Don't be absurd!'

'It would have saved a lot of time if you had told me about Stella during our interview in Great Barrow.'

'So that's what this is about! Making me wait here like some criminal, with beggars and,' he directed a look of pure poison at the Dutch couple, 'Baptists!'

Something at the very centre of Pilgrim went absolutely still. 'You should have told me about your son, too,' he said.

The colour drained from Bonwell's face. His gaze slid to the other occupants of the waiting room, then slid away again. 'I have no idea what you're talking about.'

Pilgrim stepped close to the clergyman, forcing him to retreat until his calves were pressed against the bench. 'You curdle my guts.' He spoke slowly, but very clearly, loud enough for everyone in the room to hear. 'Preaching piety in public, while, in private you beat your wife and seduce your sister-in-law.'

Hendrik Appler and Blackey the mudlark stared at him.

'You didn't even have the decency to bury the boy properly,' continued Pilgrim. 'He was your son, damn you.'

Bonwell opened his mouth, closed it, and then opened it again. 'This is outrageous ... you have no proof ... I demand to see your superior.'

'Are you certain about that?' Pilgrim refused to step away. 'I daresay he would be extremely interested to hear about you and your familial relations.'

Bonwell sat down with a thump. The fight went out of him. 'No.'

'I beg your pardon?'

'No.'

Pilgrim turned away in disgust. 'Let's get this finished.'

The sight of Stella Drake's broken body at St Bartholomew's took the last vestiges of resistance from Bonwell. He signed the paperwork without another word to Pilgrim, or to Townsend, who completed the forms on behalf of the Coroner. Then he took possession of Stella's sorry bundle of clothes, and left.

Pilgrim returned to the mortuary where Fairweather was waiting for him. The cigar box was open on the table, the severed finger in his hand.

'I see you brought me something,' said Fairweather. 'It looks like Clara Donald's – it's been severed on the knuckle with a sharp knife. I'll double-check, of course.' He put the finger back into the box. 'This one seems to be leading you a merry dance. You are certain it's the same killer?'

'What makes you ask?'

'In my experience of multiple murderers, they tend to favour one method – the knife, say, or strangulation. This man appears to be going out of his way to make all the deaths as different as possible: a blow to the head, a cut throat, disembowelment, and now poison. It's odd.'

'As if he's trying to find which method he prefers.'

'Practising.' Fairweather's eyes locked with Pilgrim's.

Practice makes perfect. The phrase rang in Pilgrim's head.

Wainwright burst through the door, startling them both. 'Inspector Field sent me to fetch you post-haste, Dr Fairweather, sir,' he gasped. 'We have a prisoner in the cells what's havin' the most fearful fit!'

'A fit?' asked Fairweather. 'What symptoms?'

'He's thrashin' about on the floor, sir.'

'Is he making a noise?' Fairweather saw Wainwright's blank look and elaborated. 'Is he screaming, or shouting?'

'He's gruntin' sir, something dreadful. Enough to raise the hairs all over your body.'

'I'll get my bag.'

After the doctor had fetched his medical bag, the three men hailed a cab that bowled them along the Strand towards Whitehall.

'Why has Field sent for me?' asked Fairweather. 'Don't you have a doctor on the premises?'

'Yes, sir, Dr Cruikshank, sir. But the Chief Inspector thinks it's poison,' said Wainwright. 'That's why he sent for you.'

'Who's been poisoned?' asked Pilgrim.

'Mr Trinkle, the suspect Sergeant Tanner brought in for the Countess.'

Pilgrim frowned.

Fairweather turned to Wainwright. 'Has he any other symptoms, apart from the convulsions? Is he cold to the touch?'

'I didn't get that close, sir. Didn't want to.'

190

The noise hit them as soon as they arrived at Whitehall; a bestial moaning coming from the direction of the cells, more suited to an abattoir than a police station.

'Hector. Thank God.' Field was waiting for them. 'This way.'

'I can hear that,' muttered Fairweather. Pilgrim followed.

Angus Trinkle lay on the floor of his cell; his body arched backwards, heels drumming on the stones. Bloody spittle flecked around his mouth. As soon as they entered the cell, however, he went limp and silent. His eyes rolled up to look at them in agonized entreaty. The police doctor, who was kneeling beside him on the floor, patted his shoulder ineffectually.

'Have you given him anything?' asked Fairweather.

'I've tried to administer laudanum, but his jaw is locked.'

Fairweather knelt to open his bag. 'I should have brought chloroform. Ether will have to do.'

Trinkle began to twitch and then to jerk again. Spittle flew, and the inhuman moaning resumed. The crowd that had gathered in the tiny cell gawked at the thrashing figure.

'Hold him still, Cruikshank.' Fairweather poured liquid onto a cloth.

Trinkle possessed an inhuman strength. It took both Cruickshank and Pilgrim to keep him still enough for Fairweather to clap the cloth over his mouth and nose. After a minute, Fairweather signalled for the men to step back. Trinkle's convulsions didn't lessen, nor did his eyes close. Fairweather wiped his own forehead with his sleeve.

'It hasn't worked,' said Field.

'It has,' said Fairweather. 'He's unconscious, thank God.'

The moaning had stopped. It had been replaced by grunting, mechanical exhalations, as Trinkle's lungs were squeezed by his spasms.

Fairweather stared at his patient. 'There's nothing else I can do.'

Trinkle continued to jerk as if he was a puppet under the control of some sadistic puppet master. His whole body stiffened and arched backwards, until it could bend no more. And then it did. Another muscle spasm seized him and there was an audible 'crack'. The body continued to thrash for another minute, before it lay still at last, twisted grotesquely on the stone floor.

Pilgrim closed his eyes.

CHAPTER THIRTY-THREE

'Strychnine?'

'I believe so, Charley,' said Fairweather, 'although I won't be able to confirm it until I get him to the mortuary.'

'Rat poison, do you think?' Field dropped into the chair behind his desk.

'I doubt it. From the violence of the convulsions and the speed of death it had to have been a massive dose. I would say it was probably strychnia in its purest form.' Fairweather frowned. 'God knows where he got it from.'

'I'm more worried about how it got into the cell,' muttered Field. 'His pockets should have been emptied. Has he had any visitors, Dolly?'

'Not that I'm aware of, sir. I can check with Sergeant Phelps.'

Field rubbed his chin. 'I don't understand why he would do such a thing.'

'Perhaps he was guilty, sir?' suggested Dolly. 'Perhaps he did murder the Countess?'

'And killed himself in a fit of remorse?' Field snorted. 'That kind of thing only happens in novels. But we'll see what Tanner has to say about the gloves.' He nodded to Fairweather. 'I'm grateful for your coming so quickly, Hector. I'm sorry there was nothing you could do. Harry will see you out.'

Pilgrim and Fairweather went down the staircase together. The entrance hall had resumed its usual noise levels, its inhabitants swearing, singing, and shouting threats.

When they got to the door, the doctor turned to Pilgrim. 'It makes no sense,' he said. 'The lad could have chosen any number of poisons that would have done the job cleaner. It's a hell of a way to kill yourself.' He rammed his hat onto his head and stepped out onto the street.

Pilgrim watched him go. *A hell of a way to kill yourself* … or a hell of a way to be killed? Why did everyone assume Trinkle had committed suicide, when another prisoner had already been murdered under their noses?

Dolly accosted him at the top of the stairs.

'I've been trying to get hold of you, sir,' he said. 'I came to your lodgings last night, but you weren't there. Didn't Lotte tell you I needed to speak to you urgently?'

'Lotte?'

'Mrs Piper.'

Pilgrim shook his head, distracted. His thoughts still lay in Angus Trinkle's cell.

'It's about Clara Donald, sir,' continued Dolly.

'Who?'

At that moment Charley Field stuck his head out of his office door. 'Harry!' he snapped. 'Can I see you in here a minute? You too, Adolphus.'

When Dolly saw that Wainwright was already in Field's office, his face drained of colour. Wainwright studiously avoided his stare, while Pilgrim looked at him, curious.

'Sorry, sir,' mouthed Dolly.

'Sit down.' Field marched behind his desk and leaned on it, as if to gather his strength. 'Just when I thought things couldn't possibly get worse, young Wainwright here tells me he found something belonging to you, Harry, in Clara Donald's effects.'

Pilgrim frowned, his thoughts whirring. Clara Donald? Hadn't Fairweather mentioned a Clara Donald? Clara Donald's finger.

Clara. *The name's Clara, since you ask. Be sure to tell your friends about me.* The words rang in his memory, left him nauseous.

'The prostitute? She's dead?'

Field glanced at Dolly and then at Wainwright. Dolly was as pale as Wainwright was scarlet. Field snatched up the portrait and thrust it at Pilgrim.

'Recognize this?'

Pilgrim didn't need to look. He'd been in such a hurry to leave Clara Donald's room that he'd forgotten Martha's portrait. He'd planned to go back for it.

'Of course I do.'

'Well?' Field glared at him.

'It was Clara who told me where to find Martha Drewitt. She recognized her, after … ' Pilgrim realized he could say no more. Field glared at the other detectives.

'Out. Both of you.'

The young men bolted for the door. Field grabbed Dolly's sleeve as he passed.

'I'll speak to you, later,' he hissed.

Dolly threw himself out of the door, and slammed it shut behind him.

'What's he done?' asked Pilgrim.

'Tried to cover your arse. Silly bugger. I know from experience what a thankless task that is.' Field sank onto his chair. 'Buggering hell's flames, Harry. It's one thing to know, unofficially, that you've been visiting tarts, and another to have my bloody nose rubbed in it.'

'Mea culpa,' said Pilgrim.

Field's head whipped up.

'Of having sexual relations with Clara Donald. Nothing more.'

'Of paying for sexual relations with Clara Donald, who then turns up dead in our investigation.'

The two men looked at each other. A world of recrimination, regret, and resignation passed between them. Field sighed.

'I can handle Wainwright. But I'm telling you now, Harry, this is your last chance. Cock-up again, and I'll not only take you off the case, I'll send you to the provinces. If, by some miracle we still have a Detective Force when this is over, I'll transfer you to bloody George Moxton in Essex. I swear.'

CHAPTER THIRTY-FOUR

'I hope you'll excuse me, gentlemen, but I have agreed to let the Phrenology Association of Edinburgh take my measurements for posterity. Dr McPherson here tells me I have the most pronounced faculty of benevolence.'

'Indeed you do, sir.' The Scotsman applied his callipers to the writer's jaw. 'Now if you could just hold still another wee moment?'

'He also examined the skull of William Burke after he was hanged,' continued Dickens, ignoring the doctor's request. 'Tell the Sergeant and Constable what you discovered.'

McPherson removed the callipers with a sigh. 'A pronounced enlargement of the temporal bone that signals destructiveness, and the propensity to commit murder. And an underdeveloped zone of empathy.'

Dickens's eyes gleamed with an evangelistic fervour. 'Only imagine, Sergeant Pilgrim, how useful it would be to be able to identify potential murderers by measurement alone!'

Pilgrim thought it best not to point out the drawbacks of such a policy. He hadn't brought Dolly to Devonshire Terrace to be drawn into a debate. They had only stopped off as a courtesy, on their way to investigate a pawn ticket that Dolly had found between the pages of Clara Donald's bible.

'Mena Levy's brother identified her body this morning,' Pilgrim

197

told Dickens. 'Thank you, sir, for giving me the introduction to Isaac Simmons.'

Dickens nodded, dislodging the callipers again. 'Delighted to be of assistance. Was Mr Levy able to give you any information?'

'He told me about a man who had taken to following Mena around, and had written her letters. Unfortunately, the letters have been burned. Mena's friend Amalia read them, but cannot remember anything of the contents. She also saw the man several times but is unable to give us anything but the vaguest description.'

'Nothing useful at all?'

'No.' Pilgrim ran a hand through his hair. 'If there was only one thing, one tiny thing she might remember.'

Dickens fell silent. Dr McPherson made the most of his subject's uncharacteristic stillness, and flew around him with the callipers, measuring and making notes. At last he gave a sigh of satisfaction. 'My examination is complete, sir.'

Dickens waited for him to pack up his equipment, and then led him to the door. 'Mrs Herring will see you out. I will call on you in Edinburgh in June.' He waited until McPherson's footsteps had gone before speaking again. 'I wonder,' he said, 'are either of you gentlemen familiar with the practice of mesmerism?'

'Isn't that where you speak to spirits?' asked Dolly. 'My ma and Lotte have been to some of those meetings … seances, I think you call them.'

Pilgrim raised an eyebrow. It didn't sound like the kind of thing Charlotte Piper would do. But, there again, what would he know? Perhaps she'd been trying to get in touch with her late husband.

Dickens shook his head. 'Mesmerism is quite different from spiritualism, Constable, although the two are most definitely linked. It is a means of putting someone in a state of deep relaxation, for healing purposes, or for soothing mental agitation. I have had some modest success with it in the past.' He eyed the two detectives speculatively. 'And I have found memory recall to be much improved in a mesmeric trance.'

There was a beat of silence.

'I can't see her father agreeing to it,' said Pilgrim.

'Her name is Cohen?' asked Dickens. 'Her father is Reuben Cohen the tailor? Is she a pinch-faced little thing with a heavy brow?'

Pilgrim nodded, although he doubted she would recognize herself from the description.

'I was introduced to Amalia and her father a few weeks ago, at a Chamber of Commerce dinner. That might be useful, don't you think?'

'I don't see how,' said Pilgrim. 'I can't imagine she would let you put her in a trance.'

'What if,' mused Dickens, 'she was unaware of it?'

Dolly's round gaze flashed from Dickens to Pilgrim.

'No,' snapped Pilgrim. 'Absolutely not.'

The bell jangled as Dickens pushed it open. The shop was almost as chilly as the street outside, and the air smelled of dust and tailor's chalk. Amalia Cohen emerged through the curtain, bundled in a muffler, the tip of her nose rosy with the cold. Dickens stifled a sigh. She presented an unpromising mesmeric subject, her body hunched and defensive.

'Good day to you,' he said. He gave a start. 'Good heavens. It's Miss Cohen, isn't it?'

The girl nodded, suspicious.

He removed his hat and unwound his scarf. 'We were introduced at the Mayor's reception. You do remember me?'

'Mr Dickens!' Her heavy brows rose in astonishment. 'Of course I remember you.' Taken unawares by her famous visitor, the girl's features lost much of their sharpness. She flushed.

'How are you, my dear?' he asked. 'Well, I hope?'

'Quite well, thank you. But … my father is out at present.'

That came as no surprise to Dickens: he had seen Reuben Cohen leave the shop a few minutes before. 'I haven't come to call on your father, although it is a pity to have missed him.' He favoured her with his most disingenuous smile. 'I am, in fact, looking for ribbon. I trust you can help me?'

'Of course.' Her surprise gave way to a businesslike demeanour. 'What kind would you prefer? We have satin, taffeta, grosgrain, and American cotton.'

'Blue?' He shrugged. 'Forgive my ignorance. It is a gift for my wife. She has blue eyes. I thought to give her some ribbon to match that she might use to trim whatever takes her fancy. A bonnet, perhaps.'

Amalia crossed to the shelves and lifted down several reels of ribbon. She put them on the counter, unravelling a length of each for Dickens to inspect. He pointed to one.

'What do you think of this?' he asked her.

'The satin? It is pretty.' She ran her fingertip down it. 'Very soft.'

'It is pretty,' he agreed slowly, caressing her with his voice. 'And beautifully soft.' He ran his finger down the length of it. Once. Twice. 'Very soft. What shade would you call this?'

'Bluebell.'

'Yes. Bluebell.' He leaned towards her a little and ran his fingertip down the ribbon again. 'Bluebell.'

'But I'm not sure it's right for a bonnet.'

He hid a flash of annoyance as she picked up one of the other reels.

'This might be better,' she said. 'It's more hardwearing.' She rubbed her forehead.

'Better. More hardwearing.' Dickens rubbed his forehead.

'And almost as soft.' She touched the ribbon.

'Almost as soft.' He touched the ribbon. 'What colour would you say this is?'

'Azure.'

'Azure. Exactly so. You have an eye for colour, Amalia.' He used her first name deliberately. She didn't react to the overfamiliarity, but continued to stare down at the ribbon. He tapped it thoughtfully with his forefinger. Once. Twice. She reached out her finger. Tapped the ribbon. Once. Twice.

200

'Azure,' he repeated. 'That is the colour of my wife's eyes exactly.'

'Exactly, yes.'

He smiled. It was going better than he could have hoped. For all the girl's prickly exterior she was remarkably magnetic.

'Azure is a beautiful colour. The colour of my wife's eyes exactly. What colour are your eyes, my dear?'

She lifted her chin to look at him.

'Brown,' he said. 'As brown as autumn leaves. Like your friend Mena's.' He held his breath.

'Yes. Like Mena's.'

'And Mena's admirer? The man who wrote her letters. His eyes are …'

'Brown.'

'Brown. And his hair is …'

'Brown.'

'How old is he?' He had been trying to avoid asking a direct question. In this case it couldn't be helped, but he kept his tone as soothing as possible.

'She thought he was foolish,' said Amalia. 'She laughed at him.'

He smothered a snort of impatience. He had no idea how long he would be able to sustain the trance.

'This man with the brown hair,' he continued smoothly, 'with hair as brown as autumn leaves. He wrote Mena letters?'

'Yes.'

'You read them?'

'She read them to me. She knew I was jealous.'

'The letters were signed?'

'No. We called him the Scribbler.'

'And he wrote to her, didn't he, he told her …'

'How beautiful she was … her hair … her eyes. She was beautiful … it was always Mena men noticed. Never me.' She paused. 'I was glad when she went away. I'm glad she's dead.'

Her words were matter-of-fact, her expression blank. A chill swept through him, scattering his thoughts.

201

The shop bell jangled. Amalia Cohen's gaze focused again, and fixed on her father who had entered. She frowned at Dickens, as if trying to remember what he was doing there.

'I'll take a yard of this one, Miss Cohen.' Dickens picked up the satin ribbon and gave it to Amalia. 'If you would be so good to wrap it for me?'

'Mr Dickens!' said Reuben Cohen. 'What a surprise to see you here. A pleasure, of course, but a surprise.' He pumped his hand.

'I was just passing, on my way to see Isaac. I needed ribbon.'

'Ribbon?'

'Indeed. And I'm pleased to say your daughter has been most helpful.' He continued to make small talk with the tailor while Amalia measured the ribbon, cut it, and wrapped it. 'Thank you.' He took the package. 'Will you see me to the door, my dear?'

Amalia led him out.

'Goodbye, my dear.' He tapped her on the forearm with his finger. Once. Twice.

She frowned and opened the door for him. 'He wanted to see her dance,' she said.

'Dance?' He was acutely aware of her father, watching them.

'Yes. He wanted Mena to dance for him.'

'Thank you.' His voice was deliberately loud. Amalia Cohen's eyes snapped back into focus. 'You've been most helpful.'

'An absurd waste of time.' Dickens delivered his verdict as he slid into the coffee shop booth, where Pilgrim and Dolly were waiting for him.

'You couldn't put her into a trance?' asked Pilgrim.

'On the contrary. The transference of ethereal fluid was remarkably easy. She was one of the most magnetic subjects I've ever encountered.' He snorted. 'But she was also one of the least observant persons on this earth. All she could tell me was that Mena Levy's admirer had brown hair and brown eyes.'

'That's it?' asked Pilgrim.

'And that he wanted to see her dance.'

'Dance?'

'Indeed. No use whatsoever.' Dickens turned to Pilgrim with an expression of disgust. 'Do you have use for a blue ribbon, Sergeant? I can't see my Kate wanting it.' He pressed the packet into Pilgrim's hand.

'She could tell you nothing more?' Dolly was in a froth of disbelief. 'Not how old he was? Or how tall? Or where he lived?'

'Nothing.' It crossed Dickens's mind to mention Amalia's animosity towards her so-called friend, but he dismissed the thought. The girl was entitled to some privacy, after all. 'I would have pressed her further about him, but her father interrupted us.'

'Dolly,' Pilgrim grasped the constable's sleeve, 'I want you to go back to Reuben Cohen's shop, right this minute.'

'Me, sir? Whatever for?'

'To ask him where he buys his wrapping canvas.'

CHAPTER THIRTY-FIVE

'It's exactly the same.' Charley Field turned the packet of ribbon over in his hand, comparing it to the wrapping that had contained Clara Donald's finger. There were another three samples of the canvas on Pilgrim's desk – one from Mena Levy's body, one from Eliza Grimwood's necklace, and the last from Mena Levy's ear – all with the same distinctive coarse weave.

'Where did Cohen say the shop was, Adolphus?'

Dolly hurried to the map on the wall and tapped it. 'Right here, sir. On Aldgate High Street: Hatchell and Manson, the stationers, sir, selling paper supplies, canvas, and pens.'

'What do we do now, Harry?' asked Field.

'There's no point watching the shop. We have no idea who we're looking for.'

'A brown-haired man with brown eyes,' said Dolly.

'That's almost everyone in this room,' said Field. All five of the detectives were present and only Dolly, whose hair was blonde, didn't fit the description.

'However,' began Pilgrim, 'if someone wished to describe me, they would say I was … disfigured. And if someone wished to describe you, Chief Inspector, they would say you were … ', Field shot him a warning glare, 'anything but nondescript.' Pilgrim finished with a half-smile. 'Only Tanner and Wainwright actually fit the description of Mena Levy's admirer.'

'My eyes are blue,' said Tanner. A muscle jumped in his jaw.

'Witnesses have been known to be unreliable, particularly when it comes to eye colour. The man we're looking for is distinguished only by his lack of distinguishing marks.'

'I take your point,' said Field, 'but it still doesn't give us a lot to work with.'

'The real problem is not so much that we don't have a clear description, but that we have no way of knowing for certain that Mena Levy's admirer is her killer,' said Pilgrim. He frowned. 'Mr Dickens should have asked Amalia Cohen if she had seen him since Mena's disappearance.'

'Mr Dickens?' Field was immediately alert. 'Mr Dickens has been questioning witnesses?'

'Only in passing,' soothed Pilgrim. 'He's friends with her father.'

Dolly had been listening carefully to the exchange. 'A thought occurs, sir,' he said to Field. 'The killer has obviously been watching us. Leaving packages and the like. What if he knows we've been talking to Miss Cohen? If he is the anonymous admirer, he knows she can identify him. The last person who could identify him got his throat cut.'

'By God, you're right, Adolphus. Could the girl be in danger, Harry?'

Pilgrim frowned. 'I hadn't thought of that, but I have to admit it's a possibility.'

'This could be the perfect opportunity to catch the bugger!' crowed Field. 'We'll take it in turns to watch the house. He thinks he's so clever, but this time we might outwit him.'

'Should we warn her father?' asked Pilgrim.

'And have the whole of London Jewry in a froth on the strength of mere conjecture? No.'

Pilgrim pressed his lips together, but he said nothing. He went to study the map. 'She and her father live above the shop. There's a lane runs round the back of Artillery Lane from Bishopsgate Street. We'll have to watch in pairs: one at the front and one at the back.'

'I'll work out a roster,' said Dolly.

'Splendid idea.' Field nodded. 'But don't include Wainwright in your plans this afternoon. He's going to St Bartholomew's. Hector Fairweather wants a sketch of Angus Trinkle's body before the autopsy.'

'Before the autopsy?' said Pilgrim.

'The contortions.' Field rubbed his nose. 'A record for medical posterity.'

All the men fell silent, remembering the scene in the cells.

Tanner was studying the map. 'Did you say this girl lives in Artillery Lane? We'll stand out like pricks in a nunnery.'

'The Sergeant's right, sir,' said Dolly.

'Then we'll have to employ our imaginations. And the extensive contents of the Whitehall lost property department.'

'Aren't we supposed to ask permission before we use disguises?' asked Pilgrim.

Field scowled. 'Let me worry about that.' He dismissed them.

Pilgrim caught Dolly's eye as they left the room. 'Do you still have the pawn ticket you found in Clara Donald's things?'

'It's in my pocket.'

'Let's see to that, before you start drawing up rosters.'

Ma Jellybelly's shop in Chick Lane was an Aladdin's cave of unredeemed goods – china cups, vases, flutes, fiddles, prayer books, ivory ornaments, silver watches, spoons, rings, brooches, chess sets, blankets, clothes, and carpenters' tools – all stacked on shelves or displayed in dirty glass cabinets. The shop window and main door fronted the lane itself, but the entrance that was used the most lay in the side alley. It led directly to a row of wooden booths, facing a counter, an arrangement that ensured the anonymity of anyone not wishing to be seen hocking the family silver.

Pilgrim and Dolly slid into one of the cubicles and waited to be noticed. On the counter, in a column in front of them, three tickets were held in a frame beside three little inkpots. A special pen holder with three nibs allowed three tickets to be written simultaneously with one dip in the ink: one for the record, one to be pinned to the goods, and the other for the customer. The tickets were not the same as the one Dolly had found in Clara Donald's box, which had probably only escaped the notice of the Widow Kelly because it had been tucked between the pages of a bible. They could hear voices from the neighbouring cubicle.

'I'll give you two shillings for it.' A woman's voice, harsh and rasping.

'That's solid silver, that is.' Another woman, with a pleading tone.

'It's plate. Two shillings. Take it or leave it.'

The second woman evidently took it, for there was silence, followed by the clink of coins, and the scrape of a stool.

Mrs Edinburgh, the shop owner, plonked herself on the stool opposite Pilgrim and Dolly. She was known by locals as Ma Jellybelly, for reasons not immediately apparent, for she was a wizened little woman with a tongue like the sting of a wasp.

'Evening, Ma,' said Pilgrim.

She blinked and her features smoothed. 'I ain't got nothing for you, Sergeant. Not today. Things is quiet at the moment. The lads 'ave been takin' a breather.'

'I'm not after information, at least not the usual kind. Can you tell me whose ticket this is?' He passed Clara Donald's pawn ticket to her over the counter. 'There's no shop name on it.'

She dismissed it with a sniff. 'It's plain enough. See them two marks? Them's wings. This ticket's from the Angel Leaving Shop, in Islington. Angel, ha! Devil more like. You want to be careful, doin' business with Bert Tanner. He'll have the shirt off your back soon as look at you.'

Dolly flashed a round-eyed look at Pilgrim.

'Tanner?' repeated Pilgrim.

'The son. The old man died last year.'

'Did he have more than one son?'

'Not that I knows of. All I knows is that Bert Tanner took over the shop, and he's been stealin' the meat out of my mouth ever since.'

Pilgrim took the ticket from her.

'I'll be back next week,' he said, getting to his feet.

'I don't know that I'll 'ave anything for you next week. Like I says, things is quiet presently.'

'Let's hope they don't get too quiet, Ma,' said Pilgrim mildly, 'or I might take the time to look around your shop.'

The woman glared at him.

'Next week,' he said again, then left her with a nod.

Dolly followed him out of the shop.

'Is it Sergeant Tanner's brother, do you think? He said his father used to have a pawnshop.'

'What if it is?' Pilgrim shrugged. 'It's a small world.'

'It's something of a coincidence, though sir, isn't it? And Islington's a long way from Worship Street.'

'What are you suggesting?'

Dolly's eager expression turned crestfallen. 'I'm not sure, exactly.'

'No.' Pilgrim eyed him. 'Neither am I.'

Dolly changed the subject. 'I take it you have an arrangement with Mrs Edinburgh, sir?'

'You could say that.' In fact it was a highly satisfactory agreement, on his part at least.

Ma Jellybelly was the brains behind the Dancing School, an elite gang of burglars whose entrance to properties was usually effected over a roof top, or through an apparently inaccessible window. They were supple and crafty, targeting only the most affluent neighbourhoods, which meant that Pilgrim's conscience was not troubled in the slightest by turning a blind eye to their activities. In exchange for his short-sightedness, Ma Jellybelly kept him informed of any criminal activity of the non-thieving kind that took place on her patch.

It had already borne fruit on several occasions, and had led to convictions in all but one. That case still vexed Pilgrim whenever he thought of it. One of Ma Jellybelly's younger boys, crouched on a rooftop in Mayfair, had watched through a window as a banker throttled his pregnant mistress with one of her own stockings. The boy had had the presence of mind to hotfoot it straight to Ma's in Chick Lane, and Pilgrim had been able to lead other police officers to the girl's body before the banker had the opportunity to hide it.

Unfortunately, it had all been in vain. The banker had several influential friends who all swore he was drinking with them when the murder happened. Even if Pilgrim had been able to persuade the young thief to testify, it would have been the boy's word against theirs, and so Pilgrim had been obliged to chalk that particular episode down to experience.

'Sir?' Dolly broke into his thoughts.

Pilgrim judged it wise to change the subject. Arrangements of the kind that existed between himself and Ma Jellybelly were frowned on by the Joint Commissioners. It was better if Dolly didn't know about it, officially at least.

Instead, he asked, 'What time is it?'

Dolly took out his pocket watch. 'Two o'clock, sir.'

'We have time to catch a cab to Islington before we go back to Whitehall.'

'I promised the Inspector I'd make up that roster.'

'You'll have time. Come on.'

Three brass balls, the usual sign of a pawnbroker, hung over the main door of the Angel Leaving Shop in Islington. There was a second sign above the side door in the alley, a pair of carved angel wings, the paint cracked and peeling. Pilgrim and Dolly passed beneath them, into a room of cubicles similar to the one at Ma Jellybelly's. They took a seat in one of them.

The man who appeared almost immediately couldn't have been anything other than Dick Tanner's brother. He was shorter, and the grooves that ran from his nose to the corners of his mouth were more pronounced, but otherwise he might have been the detective's twin. He glared at them and cracked his knuckles. Pilgrim handed him Clara Donald's ticket. He stomped off.

Dolly turned, triumphant, to Pilgrim. 'It's uncanny, sir.'

Pilgrim didn't respond.

They heard Bert Tanner returning before they saw him, his boots loud on the floorboards. He tore a ticket off a small package, and thrust the package at Pilgrim.

'Three shillin's,' he grunted.

Pilgrim nodded at Dolly. He never put his hand in his own pocket if he could avoid it: the Chief Clerk was notoriously tight-fisted when it came to expenses.

Dolly flushed. He fished in his pocket. He put the coins on the counter, and the pawnbroker scooped them up.

'When was this left with you?' asked Pilgrim.

The big man glared at him. 'You should know.'

'I'm collecting it for my sister.'

Bert Tanner read the ticket he had torn from the package. 'Eleventh January.'

Pilgrim nodded his thanks. He waited until they were back out in the alley before giving the package to Dolly.

'Open it.'

Dolly tore off the wrapping. 'It's just a picture frame. Plate, by the look of it. There's no picture in it.' He grimaced, disappointed.

Pilgrim took it from him. 'Another false trail.' He sighed. 'I'm not sure what I was expecting.' He handed it back.

'It was worth checking, though, sir. What shall I do with this now?'

'Whatever you want. You paid for it.'

Dolly sighed and pocketed the frame.

They turned left on the High Street to pass in front of the shop's window, where a selection of unredeemed items was displayed for sale. Pilgrim stopped. Dolly stopped beside him, and peered through the window to see what he was looking at.

'Something caught your fancy, sir?'

*

'In a manner of speaking.'

In the middle of the window, between a crystal decanter and an oil painting of cattle, were three silver goblets, engraved with a distinctive heraldic design. Something slid in Pilgrim's guts: it felt very like disappointment.

'Come on,' he said to Dolly. 'We're late.'

CHAPTER THIRTY-SIX

Charlotte Piper opened the door and blinked.

'Yes?' Her eyes were wary.

Pilgrim lounged on her step, outlined by the fog, wearing a gaberdine coat, a wide brimmed hat, a heavy beard, and side locks.

'Don't you recognize me, Mrs Piper?' he asked. 'I thought it best to knock, rather than letting myself in. I didn't want to give you a fright.'

'Sergeant Pilgrim?' She opened the door to usher him inside. Once in the hall she inspected him from head to toe. He opened his mouth to speak, but she lifted a hand to stop him.

'I'm sure you have your reasons. Your dinner's on the table in half an hour.' She turned on her heel and went back down to the kitchen.

He removed his hat. The side locks came off with it, but not the beard, which was attached by a ribbon that ran up and over his head. He untied it and put it on the hook, where it hung like a gamekeeper's trophy. He had spent a weary afternoon at the back of Artillery Lane, doing nothing more than standing still. The fog had returned, enough to penetrate the thick gaberdine of his overcoat, but not to melt the ice underfoot, so that the cold struck through the soles of his boots and up his legs. He felt as if he'd never get warm again. He was taking off his boots when there was a knock at the door.

Henry Wainwright stood to attention on the step outside, carrying a carpet bag. 'Reportin' for duty, sir.'

'Take off your boots and come on up.'

Pilgrim sent a silent prayer of thanks to Charlotte Piper when he saw the fire burning in the grate of his room. He shrugged himself out of his clothes, and shivered on the hearthrug in his undervest and drawers. Wainwright stripped off his own clothes and started to put on the ones Pilgrim had discarded.

'Everything quiet, this afternoon, sir?'

'Miss Cohen didn't leave the house or the shop all day, except to go to the synagogue.' Pilgrim smothered a smile, remembering Dolly's look of panic when he realized he was going to have to go into the synagogue with Amalia Cohen and her father. Pilgrim had lingered on the street outside, where he had seen Aaron and Woolf Levy also on their way into the building. The younger man was pale, and the older walked as if carrying a burden, his shoulders slumped, his whole frame diminished by grief.

'Dolly's taken over from me at the front of the shop,' said Pilgrim to Wainwright. 'You're to go to the back lane to relieve Sergeant Tanner.' This time his smile broke through. Tanner had only submitted to wearing a beard and side locks under threat of dismissal from Field.

'Mr Pilgrim!' Mrs Piper called up from the bottom of the stairs. 'Could I have a word?'

'One moment,' he shouted. He tugged on a pair of trousers and a shirt and went out onto the landing. Charlotte Piper frowned up at him.

'Have you got someone up there with you?'

'One of my constables. He'll be gone in a minute.'

'Oh.' Her frown relaxed. Her gaze travelled from his face to his unbuttoned shirt and lingered there. 'Do you like Brussels? The grocer had them at a special price today.'

'Yes.' The skin at his throat felt warm where her gaze rested.

Wainwright emerged from the door behind him, carrying his carpet bag. Pilgrim had to hide another smile. The gaberdine overcoat swamped the constable's shoulders and brushed the top of his stocking feet, making him look like a schoolboy dressed in his father's clothes.

'It'll have to do,' said Pilgrim. 'The beard and hat are downstairs. This is Mrs Piper, my landlady. Mrs Piper, this is Constable Wainwright.'

'Pleased to meet you, ma'am,' said Wainwright. He blushed.

Charlotte nodded at him. 'Would you like to stay for dinner? There's more than enough to go round.'

'No, thank you,' Pilgrim answered for Wainwright. 'He has to be on his way.'

She nodded again and disappeared from view. They heard her feet clomp back down the kitchen stairs. Pilgrim fastened his shirt and went downstairs, followed by Wainwright. At the door, he helped the constable to don the hat and wig, arranging the side locks so that they covered the ribbon of the beard.

'You have your whistle?' he asked.

'Yes, sir, snug in my pocket.'

'The signal is three loud blasts. If you see anything suspicious, don't try to be a hero. Blow the whistle. Dolly and the constables on the beat will be with you in an instant.' He hoped. Artillery Lane was in H Division, but Field was so determined to maintain control of the operation that he'd decided not to tell the Superintendent of H Division about it. Pilgrim thought it was a mistake, and had told him so, but Charley wasn't in the mood to listen.

Pilgrim opened the door and Wainwright melted into the fog and darkness.

'Your dinner's ready.'

He followed Mrs Piper's summons into the dining room. He looked forward to meals in his new lodging, but it wasn't because of the food. Thanks to his anosmia he had no subtlety of palate. In fact, he would go so far to say he had no sense of taste at all.

And it was just as well, because Charlotte Piper was an indifferent cook: she boiled, coddled, and roasted everything to within an inch of disintegration. No, the attraction was definitely not the food.

He liked to watch Mrs Piper as she brought his plates and took them away again. He liked the quick movements of her hands, the way she would brush a stray lock of hair away from her face with her forearm if she were carrying something, the sway of her hips beneath her black skirts. Harry Pilgrim looked at Charlotte Piper the same way he had looked at the confections in the bakery in Gray's Inn Lane as a boy; not in expectation, nor even real desire, but with an aesthetic appreciation of something beyond his reach.

'I thought I would give your rooms a sweep out in the morning,' she said. She plonked a suet pudding in front of him. The meat filling was almost as grey as the suet, spilling onto the plate to lap greasily around a mountain of sprouts. He picked up his knife and fork and started to chew his way through them.

'Do you like egg custard?'

He nodded. She disappeared through the door.

'Mrs Piper!'

She came back.

'Dolly will be coming for me at midnight. I have to go out again. I thought I should let you know, in case we disturbed you.'

'Try not to make too much noise.'

After his meal he thanked her and headed back to his room. He threw a shovelful of coal on the fire and sat on the sofa, stretching his toes to the flames. He was full and warm. He told himself not to get too comfortable, or it would be doubly difficult to go back out into the fog at midnight. That thought inspired another. Had he grown too comfortable in his new lodgings? His life so far had taught him to expect very little, which meant that he was rarely disappointed. As a philosophy it served him well enough, but was it any way for a man to live?

*

He jerked awake as the clock in the hall sounded the last chimes of midnight. He had fallen asleep on his bed. So much for his determination not to get comfortable. Realising that Dolly would be there any minute, he decided to go down and wait in the hallway, to catch him before he knocked at the door. He padded down the stairs, put on his boots, and opened the door onto the street. The fog had thickened to such an extent that he could barely see the bottom of the steps. He waited.

The clock struck quarter past midnight. Then half past. Where the hell was Dolly? He waited another five minutes then decided to head for Artillery Lane anyway. He set off into the fog at a smart pace, and then, after a couple of minutes, broke into a run. He had a very bad feeling.

CHAPTER THIRTY-SEVEN

Artillery Lane was in an uproar. The inhabitants had turned out into the street in their nightclothes – dozens of men, women, and children, all milling around, talking excitedly and exclaiming over the damage that had been done. Broken glass from windows sparkled in the mud, and there were eggs and animal dung splattered on several of the doors. Pilgrim headed for a knot of police uniforms at the far end of the street, gathered around a figure on the ground. He elbowed his way through.

Dolly Williamson was barely recognizable under the blood and beard. His hat had come off and the gabardine overcoat was ripped apart. One of the other constables knelt beside him. He looked up and recognized Pilgrim.

'They've beaten this poor fellow pretty bad, sir.'

'Dolly, can you hear me?' Pilgrim bent to examine him. It was hard to tell if he was breathing. 'Has anyone sent for a doctor?'

The constable got to his feet and called out into the milling crowd. 'Is there a doctor here?'

Pilgrim caught his sleeve. 'Fetch Cruikshank from Whitehall.'

The man's gaze dropped, uncomprehending, to the figure on the ground.

'Get him now!' snarled Pilgrim. 'What are you waiting for?'

He took off through the crowd.

'What the hell happened?' Pilgrim turned to another of the uniformed policemen.

'A disturbance, sir. Apprentices, looking for trouble. They do it periodically. They took off when one of the residents found this and blew it.' He showed Pilgrim Dolly's whistle. 'Lord knows what it was doing here.'

Pilgrim felt for a pulse at Dolly's neck, but couldn't find one under the beard. Dear God! Was he dead?

'Help! Help me!'

Pilgrim tore his gaze from Dolly and saw a nightshirted figure gesticulating in the doorway further up the street. His feet were bare and a halo of hair blew wild about his head.

'My daughter!' Reuben Cohen waved his arms.

'Do not leave this man, under any circumstances,' said Pilgrim to the officer. 'When Dr Cruikshank comes make sure he attends him straight away.' He ran to the old man.

Cohen gripped the front of Pilgrim's shirt. 'Help her,' he gasped.

Pilgrim pushed past him into the building, through the curtains at the back of the shop, and up the stairs. Reuben Cohen followed.

'In there.' The tailor pointed to a door half way along the landing, at the back of the house. Pilgrim went in ahead of him. At first he could see no sign of Amalia; the bed was rumpled, but empty. The window was open and the curtains and pole had been torn down. Then he saw a bare foot sticking out from under the curtain. He pulled the fabric away.

Amalia Cohen stared back at him. There was no blood, but her head was caved in at the temple as if some giant's thumb had crushed it for sport. Her expression was one of surprise rather than fear. He didn't need to check for a pulse. There was a noise, a sigh behind him, and then a thud as Reuben Cohen dropped to his knees.

Someone else crashed into the room. Dick Tanner took in the scene at a glance, ran to the window, and thrust his head out. 'Wainwright! he bellowed. 'Wainwright, you useless cunny, can you hear me?'

'Stay here,' ordered Pilgrim.

For once, Tanner didn't argue.

Pilgrim tore out of the shop, past Dolly's prone figure, scattering two of the uniformed policemen like skittles. 'You two!' he shouted. 'Come with me.'

They charged after him, out of Artillery Lane and right on Bishopsgate Street, then took another sharp right into the lane that ran behind the tailor's shop. Pilgrim skidded to a halt and pointed at one of the policemen.

'You, stay here. Don't let anyone in or out.'

The lad puffed out his chest and nodded. The other officer followed Pilgrim further into the lane. Pilgrim found the spot he had occupied himself earlier in the evening, in the shadow of the wash house that served the street.

'Look there sir!' The young constable pointed to a shape lying on the ground only a few feet away.

'Wainwright!' As Pilgrim reached him, the constable stirred. Pilgrim helped him to sit up.

'What happened?' Wainwright put his fingers to the back of his head and they came away sticky with blood. 'The bugger hit me!'

He tried to get to his feet, but Pilgrim pushed him back down again.

'Stay there,' said Pilgrim. 'Cruikshank's on his way.'

'I heard a commotion in the street, sir, but didn't hear no whistle. The bugger must have crept up on me.' Wainwright glanced up at Amalia Cohen's window and flinched when he saw Tanner glaring down at him. He swivelled his eyes back to Pilgrim. 'He didn't ... he didn't get her, sir, did he?'

'It's not your fault.'

CHAPTER THIRTY-EIGHT

'It's all my fault.' Charley Field stared morosely into his glass. 'I should have told Reuben Cohen his daughter's life was in danger. And I should have told the uniforms what was going on.'

'No one could have predicted what happened tonight.' Pilgrim was almost too tired to speak.

'No?' Field looked at him. 'Not even the murderer? What if he set the apprentices up as a diversion? The bastard's clever, Harry. Too clever.' He took another gulp of port. It was only six o'clock in the morning but he was already on his second glass. 'We're no closer to catching him now than we were three weeks ago. I might as well fall on my sword before they put me out of a job.'

Pilgrim sighed and stood up. He couldn't deal with Charley Field's self-pity now.

'I still haven't told Mrs Piper about Dolly. I'll have a wash and an hour's sleep then take her to the hospital.'

Field turned to him, his expression bleak. 'What if he dies, Harry? What if the boy dies?'

Pilgrim shrugged. He had no answer. A tap came at the door. Field hid his glass under a pile of papers.

'What is it?'

A head appeared, tousled with sleep. Pilgrim's spirits slid even lower as he recognized Sir Richard Mayne's clerk.

'The Joint Commissioners would like to see you, Chief Inspector, sir.'

Field sighed and raised his eyebrows at Pilgrim. 'Both of them, God help me. Bad news travels fast.' He stood up and straightened his clothes.

'I'll come with you,' Pilgrim offered.

'There's no need. It's my head they're after.'

'I'm coming.'

To their surprise, the clerk didn't stop at the third floor of Number Four Whitehall Place, but he continued up to the fourth to where Sir Charles Rowan had his private apartments. A housekeeper opened the door and dismissed the clerk. She saw they had no hat or coats to take, but made them wipe their perfectly clean feet on the doormat before leading them deeper into the apartment. She showed them to a room lined with books.

Sir Richard Mayne stood by the mantel, staring into a hastily lit fire. He was unshaven and wore no cravat, although Pilgrim noticed he had still had time to pin the Order of the Bath to his jacket.

Sir Charles Rowan sat in a fireside chair, wearing a green flannel dressing gown. It had been several months since Pilgrim had seen the senior Joint Commissioner and he was shocked at the change in him. Once the image of a hearty country squire, Sir Charles' skin hung on his frame. He seemed to have shrunk several inches.

'Detective Chief Inspector Field and Detective Sergeant Pilgrim, sir.' The housekeeper bobbed a curtsey and retreated, leaving them marooned in the middle of the rug.

'Good morning, gentlemen.' Sir Charles sat stiff-backed in his chair. 'Sir Richard and I have heard about the night's events. We're disappointed, Chief Inspector, very disappointed.'

Pilgrim didn't look at Field, but he sensed the fight draining out of him. Sir Charles' words were worse than any of Mayne's thunderings.

'Perhaps you could tell us exactly what your men were doing in Artillery Lane?'

Field took a breath and began with Appler's arrest and the earring in the Hackney cab. Sir Charles listened without comment, until Field reached the part where they had discovered Appler's suicide was murder.

'Good God! You mean the fellow had his throat cut right here in the cells?'

'I'm afraid so, sir.'

'Why weren't we informed?'

Field glanced at the other Commissioner. 'Sir Richard knew, sir.'

'I see.' Sir Charles's expression tightened. 'Go on.'

Mayne grew redder and redder as Field continued his narrative. Field was crafty, editing the tale so as to leave no opening for Mayne to have his revenge. He made no mention of Dickens, mesmerism, or Pilgrim's visit to Clara Donald, but improvised instead on the resourcefulness of his detectives. Finally, however, he had no choice but to confess the details of the surveillance in Artillery Lane.

Mayne seized his chance. 'Your men were in disguise?'

'Yes, sir.'

'As what?'

'As Hebrews, sir.'

He looked as if he might have apoplexy.

'The nature of the disguise is immaterial,' said Sir Charles. 'The point is that no policeman should disguise himself without express permission.'

'Such subterfuge is objectionable, on every possible level!' said Mayne.

Pilgrim couldn't remain silent. 'We had no choice but to disguise ourselves, our surveillance would have been obvious otherwise.'

Mayne widened his eyes. 'It is not your place to …'

'We were trying to save a girl's life.'

'That may well have been the case, Detective Sergeant,' said Sir Charles with a wave of his hand, 'but you appear to have missed the point.' He turned to Field. 'Is there some reason you didn't ask permission from Sir Richard before following this course of action?'

Field was silent. It was clear to everyone that Mayne would never have given his permission, everyone, apparently, except Sir Charles.

'Our position with regards to disguise is not a whim, Chief Inspector, but policy. We shun the use of subterfuge because it leaves us open to the accusation of policemen being employed as spies, or in other improper ways. However, there may be times, a few exceptional circumstances, when it can be justified.'

'Exceptional circumstances,' Mayne agreed, 'but … '

Sir Charles held up his hand. 'The Chief Inspector is aware of his transgression, there's no need to rub his nose in it. Carry on, Field.'

Field took up his story again, ending with Dolly's beating and Amalia Cohen's murder. When he had finished there was a long silence in the room.

Sir Charles gave a gusty sigh. 'It's a mess, gentlemen, and no mistake. The Home Secretary will have to be told, I see no way around it.'

Mayne bit his lip. He had gone from red to white, and no wonder: the Home Secretary's involvement was a nail in the coffin of his ambition. It was unlikely now that he'd get the chance to run the Force on his own. Sir Charles shifted in his chair and winced. Pilgrim realized he was only managing his pain with the utmost self-control.

'I cannot go to the Home Office empty handed,' said Sir Charles. 'I need a sacrificial offering. Either an arrest, or … ' he looked meaningfully at Field.

'I understand, sir.' Field nodded. 'I will tender my resignation to Sir Richard within the hour.'

Mayne flashed him a look of malignant triumph.

But Sir Charles shook his head. 'There's no need to be hasty. I can put off my visit to the Home Secretary until tomorrow.' He gave the detectives a tight smile. 'You have twenty-four hours to catch your murderer, gentlemen. Use them wisely.'

CHAPTER THIRTY-NINE

The library of the Royal College of Surgeons in Lincoln's Inn throbbed with masculine self-congratulation. Dickens listened to the voices – plummy, querulous, strident, declamatory – all raised in competition with each other in what passed for conversation. He sighed inwardly. As Guest of Honour for the Hunterian Oration he could hardly make his excuses and leave.

'I can safely say we may look forward to Mr Hawkins' speech, in fact ... ' Dr Feargal Cuthbertson mumbled on and on. The Dean of St Bartholomew's was dressed in a smock coat, knee shorts, and a wig that wouldn't have looked out of place sixty years earlier. He had monopolized Dickens ever since his arrival half an hour before, not so much trying to engage him in conversation, as lecturing him. Dickens didn't mind: it was something of a relief, for once, not to be expected to perform. He took the opportunity to admire the impressive double height room, with its graceful columns and rows of books, and the decorative balcony that ran around it. If only those books were on something other than medical subjects ...

'Museum?' asked Cuthbertson. Dickens gave a start. Was an answer expected? Apparently not. Cuthbertson ploughed on. 'I must show you around it some time. It is full of the most fascinating curiosities ... hundreds of anatomical specimens, including the Evelyn tables, bequeathed to the College in the seventeenth century. Have you heard of the Evelyn tables, Mr Dickens?' Dickens shook his head. 'They are fascinating, quite fascinating. Each one displays a different part of the human body: arteries, nerves, and veins dissected from a human specimen and glued to a wooden board made from pine planks. When they had finished, they covered everything with varnish. Remarkable, is it not, to think that organic matter could be preserved in such a way?'

Dickens nodded and smiled. Cuthbertson looked as if he had been similarly preserved himself. He reminded Dickens of a skeleton he had once seen, dug from a vault under one of the old marsh churches near Rochester: a mixture of a cadaver and a horrid waxwork, with dark eyes moving in his eye sockets. Dickens made a note of all these things and stored them away for future usefulness.

'Yes, I believe we can safely say we have a treat in store this afternoon. What do you think, sir?'

This time it seemed some response was expected. 'What is the subject of Mr Hawkins' lecture?' he asked.

The Doctor rubbed his bony hands together. 'The Excision of the Ovarium. It promises to be most illuminating. Do you know, sir, how many diseases of the ovarium there are?' Cuthbertson didn't wait for Dickens to guess but plunged on. First there are the common malignancies, such as ...' He started to count them off on his fingers.

Dickens gave an inward groan. Was he expected to listen to this lecture with a full stomach? The college was well known for its largesse, and there were rumoured to be eight courses at luncheon. Eight courses, followed by a surgical lecture. He hoped they wouldn't serve the meat rare. He became aware of a looming presence at his shoulder.

Dr Cuthbertson broke off his enumeration. 'Ah, I wondered where you had got to,' he said. 'Mr Dickens, may I present Dr Hector Fairweather, Chief Coroner, and our Head of Pathology at St Bartholomew's.'

225

Fairweather was an imposing man, with a bald head and whiskers. The expression in his eyes was at once self-deprecating and sardonic. As they shook hands, Dickens noticed his wooden leg.

'An honour,' said the pathologist. He nodded at Cuthbertson. 'Caesar Hawkins has arrived, Feargal. He's asking for you.'

'Is he … ?' Cuthbertson looked surprised, but delighted. 'Pray excuse me, Mr Dickens; I will no doubt see you later.'

'No doubt.'

They bowed to each other and Cuthbertson dodged off through the crowd.

Fairweather snorted. 'Caesar Hawkins wouldn't know Feargal if he fell over him, but you looked in need of rescuing.'

Dickens grinned.

'He insists on dragging me to these damned functions,' continued Fairweather. 'So much hot air. But at least they serve a decent dram.' He raised his glass in a silent toast.

Dickens did the same. 'You're the Coroner at St Bartholomew's? Then you'll be acquainted with Charley Field and his men?'

'On a daily basis, I'm sorry to say.' He saw his expression. 'Don't mistake me. They're all fine fellows. But I regret their necessity.'

The two men fell silent, but it was a thoughtful silence rather than an uneasy one.

'How long have you been a pathologist?' asked Dickens at last.

'Five years. But I've been a surgeon for much longer, of course.'

'You must be hardened to death in all its forms?'

'I'm not sure I am. But I enjoy my work.' Fairweather swirled the liquid in his glass. 'Pathology has its own, subtle satisfactions. A cadaver speaks to me. It whispers its secrets on the autopsy table, and together we discover the journey it has taken to arrive there. On the whole, the dead make obliging company.' He emptied the glass in a single gulp. 'Charley Field and his men have to deal with the living. I'm surprised they can sleep at night.'

Dickens nodded. 'I've been observing their investigation into the murder of Eliza Grimwood. A terrible business.'

Fairweather's eyes narrowed. Dickens guessed he was assessing him, wondering how much he knew.

'A rare guddle,' was all he said.

'That's one way of putting it,' said Dickens. 'Five victims already, but Sergeant Pilgrim and his team seem to be making little progress in catching the murderer.'

'Six victims,' corrected Fairweather. 'Another one arrived in the morgue this morning. A Jewish girl. Can't have been more than twenty. Damn shame.'

A chill trickled down the writer's spine. He placed his glass on a side table. 'I don't suppose you can recall her name?' he asked, as casually as he could.

Fairweather shook his head. 'I daresay it will be in the paperwork, providing anyone at Whitehall had time to fill it in. They were all at sixes and sevens this morning.'

'Why was that?'

'Do you know Detective Constable Williamson?'

'Adolphus?' Dickens nodded. 'Yes, I do.'

'The lad was badly beaten last night. I've heard he might not pull through.'

CHAPTER FORTY

A nurse showed Pilgrim and Charlotte Piper into an airy, well proportioned ward, lit by gothic windows. The new hospital at Westminster was a model of cleanliness and convenience; each ward with no more than eight patients, and its own water closet. Unfortunately, no amount of modern convenience could conjure away the sounds of suffering that came from the beds. Pilgrim tried to ignore the piteous cries and groans as the nurse took them towards a bed at the far end of the row.

'I can only permit you to see Mr Williamson for a moment,' she said.

'There's Winnie,' said Charlotte.

Pilgrim had caught a glimpse of Dolly's face and he was glad of a moment to master his shock. He turned to the woman sitting at the bedside who was plainly his mother. She had round red cheeks and round eyes, dulled by anxiety. Her face was wet. Charlotte embraced her.

'Lotte. I'm glad to see you, love. You've just missed the girls. I persuaded them to get a bite to eat.' Her eyes moved to Pilgrim.

'This is Sergeant Pilgrim,' said Charlotte. 'He brought me.'

Winnie Williamson clasped his hand. 'Oh, Mr Pilgrim, sir, my boy talks so much about you. He admires you so very much.'

Charlotte approached the bed. 'Dear Lord, what have they done to him?' Tears sprung to her eyes.

Pilgrim braced himself to look again. The left side of Dolly's face was swollen almost beyond recognition, his eye split like an overripe fig. The rest of his face had none of its usual colouring. His head and one ear were swathed in a bandage and his eyes were closed. He looked more dead than alive, but Pilgrim could see his chest rising and falling beneath the blanket. 'How is he?' he asked Winnie. His mouth was dry.

'The doctors don't know if he'll live, sir. But we're hopeful.' She dabbed at her eyes with a handkerchief. 'They've given him laudanum, for now. Sleep is a great restorative, they say. He has bruises ... the most terrible bruises ... and some broken bones. But bones mend. Bones mend.' She repeated her words as if trying to reassure herself of their truth.

'He's a strong boy,' said Charlotte. 'We'll pray for him, Winnie.'

Pilgrim curled his lip. He couldn't help himself. But Dolly's mother had caught it.

'You're not a Christian, sir?'

'No.' He avoided the eyes that bored into him, intelligent and compassionate. 'I once believed in a God who rewarded virtue and punished trespass, but not any more.'

'Life can be hard.' Winnie Williamson nodded. 'I lost Aldolphus' father, and three of my boys when they were no more than babes. I lost my way for a while too. But I still have my girls. And Dolly.' She clasped Dolly's hand, lying inert on the sheet. 'Pray for him, sir, in any case. He needs every scrap of help he can get.'

The nurse approached them. 'I'm sorry,' she said to Pilgrim and Charlotte, 'but you must leave now.' They left Mrs Williamson clinging to her son as if she might haul him bodily back from the brink of death.

Pilgrim handed Charlotte into the Hackney cab that was waiting for them, noting her bloodless cheeks and shuttered expression. 'Shall I drop you back at Holborn?' he asked.

She nodded. 'I'm going to sweep out your room. Keep myself busy.' She looked as if she might say more, but fell back into silence.

They had almost reached Greville Street when she spoke again.

'I've been meaning to say something to you, Sergeant.' She was twisting a handkerchief in her fingers.

'Oh?' Apprehension gripped him.

'I should have said it a while ago, but … ' she tailed off. She refused to meet his eye and continued to throttle the handkerchief. 'I wanted to apologize, for the things … for the thing I said, when we first met.'

He cleared his throat. 'Mrs Piper …'

'No, please, let me finish.' She lifted her chin, crimson with embarrassment. 'It was unforgivable … and inaccurate, besides. I don't think of you as … disfigured.' She swallowed. 'I only said that to wound you because you'd hurt my pride.'

He squirmed, mortified. He didn't know what to say.

'Can you forgive me?'

He opened his mouth, but finding no words there, nodded instead. Then he saw with relief that they had arrived at the house.

He dropped her there, and continued on to St Bartholomew's in a painful daze. He had found her apology almost as excruciating as the original insult. To his mind there had been more than a whiff of *noblesse oblige* about it, as if he was some pitiful creature she knew she had treated unfairly. His pride burned at the thought. But at the same time he knew himself well enough to realize he was probably being over sensitive.

He didn't want to think about Charlotte Piper. Or Dolly. So he decided he would keep his mind occupied by taking take a look at Amalia Cohen's body, to see if it could tell him anything. He wanted, if possible, to see it in its original condition before Dr Fairweather conducted his autopsy.

To his surprise he found Charles Dickens in the entrance hall of St Bartholomew's, squaring up to the medical assistant, Townsend.

'I don't care if you're Thomas Jefferson himself,' Townsend was saying, 'you're not going in there.' He scowled at the writer.

'But I need to discover the young lady's identity,' retorted Dickens.

'The doctors are all out.'

'I am well aware of that.' From his tone it was clear Dickens was barely holding his temper in check. 'They're at the Royal College of Surgeons. I've just come from there. But I still say it can do no harm to let me see the girl, or at least confirm her identity.'

'I don't have that information.' Townsend's expression grew even more truculent when he saw Pilgrim. 'You can't go in either.'

'Sergeant Pilgrim!' Dickens rushed over to him. 'The girl who was killed this morning, please tell me it was not Miss Cohen.'

'I'm afraid it was.'

Dickens sank onto one of the padded benches and ran a hand through his long hair. 'She was selling me ribbons not twenty four hours ago.'

Townsend was still watching them through the thick lenses of his spectacles. Pilgrim took Dickens by the elbow and steered him to the door. 'We'll come back later,' he called back to Townsend. The young man remained at his post, watching them intently, until they were safely outside, on the street.

'I heard about Adolphus, too,' said Dickens. 'What in heaven happened?'

'Do you have your carriage nearby?'

Dickens nodded.

'Give me a lift to Aldgate and I'll tell you about it.'

It took longer than the short ride to Aldgate to tell Dickens everything that had happened in Artillery Lane. While Pilgrim finished his tale, the coachman pulled into the kerb beside a dray, which was being unloaded on the High Street. He had to raise his voice to be heard above the sound of barrels being bumped down onto the pavement.

'What do you intend to do now?' asked Dickens.

Pilgrim nodded out of the carriage window to a shop with a green and yellow awning on the opposite side of the street.

'You remember the wrapping canvas? Reuben Cohen buys it from Hatchell and Manson. It can't hurt to take a look.'

*

The stationary shop was quiet. A solitary customer, a housekeeper, judging by her sober clothes and the basket on her arm, was being shown an assortment of ebony handled seals by the older of two attendants. Both attendants wore waistcoats of green and yellow stripes, the same colours as the awning outside. The younger attendant, who was stacking shelves with rolls of paper, sealing wax, penknives, and quill pens, hurried to greet them. Pilgrim saw him note the writer's expensive clothes.

'Good afternoon, gentlemen,' he said with an unctuous smile. 'May I be of assistance?'

Dickens moved off to inspect the shelves. Pilgrim took the wrapped ribbon from his pocket.

'I believe you sell this wrapping canvas,' he said.

The assistant took it from him. 'Yes, indeed. It's American. Stronger than English canvas, but still wonderfully pliable.'

'Who else in London stocks it?'

'No one, sir. We're the sole supplier. We buy it by the ton, and so we are able to sell it cheaply.'

'Do you keep a record of sales?'

'Detective Sergeant!' Dickens called out from the back of the shop.

The shop assistant looked sharply at Pilgrim. The older attendant and the housekeeper stopped what they were doing to stare at him as well. Pilgrim sighed. He had wanted their enquiry to be discreet, but he should have known that nothing with Dickens was ever that. He joined the writer who was surrounded by stacks of blotting books and canvases.

'Red ink!' Dickens held a jar triumphantly to the light. The contents looked like blood. 'Exactly like the ink on the notes.'

The young attendant had followed Pilgrim. 'We stock ink in several shades, sir, both Indian and Chinese. Lavender is popular with the ladies, and red with accounting firms.'

'Do you keep a record of sales?' Pilgrim repeated his question.

'Of course.'

'And customers' details?'

'Most of them. Those we deliver to and the ones that hold an account with us. Only a small proportion of our custom is passing trade.'

'How many people might buy both the canvas and the red ink?'

'I have no idea.'

Dickens replaced the ink on the shelf. 'Our murderer must buy both here.'

'Murderer?' squeaked the attendant.

'Excuse me one moment, madam.' The senior attendant abandoned the housekeeper to join them. 'I am Frederick Manson, co-owner of this establishment. Is there a problem?'

Pilgrim submitted to the inevitable. 'I'm Detective Sergeant Pilgrim of the Metropolitan Police. I need to take your sales ledgers for the last year.'

'I beg your pardon?'

'Your sales ledgers.'

'What, all of them?'

'I will provide a receipt, and return them as soon as possible.'

There were six ledgers in total: hefty, leather-bound volumes, too heavy to carry more than two at a time. Dickens's coachman helped Pilgrim manhandle them into the station at Whitehall, and to stack them on the floor beside Sergeant Phelps' desk.

'Thank you, John. Tell Mr Dickens I'll let him know if I find anything.'

'Right you are, sir.' The coachman tipped his hat and left.

'Evening, Sergeant Phelps,' said Pilgrim. 'Could one of your boys give me a hand up the stairs with this lot?'

'Actually, sir,' the Sergeant gave him an ambiguous look, 'I think it best if you wait here a moment.' He whispered into the ear of the uniformed officer beside him, who darted a glance at Pilgrim before hurrying up the stairs.

'What's going on?'

The Sergeant wouldn't meet his eye.

'Is Dolly … ?' Pilgrim felt the blood drain from his face.

'No, sir. We've had no news of Constable Williamson.' For an instant, Phelps looked as if he would say more, but then he clamped his lips together.

Pilgrim's mind whirled. Perhaps Charley had decided to resign after all, ahead of the deadline Sir Charles had given them? But that wouldn't explain Phelps' peculiar behaviour. The Sergeant was practically rigid with tension as he stared up the staircase. His expression changed to relief as Dick Tanner, followed by Wainwright, thumped down the stairs.

Tanner stopped in front of Pilgrim, his expression oddly blank. His eyes seemed to look through him rather than at him.

'Henry Pilgrim,' he said. 'I'm arresting you in the Queen's name on suspicion of the murder of Mena Levy, Johannes Appler, Eliza Grimwood, Martha Drewitt, Clara Donald, and Amalia Cohen.'

CHAPTER FORTY-ONE

Dickens sat down to his breakfast: fresh sausages, boiled eggs, ham, porridge with fresh cream and butter, Whitby kippers, and pheasant pie. A pot of tea and a teacup waited beside the congested plates, and, as instructed, the tablecloth was plain, rather than patterned: he found patterned fabric upsetting to his digestion in the morning. Everything was exactly as it should be, and yet he felt … dissatisfied. Ill at ease. Yes, distinctly ill at ease.

'What are your plans for today, dear?' His wife Kate eyed him nervously over the rim of her own teacup. She was still in her wrap and curlpapers. At the age of thirty-five she looked fifteen years older, with deep grooves running from her nose to her mouth, and a perpetual expression of weariness. It was hardly surprising: nine children in thirteen years would take a toll on any woman's looks and nerves.

'I thought I might press on with my new novel.'

'Oh?'

'I've written the first instalment, but don't have a title for it yet. I have two possible ones …' he tailed off. Tapped his fingers on the table. Was there something else he was supposed to be doing today? He knit his brows together. If there was, he couldn't think of it.

'And what are they?'

'I beg your pardon?'

'The potential titles. For your new novel. What are they?'

'I thought either "Bleak House" or "Hard Times, for these Times".' He peered at her. 'What do you think?'

'I like Hard Times. I imagine it would be in the vein of *Oliver Twist*?'

'Yes. But I think I prefer "Bleak House". I'm going to make it a mystery … a proper mystery, with a police detective …' he tailed off again. 'His mother worries about him … we live in hard times.'

Kate put down her cup. 'If you don't mind me saying so, Charles, you seem a little distracted. Why don't you take a walk after breakfast?'

'Capital idea.' He nodded and helped himself to a slice of pheasant pie. Looking at the dark meat inside the crust, he put it down again. 'Actually, no. I rather think I need to go out now. Could you please ask John Thompson to bring the carriage around while I dress?'

When Dickens arrived on the ward at Westminster Hospital he could hear raised voices. He walked down the room towards the bed he had been directed to, and saw that Dolly was not only alive, but apparently in the middle of an argument.

'I need to speak to Sergeant Pilgrim, of Whitehall.'

'If you don't remain still,' said the doctor, 'I shall be forced to sedate you again.'

'But it's urgent.' Dolly struggled to sit up, but the doctor held him down. The doctor signalled to a nurse, who nodded and rushed into a side room. She arrived back at the bedside at the same time as Dickens. 'Here you are, sir.' She gave a glass of colourless liquid to the doctor.

'Drink this.' The doctor pressed the glass to Dolly's lips.

'No!' Dolly twisted his head to avoid it. The doctor took a hold of his chin. 'Get off me, damn you.'

'Adolphus, my boy!'

They froze into an absurd *tableau vivant*: the grappling doctor, the red-faced nurse, and their patient.

'Mr Dickens,' gasped Dolly.

The doctor's eyes widened. He released his grip on Dolly's chin and stepped back.

'I'm delighted to see you're not dead yet,' said Dickens. He struggled to master his shock at Dolly's grotesquely distorted features.

The doctor flushed. 'He was trying to get out of bed ... but he has broken bones and a head wound. Not to mention the possibility of internal bleeding.'

Dickens nodded and went to the bedside, trying not to betray his revulsion. He patted Dolly's hand. He took a handkerchief from his waistcoat to dab at a tear that had leaked from the boy's swollen eye. 'You must calm yourself. What is all the commotion about?'

Dolly licked dry lips. 'I need to know what happened, sir, in Artillery Lane. Is Miss Cohen safe?'

The writer's expression told him everything he needed to know. Dolly sank back onto the pillows and closed his eyes. Dickens took the glass from the doctor.

'Perhaps I might administer it?'

The doctor glanced from Dickens to Dolly, and back again. He gave a brusque nod and steered the nurse away. Dickens sat on the edge of the bed. Dolly opened his eyes.

'How?' he asked.

'The killer used your little disturbance as a diversion, knocked out poor Constable Wainwright, and slipped in at the rear of the house. He killed Amalia Cohen with a cudgel.'

'He was carrying one,' said Dolly.

'Yes, he must have been.'

'No, you misunderstand, sir. He was carrying one. I saw him, you see. In Artillery Lane. I saw the killer.'

CHAPTER FORTY-TWO

Pilgrim sat on the cot and stared at the floor. In spite of the hours the station char had spent scrubbing the flagstones there were still marks on it from Appler's blood. Pilgrim stared at the stains and tried to think, but it was as if his usual mental processes had been disconnected by shock. He dropped his head into his hands. A woman's voice, hoarse with shouting, echoed along the corridor, bouncing off steel and stone.

'I'm the daughter of a British officer, so strike me blind and dead! You can't treat me this way. I'll write a letter to the bloody Queen, so I will, and then you'll be sorry!'

Elsewhere in the cells a base voice started up.

'The Camptown ladies sing this song,

Doo-da, doo-da,

The Camptown racetrack's five miles long,

Oh, de doo-da day.'

'Keep the noise down, you sot,' bellowed a different female voice. 'You'll wake the babby!' Sure enough, the wail of an infant sliced through the air. 'See! See what you've done?'

'Goin' to run all night,

Goin' to run all day,

I bet my money on a bob-tailed nag,

Somebody bet on the grey.'

Without opening his eyes, Pilgrim curled on the mattress and pulled the blanket to his chin. The wool was threadbare, but clean. Miraculously, he slept.

He dreamed of Clara Donald's finger. He put his hand into his pocket and felt something there, tangled in the lining like a twig. He didn't realize what it was until he turned out the pocket and the finger dropped onto the floor. He looked down and saw he was soaked from armpit to ankle in blood. Fresh blood, stringy and clotting.

'It's all my fault.'

He woke with a gasp, and, for a moment, couldn't think where he was. Then he heard the coughs and snores of the other prisoners and remembered. It took a while for the horror of his dream to drain away, but by that time, the sky behind the high barred window had paled and so he gave up on any thought of going back to sleep. He sat up. His head was clear again, as if all the sediment stirred up the day before had settled.

Breakfast was skilly, pushed through the flap at the bottom of the door. He ate it quickly and sat back on his cot. There was no point getting exhausted with imaginings. Someone would tell him why he had been arrested soon enough. All he had to do was to wait.

The noise in the cells lessened as the overnight prisoners were released, one by one. The officer's daughter was the first to go, still shouting threats of letters to the Queen, then the woman and baby, and finally the singer, who had sobered into muttering resentment.

Finally, when the cells were silent, he heard footsteps approaching his cell. He sat up. The door opened, framing Charley Field.

'Good morning, Sergeant,' he said. He looked tired, but full of purpose.

Pilgrim wondered at the coldness of his tone. Was it for his benefit? Or for the constable he could see lurking in the passage? Field closed the door.

Pilgrim stood up. 'You shouldn't be speaking to me alone.'

'Don't tell me how to do my job.' Field's earlier morose mood had crystallized into something harder. Much harder. 'Sit down.'

He waited for Pilgrim to obey him before speaking again. 'We found Martha Drewitt's baby in your rooms. Or, rather, your landlady found it.'

Pilgrim's bile rose. 'The killer must have put it there.'

'This isn't just about the baby.'

Pilgrim opened his mouth to speak, but Field forestalled him with a raised forefinger.

'You were connected personally to Martha Drewitt through your niece Frances. You had intercourse with Clara Donald the night she was killed. You had access to Appler's cell. And now, of course, there's the baby.'

'It makes no sense. Why would I have stopped the Hackney with Mena Levy's body in it?'

'To set up Appler.'

'Why would I bother?'

'Because he knew who you were. Because it was you who asked him to move the body.'

'Surely it would have been easier just to move the body myself. Or kill him, rather than arrest him? And what about the notes? The finger? The ear?'

'False clues, to mislead us.'

'And what about Mena Levy's admirer? I don't fit the description.'

'You said yourself, he might not be the killer.'

'But why?' Pilgrim spread his hands. 'Why would I do all those terrible things? Even a maniac has to have a reason, even if it makes sense to no one but himself.'

'Only you would be able to answer that.'

'I didn't do it, Charley.'

Unexpectedly, Field grinned. 'I know that. But my hand has been forced, for the time being.' He sat beside Pilgrim on the cot. 'You have to admit, it doesn't look good. I've spent most of the night going through statements from witnesses, such as they are. I've talked to your landlady. She said she didn't see you after seven o'clock on the night Amalia Cohen died.'

'I fell asleep after Wainwright left.' He hesitated. 'How is Mrs Piper? It must have been a shock.'

'That foetus stank to high heaven. God knows how long it had been there.'

Pilgrim touched his nose. He wouldn't have known it was there, no matter how rank. But surely Charlotte would have smelled something foul, if it had been there long? And Wainwright hadn't commented on any smell.

'Your widow Piper is tougher than she looks,' said Field.

'I don't think she's the fainting type.'

'Just as well.' Field lifted his eyebrows, and then he continued. 'We don't know exactly when Mena Levy was killed, but Martha Drewitt died on the sixth of February, and Eliza Grimwood had her throat cut between eight o'clock and midnight on the third. You need to think hard about where you were on those nights. If you have an alibi for even one of the murders, the prosecution case will crumble.'

'I was in the barracks, both nights.'

'Excellent. No one's likely to question the testimony of a dozen policemen. I won't be allowed to interview you, for obvious reasons. They're sending George Moxton down to do it. But it will take him a while to get here, and also for Tanner to give him all the information he needs. I'd say you have a day or two to prepare yourself and to find a decent lawyer.' Field got to his feet. 'In the meantime, however, the best way to clear your name is for me to find the real murderer.'

Pilgrim managed a smile. 'You did it, Charley.'

'Did what?'

'You made an arrest. Now Sir Charles will have something to give the Home Secretary this morning.'

'Other than my resignation?' Field grinned back. 'It's true what Mother Molly says, Harry: every cloud has a silver lining.'

*

241

After Charley had gone Pilgrim lay down on his bunk again. He knew several lawyers who would be happy to help him: he would ask for writing paper as soon as someone came to take his empty breakfast bowl. He looked at the flaking paint on the ceiling and thought about Charlotte Piper. It must have been shocking for her to find the baby in his room. Did she believe he was a murderer? He hoped not. He hoped she knew him well enough to doubt it at least, but there was no real reason to think that she might.

He must have drifted off, for he was woken by the noise of the flap in the door. A mirror, a razor, a towel, and a bowl of water had been pushed through it. He heard boots clump off down the corridor, and cursed the missed opportunity to ask for paper. Then he shrugged. A shave would fill the time.

The water was lukewarm; he was only able to get a half-hearted lather with the soap. He felt the bristles under his fingers and guided the blade of the razor towards them. The fragment of mirror he'd been given could barely reflect a square inch of his face at any one time; it was like trying to fasten a shoelace through a keyhole. He was surprised they had given him the razor at all, considering what had happened to Johannes Appler. Then he thought again. Perhaps it wasn't so strange. It would probably be a relief for the police force if he were to cut his own throat.

As if the thought had guided the blade, the edge of the razor caught on a scar on his neck, nicking the skin. He dabbed at the cut with the towel, and then at a spot of blood that had splashed onto his undervest. He slowed ... then stopped, watching the blood spread like capillaries across the cotton. His heart thumped. He remembered what it was that he had seen, so many days before, that he had been trying to remember. Something that shouldn't have been there. Like the missing piece of a puzzle it slotted smoothly into place. And once it had, another piece fitted, and then another. A dreadful comprehension seized him.

He ran to bang on the door.

A squint-eyed constable appeared on the other side: one he knew by sight but not by name.

'Keep it down in there.'

'I need to speak to Inspector Field.'

'So what? I ain't goin' to bring him here on your say so.'

'It's urgent.' Pilgrim could see the doubt on the young man's face. 'Let me send him a note.'

The constable scowled.

'What harm could it possibly do for me to write him a note?' Pilgrim changed his strategy. 'It might even do you some good.'

'Make it quick, then. I ain't no messenger boy.'

It only took a moment to scribble a few words on the paper the constable brought him. He folded it carefully and passed it through the hatch in the door. As he did, a thought occurred. He held on to the paper as the constable tried to tug it off him. 'Is your name Anderson?'

'What of it?'

'Do you like gingerbread?'

The young policeman scowled. 'What kind of question is that to be askin' me? Are you tryin' to be funny?'

'Not at all. Do you?'

'It's my favourite. Not that it's any of your business. Are you goin' to give me that note or not?'

Pilgrim released the paper. 'Take it to the Inspector right away. Him and no one else.'

The constable grumbled as he took the paper. He stomped off down the passage.

Pilgrim rinsed the soap from his face and dried it. He couldn't trust himself to finish with the razor. His hands were shaking. He pulled his shirt over the blood-spotted vest, then sat down, and waited.

It seemed hours before he heard the tramp of feet back along the passage, the tread of someone carrying a burden. The key scraped in the lock and the door creaked open to reveal Constable

243

Anderson, carrying two of the ledgers from Hatchell and Manson. He thumped them down onto the floor. 'The Inspector said we was to bring you these, sir.' Another officer stepped into the cell with two more of the ledgers.

'Thank you.' Pilgrim had noted the 'sir'.

'We'll fetch the others.'

He knelt to look at the dates on the spines of the massive books. Each one covered several months and detailed hundreds of transactions. He had dreaded going through them, but that was before he knew what he was looking for.

Now he had a name.

CHAPTER FORTY-THREE

Dickens was aware that Charley Field was watching him out of the tail of his eye as they hurtled towards St Bartholomew's. He suspected that the Inspector would have forbidden him to be in on the chase, if it wasn't for the fact he had put his carriage at the detectives' disposal. He favoured the Inspector with his most disingenuous smile.

'What are we going to do if he isn't there?' he asked.

'Track him down.'

Tanner snorted. 'Just because Dolly saw him in Artillery Lane, it doesn't mean he's the murderer.'

'Dolly said he used the phrase "just for jolly" in the mortuary, the same as in the note. And he was carrying a cudgel. It's too much of a coincidence.' Field lifted a forefinger. 'Don't forget that Appler said his mysterious gambler was a foreigner, and Martha Drewitt's baby was cut from her womb with medical precision.'

Wainwright shuddered. The carriage drew up at the kerb in front of the hospital and the four men jumped down to run into the building beneath the legs of Henry VIII. The entrance hall was busy with visitors, and students on their way to late lectures.

'Wait here, Tanner,' said Field. 'If you see our man, don't let him get past you.'

'Yes, sir.'

'Wainwright, go and see if there's a back exit. Make sure he doesn't get out that way.'

The constable hurried off.

Field glared at Dickens. 'Are you sure you wouldn't rather wait in the carriage?' He read his answer in the other man's face, and sighed.

They went past the staircase, beneath Hogarth's famous paintings of *The Good Samaritan* and *The Pool of Bethesda*. Dickens studied them as they passed and decided he didn't find their grand, mock Renaissance style appealing. Hogarth, in his opinion, was at his best when showing ordinary people, in all their plain, unvarnished eccentricity. He liked to think it was something they had in common.

'This way.' Field took a left-hand turn, down another staircase, and into a corridor lined with drab painted doors. One of the doors opened and a skeletal figure in knee breeches emerged.

'Dr. Cuthbertson!' Field strode along the corridor to meet the Dean. 'Could we have a moment of your time?'

'I'm due to give a lecture in five minutes.'

'We're looking for Dr Fairweather's assistant. Do you know where he is?'

'Young Townsend?' Feargal Cuthbertson blinked black eyes. 'Certainly. He's in New York.'

CHAPTER FORTY-FOUR

Pilgrim rubbed his eyes. The words and numbers on the page were melting into a blur of vertical and horizontal lines, and the tip of his forefinger was sore and stained with ink. He slammed the fifth ledger shut. Perhaps he was wrong? Or perhaps he had missed it? He closed his eyes and pinched the bridge of his nose. Reading the ledgers in the dingy light of the cell was making his head ache, and the possibility of having to start all over again made him want to lie down and go back to sleep.

He picked up the last book and opened it. The name he was looking for leapt off the page as if illuminated by monks. He moved his finger to the column beside the name. The address was right, too, although the order wasn't quite what he was expecting.

He ran to the door and pounded it with his fists. This time it was Sergeant Phelps who came to see who was making the noise.

'I need to speak to Inspector Field,' said Pilgrim. 'Urgently.'

'I'm afraid that ain't possible.'

'It's very important.'

'You misunderstand, sir. It ain't because I won't fetch him, it's because I can't. He ain't here at present. He's gone with Sergeant Tanner and Constable Wainwright to catch the killer. Mr Dickens is with them.'

'The killer?' Pilgrim blinked.

'They took off more than an hour ago. To arrest him, they said.'

'That's not possible. You have to let me out.'

'Can't do that, sir.'

Pilgrim ran his hand through his hair. 'You say they've gone to catch the killer? The killer of Mena Levy, Eliza Grimwood, and Martha Drewitt?'

'Yes, sir. And Mr Appler, and that poor Hebrew girl.'

'So what does that make me?'

Phelps studied him for a heartbeat, then pulled a face. 'You do 'ave a point, sir.'

Pilgrim pulled his overcoat around him and hurried on through the rain. He had thought it would be faster to walk to Portsoken rather than trying to catch a cab, but he was already regretting his decision. It was further than he thought. Or perhaps it was only the rain that made it seem as if he had already been walking for hours. It slashed down like knives, obscuring the still distant dome of St Paul's. He cursed and broke into a run. The most direct route took him along the path of the old city wall, the quickest way by foot, but not popular with traffic. He heard the clatter of hooves and looked over his shoulder to see a glossy Brougham bowling towards him. On impulse, he leapt into the middle of the road and windmilled his arms. Having no choice but to stop, the coach driver hauled on the reins.

'What the devil do you think you're doin', prancin' about in the middle of the road?' He scowled down at Pilgrim.

'I'm a police officer. I need you to take me to Portsoken.'

'Why are we stopping?' A woman's voice called out from inside the carriage. The coachman swivelled in his seat.

'It's this gentleman, ma'am, 'e says 'e's a policeman.'

The window dropped with a bang and a woman leaned out to look at him. 'Are you really?' She scrutinized his dripping figure. 'Where's your uniform?'

'I'm a detective, ma'am. We don't wear uniforms. I need to get to Portsoken, urgently.'

She sniffed. 'What are you waiting for? Climb up here, man, out of the rain. Drive on, Dixon, to 'soken.'

Pilgrim hauled himself up into the carriage and squelched onto the seat as far from its passenger as was possible. 'Much obliged to you,' he said.

'A police detective. How thrilling!' She inspected him through her lorgnette. 'I've been following your adventures in *Household Words*. I don't suppose you know Mr Dickens?'

'No, ma'am.'

'How about Sergeant Pilchem? You must have heard of Sergeant Pilchem?'

'No, ma'am. I'm afraid he's just a figment.'

'A figment?'

'Of Mr Dickens's imagination.'

He jumped down from the Brougham in Bishopsgate Street and plunged into the labyrinth of streets and alleys behind Houndsditch. If he remembered rightly, the house he was looking for was at the east end of the street, behind Gravel Lane. He found it with some difficulty, for it looked quite different at the back than it did at the front. From the front it had given the illusion of affluence, thanks mainly to its generous front garden, but from the back its dilapidation was all too plain. Even though it was dark he could see holes in the roof. Many of the gutters were hanging off it. Some of the windows were also broken. Lights shone behind the curtains at ground level, but the upper floors were in darkness.

He chose a window that was open a few inches. He tested the drainpipe that ran past it. Unlike some of its neighbours it seemed to be anchored securely to the wall. Even though it was slick with rain he shinned up it easily – a legacy of his misguided youth – and hauled up the sash. It creaked like the gates of hell. He froze. But there was no responding shout, or any sound within the house. After waiting another second or two, just to be sure, he swung his leg over the sill and levered himself into the room.

It was a woman's bedroom, strewn with hatboxes and frilled garments, and every surface cluttered with knick-knacks. He crossed the room and stepped out onto the landing.

A light gleamed in the hall downstairs. He paused. If this were the domain of the lady of the house, then where would she put her lodger? There was a glazed door at the end of the corridor that led to the upper storey. He crept to it and opened it, listening for any noise from downstairs. All he could hear was a steady plop, plop, plop. The sound came from buckets positioned on the upper stairs to catch leaks. They were all full; the water lapping over the rims to splash onto the stairs, creating a miniature waterfall. He wondered how long it had been since they were emptied. He splashed between the buckets, and, after making sure that no light was showing beneath the door at the top, pushed it open.

A draught of bitter air chilled his cheeks. He could hear rain drumming on the roof and the steady drip, drip, drip of water. There was enough light from the dormer windows to make out several buckets positioned around the room and an oil lamp standing on a chest of drawers. He made his way over to the lamp and took his tinderbox from his pocket. It was a risk to light it, as the light could be seen from the street, but it couldn't be helped: he needed a few minutes to search the room. There was a narrow, unmade bed – obviously the bed of a bachelor – and a table stacked with oil paints and brushes. An easel braced in one corner was empty.

There were several canvases propped against the wall covered with dustsheets. He took the oil lamp to the nearest one and tugged off the sheet.

Venus lay on her side, her head tipped back on her pillow as if her hair was too heavy for her slender neck. She looked at him through eyes narrowed to languorous slits, the fingers of one hand curled loosely at her groin, more in invitation than denial. She took his breath away. She was anatomically perfect – strong limbed, wide shouldered, and round bellied – and unmistakably Eliza Grimwood.

He pulled the cover off the next canvas. St Sebastian's milky body bristled with arrows, contorted by the rope that bound him to the tree. He had one elbow pinioned above his head, while the other was wrenched behind his back, forcing his spine to arch unnaturally. One foot rested on a boulder, and his legs twisted away from the viewer at a torturous angle. Apart from his pale forehead very little of the Saint's face was visible, hidden by a tumble of dark red hair. Pilgrim didn't need to see his features to know he was looking at Angus Trinkle.

The girl on the next canvas was dark-haired and sloe-eyed and her expression solemn, apart from a quirk of her lips that may have betrayed the first thoughts of a smile. She wore a red robe and carried a head on silver platter. A head with mutton chop side whiskers and a beaked profile, easily recognizable as Johannes Appler. John the Baptist. And Salome. *He wanted to see Mena dance.*

He moved on. Mary Magdalene raised her eyes to heaven and parted her lips as if in expectation of a lover's kiss. Her glorious red hair rippled over her body, lapping her shoulders, and isolating the islands of her breasts. Breasts that he – Harry Pilgrim – had once kissed. The paint glistened. He touched a fingertip to it, which came away wet.

There was only one canvas left under cover, larger than the others. His fingers reluctantly twitched the sheet away. It was a Madonna and child. The composition was conventional, with the apple-cheeked Madonna smiling down at the child that lay across her knee. But something jarred. The Christ child was older than in most portrayals, and his body was limp, totally supported by the Madonna's arm. Louis Drake smiled up at his painted mother, Martha Drewitt, and she smiled back at him with the maternal love he had never known in life.

Pilgrim closed his eyes. What was it he had said to Charley Field? Even a maniac has to have a motive. He had guessed Wainwright was the killer, but hadn't realized until that moment why he had selected these particular victims. The paintings were all copies of the ones he had seen in the Royal Academy. Wainwright said he visited the Academy whenever he could. Now he knew why.

He moved to the table to look at a sketch pad resting there. On the top sheet, drawn in red chalk, there was an anatomical study of a hand. It was meticulous in its attention to detail, faithfully capturing the whorl of each knuckle, the ragged nails, some lined with dirt. A red handkerchief lay nearby. Pilgrim picked it up. Clara Donald's hand was underneath, the flesh grey, the little finger missing from the knuckle. The last time Pilgrim had seen it, Clara Donald had been combing her hair. And, just before that … He dropped the handkerchief back onto the hand and swallowed back his nausea and his rage.

Where was Wainwright now? And how long would he be gone? There was no way he could get a note to Field without arousing Wainwright's suspicion, and Wainwright could return home at any minute. Pilgrim decided to hide and wait, in the hope that the element of surprise would work in his favour. He turned out the lamp and replaced it on the chest of drawers. As he moved to conceal himself behind the door, however, he brushed past the table and knocked the sketch pad onto the floor. He snatched it up. Underneath the hand study there was another drawing, a preparatory sketch for Wainwright's next painting. He took it to the window and tipped it to catch the light.

It was Venus again, but very different from Eliza Grimwood's wanton goddess. This one sat before a mirror supported by cherubs, gazing at her reflection with haughty self-possession. It was only an outline, but it was enough for him to recognize the pose and the subject from the Royal Academy. His imagination was able to complete the details suggested by the chalk: straight brows over wide eyes, braided hair. It was a face he recognized.

CHAPTER FORTY-FIVE

'New York?' Field's face was comical with consternation.

'Indeed.' Cuthbertson nodded. 'That is to say, Townsend is on his way there, as far as I know. I believe he was due to sail some time today. Is it anything I can help you with?'

'I'm afraid not.'

'Then, if you'll forgive me ...' Cuthbertson waved a hand towards the staircase.

'Of course.' Field stepped aside to let him pass. 'Do you know where the boy was living?'

'Records will have a note of it. On the first floor.' Cuthbertson disappeared up the staircase in a flurry of wig powder.

'Bugger,' said Field.

'If we're quick,' said Dickens, 'we might be able to catch him at the docks.'

Field looked at him. 'If I'm quick. I think it best if your involvement ends here, sir. Don't imagine that I'm not grateful for your help, but I worry about the danger to your person.'

Dickens nodded. 'I quite understand, Inspector. Allow me to put my carriage at your disposal. It will be faster than a Hackney.'

'Thank you.' Field seemed taken aback by his easy surrender.

Back in the foyer, Field gathered Wainwright and Tanner to him and quickly explained the situation.

'Tanner,' he said, 'I want you to come with me to the docks. Wainwright, find out where Townsend has been lodging, and check the place over.'

'Good luck, Inspector,' called Dickens.

He watched Tanner and Field climb into the carriage and the driver whip them off at a smart trot.

'Right.' Dickens turned to Wainwright and rubbed his hands together. 'You summon a cab, and I'll find out where Townsend was lodging.'

Half an hour later, Wainwright cupped his hands on the window of a dingy artisan's cottage, trying to see through the chink in the curtains. 'Ain't nobody in there,' he said.

'This is definitely the right address?' asked Dickens.

'Positive, sir. Seventeen Yew Tree Cottages, like it said in the ledger at St Bartholomew's.' He shook the door handle again. 'Lord knows where we'll get a key.'

'We need to be certain Townsend's gone,' said Dickens. 'Break it down.'

'Eh?'

'Kick the door down, Wainwright. You have good stout boots. Don't worry, I'll answer to Chief Inspector Field if necessary.'

It only took one kick. The lock gave with a crash and the door swung open. They went inside, leaving footprints in the dust. Dickens opened the curtains, admitting enough light from the streetlamp to see that there were no sheets on the bed and no sign of any personal possessions. Wainwright stooped to touch the ashes in the hearth.

'Stone cold, sir.'

'Look here, Constable,' Dickens beckoned Wainwright to the table and nodded at the marks on the scrubbed surface.

'Bloodstains?' asked Wainwright.

Dickens shook his head. 'Ink. Red ink. I think it's safe to say that Townsend is our man.'

'Will the Inspector and Sergeant be in time to catch him, do you think?'

'I do hope so.'

'What shall we do now?'

'I suppose I should get you back to the station,' Dickens rubbed his chin, 'but we're not far from Shepherd's Bush. Would you mind if we made a small detour on the way?'

CHAPTER FORTY-SIX

The house in Greville Street was in darkness. Pilgrim banged on the door and stepped back to look up at the windows. No light came on to answer his summons. There was no sign of life at all. Was he too late? He banged again. Nothing. He leaned over the railing to peer down into the basement, to see if any of the kitchen windows had been left open, but the curtains were drawn and the windows all looked secure.

He was about to turn away when he heard a footfall in the hall. The door opened. Charlotte Piper rubbed her eyes and stared at him. Her face was slack with sleep, her eyelids swollen. Had she been crying? It took her a fraction of a second to register exactly who he was. In that fraction he saw himself through her eyes: half-shaved, soaking wet, and desperate. She whirled and ran.

He caught up with her at the top of the basement stairs, grabbed her by the shoulders, and spun her to face him. 'Let me explain.'

She brought up her knee, fast and hard, but not quite fast enough. He was able to block it with his thigh. He slammed her against the wall and held her there, his body pressed into hers. Their faces were only inches apart. She was solid in his arms and he could feel the heat of her through his wet clothes.

'Listen to me.'

She twisted her face away.

He caught her chin and dragged it back to him. 'The Inspector knows I'm not the killer. He thinks he's gone to catch the killer, but he's after the wrong man. I know who the real murderer is. I know who his next victim will be.' He looked into her eyes. 'It's you, Charlotte. He wants to paint you as Venus.'

'But ... the baby ... ?'

'He hid it here, the night Amalia Cohen died.' He closed his eyes, briefly. 'I've been blind.'

'How do I know you're not trying to trick me?'

'You don't. There's no way I can prove anything to you.' She was tall, for a woman, her eyes almost level with his. Something flickered in them as elusive as a trout in a mountain stream. He could see the pulse of her throat, the way a strand of her hair moved with his breath, feathering against her cheek. He pushed away from her. 'I don't care if you don't believe me, as long as you get out of this house. Go somewhere safe, now.'

She stood looking at him, rubbing her arms. Then she pushed past him into the vestibule, grabbed her coat and bonnet from the rack, and slammed out of the door.

He bent over, winded with relief and a fierce, renegade desire. His whole body ached with it. He wasn't a vain man, but he could have sworn something had passed between them: a sensual aware-ness, a recognition. He hoped she had somewhere safe to go. It was only then that he realized he'd been so concerned to get her out of the house, away from danger, that he hadn't told her who the murderer was.

CHAPTER FORTY-SEVEN

'This is Constable Wainwright.'

'Pleased to meet you,' Mrs Wallace nodded to the constable and then turned back to Dickens. 'We weren't expecting you tonight, sir.'

'I left some shirt collars here, on the night of the Gala. I thought I would call in for them, as we were passing.'

'I was just taking supper with some of the older girls. Would you care to join us?'

Dickens cocked his head at the constable.

'As long as we're quick, sir, I'm still on duty, after all.'

'I think we have time for a cup of tea. Thank you, Mrs Wallace.'

Four faces turned to greet them in the parlour, flashing instantly from boredom into animation.

'Pour the gentlemen some tea, Isabella,' said Mrs Wallace. 'And make some room by the fire there, Julia.'

They jumped up to obey, and, with much fussing and tutting, installed Wainwright in the fireside chair with a cup of tea. Kathleen Chalk hung back, mouth drooping open.

Dickens picked up a sketchbook that was lying on the table. 'I see you've been sketching again, Mary Ann.' It was an indifferent still life of the tea caddy and one of Mrs Wallace's bonnets. 'Constable Wainwright here is a very accomplished artist. Perhaps if you ask him prettily, he'll take your likeness.'

'Would you, oh, would you, sir?'

The policeman blushed under Mary Ann's pleading gaze.

'Well …' he began.

'No, not Mary Ann,' snapped Isabella. 'She has a big nose. Sketch me instead.'

'Isabella Gordon!' chided Mrs Wallace. 'The Constable will certainly not want to take your likeness now. He'll sketch Mary Ann … that is, as long as you're willing, sir?'

Wainwright was allowed two gulps of his tea before the sketchbook and pencil were thrust into his hands. The girls helped him to settle Mary Ann into a suitable pose, clustering round him, laughing and making suggestions.

'No, not like that! Put her chin on her hand, like this.'

Dickens and Mrs Wallace stood back and watched them, indulgent.

'How did the Lord Mayor's Gala go?' murmured Mrs Wallace.

'Well enough,' said Dickens. 'It was a pity you missed it. But hardly surprising that the girls were too upset, under the circumstances.'

They fell silent again. Mary Ann was not yet arranged to everyone's satisfaction.

'She looks like a wooden doll,' snapped Isabella. 'Smile, you lump. You ain't at a funeral.' The girls all laughed, apart from Kathleen Chalk, who frowned and tugged at Isabella's arm.

'Come away, come away from 'im, Bella.'

The other girl shook her off. 'What the devil are you pawin' at me for?'

'Don't get so close. 'E only wants to touch your bubbies.'

'Kathleen!' Mrs Wallace pulled the girl aside and shook her gently. 'For shame, Kathleen Chalk! How could you say such a thing?'

'It's what that Reverend done.'

'What?'

'It's what that Reverend done. To Becky Woods.'

The Matron locked her gaze with Dickens.

'I saw it with my own two eyes,' continued Kathleen, 'when I brought the tea tray in. 'e touched 'er bubby, like this.' She ran her index finger over her own bosom with a leering expression. If he hadn't been so appalled, Dickens might have laughed.

'Why didn't you say anything?' asked Mrs Wallace.

'No one asked me. No one ever does.' She gave the Matron a sly look. 'I know something else, too.'

'What's that?'

'Becky weren't her real name.'

Mrs Wallace gave Dickens a triumphant look.

Kathleen nodded. 'She were called Stella. She told me so.'

Dickens blew out his cheeks. Becky Woods, Stella Whatever: the girl was gone, whatever she was called, and there was nothing could be done about it.

Isabella was settled at last, and the other girls arranged themselves behind Wainwright to watch him as he sketched.

Dickens also watched, fascinated. The constable had taken on a peculiar intensity as he squinted from the paper to Mary Ann and back again, his hand moving over the page. His affable features had hardened. His posture was authoritative, his movements incisive. It was as if a mask had been dropped to reveal a different man. Dickens found it rather disconcerting. What a pity, he thought, that Wainwright was wasting his artistic talents by working as a police detective – from what he had seen, he had neither ability nor inclination in that direction.

Silence reigned in the parlour. Dickens savoured it – a rare occurrence at Urania Cottage.

Finally, Wainwright sat back. 'There you go, miss.' He signed the sketch with a flourish and gave it to Mary Ann. His face had changed back again to its usual doleful expression.

'Oh, look, Mr Dickens,' said Mary Ann, ''e's turned me into a fairy.'

She brought the sketch to show him. He noticed that Wainwright had not only captured the girl's rather heavy features, but, miraculously, something of the mercurial quality that saved them from ugliness. To his surprise he had drawn her as Diana, with a crescent moon coronet and a bow at her side.

'A fairy, you?' Isabella snatched the paper from Mary Ann's hand and peered at it. 'That ain't bad. Me next!'

Dickens thought it time to intervene. 'I'm afraid the Constable and I must be going. Perhaps he will oblige us by calling back another day? If we ask him nicely he might even agree to give some of you lessons.'

Wainwright's long face flushed to the roots of his hair. 'I'd be honoured, Mr Dickens, sir.'

Dickens turned to Kathleen. 'Would you please fetch my shirt collars? They're on the dresser in my room.'

She set off at a thump up the stairs. The other girls crowded into the hall to wait with them. Dickens caught Mrs Wallace's eye.

'We'll talk later,' he said.

Kathleen returned with the collars and the two men took their leave amid much dimpling and batting of eyelashes. The carriage was waiting at the gate.

'Thank you for indulging me,' said Dickens to Wainwright. 'I know you're anxious to get back to Whitehall, but it's good to see the girls enjoy such an innocent pleasure.'

CHAPTER FORTY-EIGHT

After Pilgrim sent Charlotte away from the house, he wondered what to do next. It made no sense to return to Wainwright's lodging on his own, with the station less than ten minutes away. If Wainwright were to go to Mrs Piper's first, he would find no one home. Pilgrim locked the house up tight and set off at a jog for Whitehall.

The rain had stopped and the temperature had fallen significantly. The air burned Pilgrim's throat as he ran and he had to watch where he put his feet on the pavements, for they had taken on a glassy sheen. He arrived at Whitehall without mishap, however, and ran into the reception.

Phelps came out from behind his desk. 'Any luck, sir?'

Pilgrim shook his head. 'Is the Inspector back yet?' he gasped.

'There's been no word. You're wet through. And frozen too. Come and sit by the fire.'

Pilgrim nodded. He didn't want to stay in full view, in case Wainwright spotted him and bolted.

The Duty Sergeant's office was cramped, more of a cubbyhole than a room, but it had a fire, and an occupant: a small boy looked up from the flames as they entered.

'He's lost,' explained Phelps. 'I get one in here at least once a week. He says if we show him Newgate Street he'll know his way home. I'm just waiting for young Anderson to be free to take him. Here, let me take your overcoat, sir.'

Pilgrim studied the solemn-eyed boy as he shrugged off his coat. He judged him to be five at the most, but he had the self-possession of a lad twice that. His jacket was thin and his shoes were scuffed at the toes. But at least he had shoes. Pilgrim thought of the little flower seller in her slippers.

'The kettle's just boiled, sir. Let me make you a brew.' Phelps spooned tea leaves into a pot with a housekeeper's efficiency, and took the kettle off the hearth. 'We was shocked, sir, when you was arrested. None of us thought you was capable of anything like murder, you being one of us, an' all. I said to young Anderson, I said, that's one arrest that'll come back to bite us, sure as mustard.'

The boy swivelled to look at Pilgrim. Pilgrim took the cup Phelps offered and blew on the tea to cool it. They all heard the tramp of boots.

'Here's Anderson now,' said Phelps.

The squint-eyed constable was clearly shocked at seeing his former prisoner taking tea with his Sergeant, but Phelps forestalled any questions with a flap of his hand.

'Never mind that now.' He beckoned to the boy. 'This here's Constable Anderson. He'll take you to Newgate Street.'

'I can find my own way from there, sir,' piped the boy.

'None of that nonsense. If you show the constable the way, he'll see you safe home.'

Pilgrim thought of Charlotte Piper. Perhaps he should have brought her to the station with him? But he hadn't wanted to risk her getting any closer to Wainwright than absolutely necessary. He hoped she'd found somewhere safe to stay for the night.

CHAPTER FORTY-NINE

'Wait for us here, John Thompson, we should only be a few minutes.'

Dickens and Wainwright jumped down from the Brougham at Westminster Hospital.

'Is Adolphus hurt bad, sir?' asked Wainwright. 'Only I'm not sure I want to see him, if that's the case. I heard he was in a grave way, if you take my meanin'.'

'He's not so bad as that.' Dickens led the way into the hospital. 'Thank you for agreeing to stop off and see him. I know he'll want to hear how we got on with Townsend. I must warn you though, he has looked better, and we're not to excite him.'

A woman sat on the bench in the corridor outside the ward, swinging a bonnet to and fro in her fingers. She rose when she saw them.

'Mrs Piper!' Dickens took her hand. 'Whatever are you doing out here?'

'They're changing Dolly's bandages. I haven't the stomach for it.'

'Isn't it late for you to be visiting?'

'Sergeant Pilgrim sent me.' She grimaced. 'Not here, exactly, but he said to find somewhere safe. This was the safest place I could think of.'

'But isn't the Sergeant … ?' began Wainwright.

'He came to the house. He said he knew who the murderer was and that I was to be his next victim.'

Dickens nodded. 'You have no need to worry, Mrs Piper. Townsend is either at the docks, or on his way to New York. We've just been to his lodgings. All his belongings are gone.'

'What made the Sergeant think you would be his next victim?' asked Wainwright.

Charlotte frowned. 'I'm not sure. I can't remember what he said, precisely.'

'Whatever it was,' said Dickens, 'there's no reason for you to remain here any longer. I'll talk to Adolphus when he's finished with the doctor. Why don't you take the carriage, Constable, and see Mrs Piper safely home?'

CHAPTER FIFTY

'What the hell are you doing in here? Who let you out of the cell?' Tanner had found Pilgrim dozing in the Duty Sergeant's office. He glared at Phelps.

'Never mind that,' said Pilgrim. 'Are you on your own?'

'I left the Inspector at the docks. I'm on my way to the telegraph office.'

'I know who the killer is,' said Pilgrim.

'Who do you think we've been chasing all night?'

'I have no idea.'

Tanner crossed his arms over his chest. 'Go on, then. Tell me who it is.'

'William Wainwright.'

Tanner blinked at Pilgrim. He grinned. Then his grin split even wider. He laughed, long and loud. Finally, he wiped his eyes with his sleeve. 'Priceless,' he gasped. 'Absolutely bloody priceless. How did you work that one out?'

'I don't have time to go into it. Where is he?'

'Home by now, I should think.' Tanner grinned again. 'Sharpening his knives.'

'I know it sounds far-fetched. But it's true. He's been murdering them to order, to use as models for his paintings. Mena Levy, Johannes Appler, Martha Drewitt, Eliza Grimwood, and Clara Donald, he killed them all. I think he poisoned Angus Trinkle too.'

'You're serious?'

'I've been to his lodgings. I've seen the paintings. And Clara Donald's hand.'

They stared at each other for a long time. Finally Tanner blew out his lips. 'Fair enough,' he said. 'Get your coat.'

'You believe me?'

Tanner gave a wry grin. 'It's no secret that I think you're a self-righteous glory seeker, but I never did believe you were the killer.'

'So why did you arrest me?'

'Just doing what I was told, like a good little boy.' Tanner watched Pilgrim shrug on his overcoat. 'Wainwright lives in 'soken, doesn't he? It'll have to be Shanks's pony to get there. I've just come all the way from the Pool without hide nor hair of a cab.'

'I want to go via Holborn,' said Pilgrim, 'to make sure he hasn't gone to my lodgings.'

'Why should he go there?' Pilgrim was about to answer when Tanner stopped him. 'Tell me on the way.'

When they reached Greville Street, Pilgrim stopped with a frown in front of Charlotte Piper's house. 'There's a light on in the kitchen,' he said.

'So?' Tanner followed his gaze to the basement, to where a glow showed through the curtains.

'It wasn't on when I left. Either Mrs Piper's come back, or … '

They crept down the steps to the basement window, where they each put an ear to the glass. They could hear voices, one male, one female. Although he couldn't hear what was being said, Pilgrim recognized them immediately. Tanner gave a grim nod. They crept back up to the street.

'That's him, all right,' said Tanner. 'And it sounds as if your Mrs Piper is with him.'

Anger flashed through Pilgrim. Why hadn't the bloody woman obeyed his instructions? Was she wilfully contrary? Hadn't he made himself clear?

Tanner watched with a wry expression as Pilgrim struggled to master his frustration. 'What now?' he asked.

'I have my key. I'll go in through the front door and down to the kitchen. You come in through the window. We'll have the element of surprise.'

'I'll give you till the count of twenty.'

'That's not long … ' He was going to say 'enough', but Tanner had already gone.

One. Pilgrim muttered a curse and hurried up the steps. Two. He slipped his key into the lock and turned it. Three. He stepped inside. Four. Closed the door carefully behind him. Five. Crept down the hall. Six, seven, eight, nine. Paused at the top of the basement stairs. Ten. Made his way gingerly down in the darkness. Twelve, thirteen, fourteen, fifteen. A stair creaked under him. He froze. He could hear the voices in the kitchen clearly now.

'What did the Sergeant say, exactly? About the killer?' Wainwright's tone was casual.

Water splashed into the sink.

'Just that you and the Inspector were after the wrong man and that I was to be the next victim. He also said that the killer hid that poor baby here the night you and he were dressed as Hebrews. Lord knows how he got it into the house.'

Pilgrim put his eye to the keyhole. He saw Mrs Piper's hand hesitate on the cupboard handle, but only for a second.

'Do you take cream, Constable?'

'Please.'

Pilgrim shifted position. Where was Tanner?

Mrs Piper took a jug from the cupboard. 'Didn't I hear you were an artist, Constable Wainwright?'

Wainwright gave her a sharp glance, but she was concentrating on pouring the cream into a smaller jug and not looking at him.

'Who told you that?' he asked.

'Dolly.'

Wainwright relaxed. 'Yes, I am an artist.' His voice took on a note of pride. 'I'm workin' on an exhibition just now, in fact.'

Charlotte took a plate from the meat safe, her hand trembling under the weight of it. She opened a drawer and took out a carving knife. Wainwright peeled it from her grip.

'Why don't you let me carve?' he said. 'We wouldn't want you to hurt yourself, would we?'

WHERE THE HELL WAS TANNER?

Pilgrim's question was answered by an almighty crash. The air filled with flying glass and splinters as Tanner swung himself, feet first, through one of the kitchen windows.

Pilgrim ran into the room, saw Tanner stagger as he landed. Wainwright whirled, grabbed Charlotte, and stepped back, pressing the knife to her throat. He clapped his other hand over her mouth.

'One more step and I'll do for her,' he said. 'I swear it. I'll do for her the way I done for the Dutchman.'

Pilgrim and Tanner stared at him. The affable young constable had gone, and a stranger stood in his place.

'You took your time,' he sneered. 'The oh-so-clever Detective Sergeants.'

Tanner's chest was heaving, but whether it was with the exertion of coming through the window or outrage it was hard to tell. Charlotte Piper's eyes locked on Pilgrim's, but the expression in them wasn't what he expected: not fear, but fury. The table stood between them: there was nothing he could do. His guts knotted.

'Move!' Wainwright growled at Tanner. 'Away from the window.'

When Tanner was slow to obey, Wainwright pressed the knife into Charlotte's throat. Blood trickled down the blade. Charlotte's eyes widened. Tanner backed away reluctantly.

'We've been leadin' you both round the garden for weeks, and you had no idea.' Wainwright's gaze flicked to him. 'The great

Sergeant Pilchem. The Prince of Detectives! Ha! If only Mr Dickens could see you now.'

His boots crunched on glass. He was almost at the window. Once he was there he had a decision to make. Pilgrim knew he wouldn't be able to take Charlotte through the window with him, which left two choices. Given Wainwright's recent actions, only one was likely.

It all passed through Pilgrim's head in an instant. Charlotte, who had never taken her eyes from his face, saw his expression change in the moment the knowledge hit him: Wainwright was going to kill her. In the next fraction of a second, Pilgrim read her intention. She bit down on Wainwright's hand with all her strength.

Wainwright howled. The blade passed a hair's breadth from Charlotte's cheek as she twisted away from him. Pilgrim heaved the kitchen table towards Wainwright, sending him staggering backwards.

Tanner threw himself at Wainwright, but the other man somehow managed to regain his balance and turned to face him. Carried by his own momentum, Dick Tanner ran straight onto the knife in Wainwright's hand.

A stunned silence. Everything moved slowly, as if the world had stopped on its axis.

Tanner had folded over Wainwright's fist. Wainwright released the knife and stepped backwards, blood on his hand. Charlotte goggled up at them from the floor, her own hand over her mouth. Then Tanner groaned.

'You bastard,' he said. He dropped to his knees.

The words released them all from the spell. Wainwright pushed past Tanner to leap up and out of the smashed kitchen window. Charlotte rushed to Tanner.

Pilgrim hesitated, torn.

Charlotte pressed her hand to Tanner's wound and glared up at him. 'What are you waiting for?' she hissed. She nodded at the window. 'Get after him!'

CHAPTER FIFTY-ONE

Glass stung Pilgrim's palms as he levered himself out of the window. He scrambled up the steps, just in time to see Wainwright vanish at the far end of the street. He ran after him.

Wainwright headed towards the Holborn Bridge, or rather, the junction where the old bridge used to stand that now marked the entrance to the Farringdon Market. The market was closed and dark, and there were few carriages and even fewer pedestrians about. Pilgrim arrived at the junction, and saw Wainwright run to the market gates and rattle them. A figure detached itself from the watchman's hut.

''Ere!' It shouted. 'What do you think you're doin'? Hook it, cully!'

Wainwright darted off.

Pilgrim ran to the gates. Old Charlie Rouse, one of the last night watchmen in the city, lifted his lantern to peer at Pilgrim's face.

'Harry Pilgrim, is that you? What's goin' on?'

'Where did he go?'

'Down there, into the Fleet ditch.' Rouse pointed to a low wall.

'Give me your lantern,' said Pilgrim. 'Your cutlass too,'

'You're not goin' down there after 'im, are you?'

In answer, Pilgrim tucked the cutlass into his belt and swung his leg over the wall. Rouse handed him the lantern, his expression saying exactly what he thought of the pursuit.

271

'Stick to the main ditch,' he advised, 'and get a move on. The sluices open at low tide to flush the tunnels. With all the rain we've had, it'll wash you right down to the river if you ain't careful.'

Pilgrim nodded to show he'd heard, and jumped down into the culvert on the other side. He landed in mud that oozed over the top of his boots. He looked to his right, along the open ditch, where thick wooden stakes propped the walls of the channel. The stakes were black, festooned with hanging debris; a barrier to anyone in a hurry. In the other direction the ditch disappeared into a tunnel that ran beneath the market as dark and hollow as an empty eye socket. He strained his ears. The sound of splashing came faintly from inside.

'Bollocks.' He looked back up at Rouse. 'Do me a favour, Charlie, fetch some of the lads from F Division. Tell them to come quick.'

'Right you are.' Rouse disappeared.

Pilgrim headed for the tunnel. The Fleet was one of the ancient rivers of the city, now used only as a sewer: fed with waste from the meat markets, tanneries, and all the households of the city, south of Hampstead Ponds. It was notorious for its stench and many parts of it had been enclosed and built over as a result. The section of tunnel ahead of him led beneath Farringdon Street, under the market, and ran, as far as he knew, all the way down to the Thames at Blackfriars Bridge; a distance of a mile or more, with no exits or access shafts.   He reached the mouth of the tunnel and ran inside. There was just enough room to stand upright. Mushrooms clustered on the roof above him, reminding him of dead things. Of Clara Donald's finger.

'Wainwright!' He bellowed into the darkness, thick as soot. 'Wainwright!' He paused. There was no noise ahead of him now: the other man had stopped, and was listening. 'Don't be a fool. You have no light. God knows what you might fall into.' He had heard that in some of the tunnels the floor had collapsed, leaving great sinkholes where decades of filth had accumulated. He was knee deep in ooze himself. He could see turnip tops, oyster shells, and potato peelings, and the occasional turd, but much of it had decomposed into an unidentifiable slime. Here and there on the surface he could see spiky prints and droppings. A thought occurred to him.

'Wainwright!' he yelled. 'There're rats down here. Hundreds of them. Stay where you are and let me fetch you.'

Silence, for a moment. Then the suck and slap of boots resumed. Pilgrim swore. He pressed forward again. It was much warmer in the tunnels than up on the street. The air was moist, like the breath of a great beast. At least he had the lantern. And yet, in some ways he wished he hadn't. He felt as if its light was pulling something towards him, something merciless and ravening. It was a fancy born of fear, he knew, but as much as he tried to reason it away, he couldn't shake off the sensation that he was being watched.

He walked on, until his thighs ached with the strain of pulling his feet repeatedly up and out of the mud. After a while he had to stop to catch his breath. He wiped the sweat from his eyes with his sleeve and frowned. The light of the lantern had revealed a hole on his left. He went to investigate and discovered that it was a side tunnel that inclined upwards, big enough for a man to climb in. A trickle of filth ran out from the bottom. He paused, trying to calculate how far he had come along the main tunnel, and guessed that the smaller one must lead up to the old Fleet Prison that stood dilapidated and half-demolished some twenty feet over his head. He doubted that Wainwright would be stupid enough to have taken it, but he listened, to be sure. There was no sound at all, from any direction.

Then came a shout. 'Help!' It echoed faintly off the brickwork and bounced towards him from the direction of the main ditch. He heaved a sigh of relief.

'Help me,' shouted Wainwright again.

Pilgrim hurried towards his voice. He walked for three or four minutes before the lantern picked out movement in the mud ahead of him. Wainwright had fallen, thigh deep, into a sinkhole, and the slurry held him fast. When he turned his head towards the light, Pilgrim could see his long face, rigid with fury.

'I can't move!' He floundered in the muck, his shadow casting grotesque shapes on the tunnel walls.

Pilgrim moved towards him. He was still several yards away when they both heard the sound: a great rumble, like a subterranean beast clearing its throat. He turned and lifted the lantern, but at first could see nothing. Then, as he stared, the mud began to ripple towards him. He heard another noise, high pitched and frantic, and he realized that it was not the mud itself that was moving, but something running over it.

Wainwright realized what it was before Pilgrim. He squawked and tried to heave himself up out of the mud. But he only sank further, up to his chest.

The rats surged towards them; a great squealing, heaving tidal wave of fur, tails, and paws. They parted to flow around Pilgrim and he could only watch in horror as they engulfed the fallen man. All he could see of Wainwright was his arms, thrashing as he tried to fight them off. He could hear him, though, gibbering and howling, a sound that made Pilgrim's blood thicken in his veins. And, all the while, the rumbling grew louder and louder, like an approaching train.

Pilgrim launched himself at Wainwright as the rumble burst into a roar. He dropped the lantern and grabbed Wainwright's collar just as the water hit them both. Pilgrim's feet went from under him. He gasped at the shock of it. Water swept over his head, but he still kept his grip on the other man. At first he thought Wainwright's weight might anchor them both, but then he felt the mud give way and release its prisoner. The two men were swept down the tunnel. The water tumbled and buffeted Pilgrim; filling his mouth, his nose, roaring in his ears, until he was no longer sure which way was up and which way was down. Swimming was out of the question, even if he'd known how. He fought down the panic, and kept his grip on Wainwright's collar.

They were buffeted against the tunnel sides, again and again. Once, Pilgrim had the breath almost knocked out of him completely. He swallowed water and thought he was done for. He reached out blindly, instinctively, with his free hand and grasped something. Something buoyant. He clung on to it. Was he imagining it, or was the noise of the water lessening? No, the current was definitely slowing. It slowed until he felt the ground scrape beneath him, and he landed with a jolt.

He opened his eyes to mud. He lay face down, still clutching the section of barrel that had kept them afloat. He pushed himself up, wincing, as pain shot through his shoulder, and looked about him. He was on a mudbank. Behind him gaped the mouth of the sewer and ahead he could see the dark rush of the Thames. He turned his head to his left and recognized the arches of Blackfriars Bridge, and behind, the great upturned pudding basin of St Paul's.

He flopped back onto the mud. Every bone and muscle in his body ached as if he'd been cudgelled, but he knew he was lucky to be alive. The thought spurred another. He sat up again. Wainwright lay facing the sky, a few feet away; somehow, Pilgrim had managed to keep his grip on him all the way down the tunnel. But his eyes were closed and he wasn't moving.

'You all right there, guv'nor?'

Pilgrim looked up. Several people gawked down at them from the embankment parapet.

'What you doin' down there?'

'Drowning.' The word rasped out without a thought. He wanted to laugh. He looked again at the faces. There was one he knew, smeared in mud, with a single snaggled tooth.

'Is that you, Blackey?'

'Yes, sa?' The mudlark blinked and looked more closely. 'Sergeant Pilgrim?'

'Go to the Whitehall station. Fetch someone. There's a shilling in it for you.'

'Right away, sa!'

CHAPTER FIFTY-TWO

'You stink. And you look terrible.'

'Thanks, Charley.' Pilgrim gripped the blanket and pulled it further onto his shoulders. 'But you're right, I'm not feeling well.'

'You've probably swallowed half the shit in the city. Here take this.' Field thrust a glass of port into his hands. 'It won't kill you, for once.'

He took a gulp and felt it burn down his throat into his belly.

'How did you know it was Wainwright?' asked Field.

'I saw blood on his shirt, the morning he cut Appler's throat. I dismissed it at the time, thinking he'd cut himself shaving. But what man shaves with his shirt on? And then I remembered the gingerbread.'

'Gingerbread?'

'Appler was left unattended because Constable Anderson had an attack of the flux. Gingerbread is Anderson's favourite.'

Field rubbed his nose. 'I'm not following you.'

'Wainwright brought gingerbread into the station that morning. Presumably he'd laced it with something, knowing Anderson was on slops duty. But I didn't know he was the killer, not for certain, until I saw his name in the Hatchell and Manson ledgers.'

'Those books you asked me for?'

Pilgrim nodded. 'Wainwright had taken delivery of American wrapping canvas and some canvases three months ago. No red ink, though.' He frowned, following a train of thought.

Field broke it. 'And you say he's done paintings of all his victims?'

'He could take all the time he needed to sketch them in the morgue. He was choosing them carefully. Eliza Grimwood for her handsome looks. Mena Levy and Johannes Appler, not only for their looks but also for their religion. Clara Donald for her hair. Martha Drewitt for her condition ...' he tailed off. 'He didn't use her baby in the end. I don't know why, perhaps it wasn't developed enough, so he was forced to improvise and use the study he'd made of Louis Drake.'

Field shuddered. 'What about Trinkle?'

'He was the perfect St Sebastian, exactly like the one in the Royal Academy. Wainwright poisoned him with strychnine so that his body made similar contortions. I don't know where he got it, though. We should ask him.'

'He won't be telling us anything. Cruikshank's had to truss him up like a Christmas goose.'

'He's mad?'

'As a Whitechapel hatter.'

'I'd like to speak with him anyway.'

'What the devil for? Anything he says isn't admissible as evidence.'

'When he was boasting about the murders in Mrs Piper's kitchen, he said "we". He said, "we've been leading you a dance". He was working with someone. Townsend, perhaps. The handwriting on the notes definitely wasn't his.' Pilgrim's eyes opened wider. 'Townsend would have had access to strychnine, at the hospital.'

Field sighed. 'Go ahead. He's in Appler's old cell.' He paused and grinned. 'Or should I say yours?'

Pilgrim tried to smile, but couldn't. The memory of his arrest was still too raw.

Dr Cruikshank was about to administer a dose of laudanum when Pilgrim let himself into the cell. Wainwright rocked backwards and forwards in his straight waistcoat, shaking his head as if trying to dislodge something from it.

'Can I talk to him before you give him that?' asked Pilgrim.

The doctor nodded. 'Much good it'll do you. Let me know when you're finished. I have to arrange for the Bedlam Asylum to come and get him.' He left the cell.

Wainwright was still rocking and muttering. 'I couldn't … no … HA!'

'William.' Pilgrim knelt beside him. 'William, look at me.'

Wainwright's eyes slid over him, without recognition. Pilgrim noticed the marks on his face; scratches, and a scabbed crescent.

'Rats,' muttered Wainwright.

'There are no rats here. I need to ask you something.'

'Always such a mess … I told him … I told him straight … IT AIN'T SALOME WHO HAD HER HEAD OFF! HOW CAN I PAINT SALOME IF HER HEAD'S OFF?' He subsided again. 'He cut them up. Cut all of them up. They never looked right.'

'Who?' asked Pilgrim. 'Who cut them up?'

'He wanted her, you know … my Magdalene. But I wouldn't give her to him … I found him another one.'

'Who wanted her?' Pilgrim fought the urge to shake him.

'Francis Townsend. Who else?' Wainwright gave him a scornful look. 'You shouldn't feel sorry for them. We did them a kindness. They were nothing … less than nothing. But now they'll live forever.'

Pilgrim clenched his fist.

'FILTHY CREATURES!' Wainwright shrieked and jumped up onto the cot. The metal frame squeaked under him and he shrieked again. 'RATS' He caught his foot in the blanket and crashed onto the floor, squirming and thrashing beside Appler's faded bloodstain. 'KEEP THEM OFF!' He began to cry; a dreadful, rasping noise that sounded as if it was being ripped from his chest.

Pilgrim left him there. He found Charley with his coat on, ready for home. 'Wainwright was working with Townsend,' he said. 'When I found Mena Levy's body it must have been Townsend I followed through the sewers. I think Wainwright was choosing the victims, but Townsend was killing them, apart from Appler and Trinkle.'

278

Field rubbed his nose. 'That makes sense. I can imagine Wainwright cutting Appler's throat … just about … but not decapitating Mena Levy, or excising Martha Drewitt's baby. Wainwright must have let Townsend bash him over the head the night Amalia Cohen was killed.'

Pilgrim considered the possibility. He could hear Wainwright's incredulous words: *the bugger hit me*. No. He hadn't expected Townsend to hit him. But it was no more than he deserved for putting his trust in a killer.

'We could do with proof that Wainwright and Townsend knew each other,' said Field.

'I'll go back to their lodgings tomorrow, see if I can find anything.'

'When are we expecting news from Liverpool?'

'Tomorrow afternoon, if the Princess Alice makes good time on her way to New York. If not … God only knows.'

'You'll be sending someone up there, though, to bring Townsend back?' asked Pilgrim. 'Let me go. He probably doesn't know we've caught Wainwright. Even if he does, he won't know that Wainwright can't legally tell us anything. He might confess.' He paused. 'I hear that Dick Tanner will be out of the hospital by Friday.'

Field nodded. 'I swear the bloody man is invincible.'

Pilgrim hesitated. Did Charley suspect that Tanner was crooked? That he was turning stolen property into cash through his brother's pawnshop?

'What?' asked Charley, piqued by Pilgrim's expression.

'Nothing. What do you think? Can I go to Liverpool?'

Field rubbed his nose, and then shrugged. 'Very well. But bring Townsend back as quickly as you can. I have to make my report to the Joint Commissioners.' He grinned at Pilgrim. 'Sir Charles has announced his retirement at last, and the appointment of someone to replace him. Before he bows out I want to remind him and that prick Sir Richard why this city needs us. But first, I need some sleep.' He headed for the door. 'Aren't you going home?'

Home. Pilgrim thought about his rooms at Greville Street. About Charlotte Piper. Was she asleep, he wondered, or waiting for him? He looked down at his clothes, almost dry now, but streaked with mud, blood, and worse. Charley was right, he needed a bath, but it would have to wait until the bathhouse opened. He didn't want Charlotte to see him like this.

Field was still watching, still waiting for an answer.

Pilgrim shook his head. 'I have some things I need to do first.'

CHAPTER FIFTY-THREE

His office was dark. He lit the oil lamp and turned it up. It seemed a lifetime since he had last stood there. Dolly's desk was in chaos, as usual, and the travelling valise with its stickers was still on Tanner's desk. How long had it been since he and Dolly had visited the laundry in Limehouse? A week? Ten days? He remembered the Chinaman's warning; *something bad has passed close to you. It will come again.* He shook his head. The old man had been wrong: there was something bad beside them all along.

Wainwright's desk was clear of everything save a notebook, left open as if the young constable might stroll in and pick it up at any moment. Pilgrim sighed and looked around. The same pile of letters from *Household Words* waited, unopened, on his desk, topped with the stale beef pie. Nothing had changed. Almost nothing. He felt the familiar tightening behind his eyes.

A small package lay on his desk, wrapped in American canvas, addressed in red ink to 'Sergeant Pilgrim'. He picked it up and ripped it open. There was a note inside, wrapped around something small and hard. He unfolded the paper and read the message:

How now, Harry?
I daresay you'll have figured it all out by now. Or most of it, at any rate. Sorry to disappoint you, but you won't catch me

on the ship. I made other arrangements. Ha ha.
Pity I have to go away for a while, 'cause I was just getting
into my stride, but I hope you don't mind I left a little
present for you. Something to remember me by. I will miss
you all, I imagine, but 'the devil finds work for idle hands'
or so they say.

It was wrapped around an earring, made of jet, carved into the shape of a rosebud; the perfect match to Eliza Grimwood's choker. *I've left a little present for you.* Did Townsend mean the earring? Or something else? Pilgrim looked more closely at the earring. Was it familiar to him because it matched the choker? Or had he seen it before?

Suddenly the effort of thinking was too much for him. He needed to sleep. In a bed. Dirty or clean, he no longer cared.

He put the earring on his desk and turned off the oil lamp. The note meant nothing. A final act of defiance. Wainwright must have left it there earlier that morning. As for Townsend ... they would catch up with him. He didn't know how, yet, but he would put his mind to it in the morning. He would find a way.

He trudged down the staircase. Phelps was nowhere to be seen, but Anderson squinted at him from behind the desk.

'Did you get the lad home safe?' asked Pilgrim. He saw the constable's blank look. 'The lost boy.'

'If you can call it home,' said Anderson. 'A pit of a place behind the Newgate Prison, no fire, no door even, and seven of them in there, like rats.'

Pilgrim nodded goodnight and went out into the street. The wind had risen; a gnawing wind straight off the river. He folded his collar up to his chin and set off towards Holborn. No doubt Wainwright was on his way to Bedlam, if he hadn't arrived there already. He hardened his heart to pity. Bedlam was better than Wainwright deserved, for as long as his mind had gone, he would barely be aware of the constraint. *He wanted my Magdalene, but*

I gave him another. In his mind's eye Pilgrim could see Clara Donald as she had appeared in Wainwright's painting, haloed in the lamplight, with her hair draped artfully over her breasts. His footsteps slowed, and stopped. Clara Donald, with her long red hair, who looked so much like his Bess.

Without consciously thinking about it, he turned on his heel and headed back the way he had come.

Why should Wainwright have changed his mind about his original choice of Magdalene? *My Magdalene.* Mine. He hadn't wanted to kill her. He had wanted her for himself. Who was his original Magdalene? But Pilgrim already knew the answer.

He broke into a run. He ran past the station to Westminster Bridge. The bridge was busy, so busy that he was forced to run on the road, dodging omnibuses, Broughams, and Hackneys, like an eel. Blood pounded in his ears as he reached the other end of the bridge and ran beneath the dark walls of Lambeth Palace to Lambeth Walk.

He stopped for a moment to catch his breath. Even though it was almost midnight, the Walk was as busy as the middle of the afternoon. The crowd, lit with gas and paraffin lamps, was badly dressed and dirty, but cheerful. Pilgrim set off again, dodging the barrows and handcarts that blocked his way, past an organ grinder and a group of dancing children. Frustration flared. The crowds on the Walk were slowing him down.

He spotted the entrance to a court that ran off to the left, away from the glare of the street into darkness, and plunged into it. The houses were low, with narrow doorways and windows that showed no glimmer of light. He leapt a pile of rubbish, ignoring the squeal of a rat as he landed on it. His footsteps rang in his ears until he burst out the other end of the court into a broader street. He had no real idea where he was now, but relied on instinct to guide him. He kept running.

He left the main street again, to dodge though a stable yard, where a dog barked and lunged at him. He was too fast for it, vaulting over a fence into another lane that he guessed ran roughly parallel to where he needed to be. He ran on, saw an alley cutting to his right, and took it.

Finally he arrived, winded, and lathered with sweat, in Gloucester Street. He found the lodgings and took the stairs three at a time, ignoring the shouts of an old man who had to leap aside to avoid him. He had almost reached the top when he stopped abruptly.

There was a splash of blood, bright as a rose petal, on one of the stairs. And then another, on the top landing, beside Frances' door. It was slightly ajar. Pilgrim pushed it open. Frances lay on her back in a pool of blood. He ran to kneel beside her. Her hair, her glorious hair, was loose, but thick with gore, plastered across her cheeks, breast, and throat. He brushed the hair tenderly from her face and saw what had killed her: a single cut, slicing her throat from one ear to the other, where a single jet earring dangled.

He gathered her into his arms, and howled.

CHAPTER FIFTY-FOUR

Mrs Wallace pushed her index finger into the soil to make a hole. The sunlight was warm on her shoulders and she could feel the dampness of the earth through her skirts; both welcome sensations after the dreary months spent indoors.

'Get away from me with that ruddy water!' shrieked Isabella, picking up her skirts and darting away from Mary Ann who was chasing her with a watering can.

'Get 'er, Mary Ann!'

The girls laughed and shrieked as each tended their own little patch of garden, their high spirits soaring at unaccustomed freedom. She knew she should reprimand them, tell them to behave more decorously, but she didn't have the heart. Let them scandalize the neighbours, for once.

'Just one in each hole.' She helped Kathleen Chalk laboriously separate a single sunflower seed from the heap in her palm, and watched as she dropped it into the ground. 'That's right. That way they'll all have space to grow.'

Kathleen's eyes drooped under the combination of the sun's heat and the repetitive action of sowing the seeds. Mrs Wallace heard a rapping sound. She looked up to see Mr Dickens at the parlour window, signalling for her to come inside.

'Make some more holes like that, Kathleen, with your finger.

But don't put any seeds into them until I get back.' She stood up and brushed the soil from her skirt.

In the parlour, Dickens already had on his overcoat. He was putting paperwork back into the bureau. 'I've brought the books up to date, Mrs Wallace,' he said. 'You should manage well enough without me for a few weeks. I'm sorry to have to abandon you like this, but I need to concentrate on *Bleak House*.'

'That's quite all right, sir. I've been following it in *Household Words*.'

'What do you think?'

'Most intriguing. I particularly admire the police detective, Inspector Bucket, and the heroine, Esther Summerson. I'm so pleased that Mr Woodcourt has not been put off by her disfigurement. Society places far too much value on appearance, in my opinion.' She hesitated. 'I also read your article in the *Chronicle* about the expansion of the Detective Force. Is it true that Sergeant Pilgrim has been promoted?'

'Yes, indeed. He's Inspector Pilgrim now. But I didn't realize you knew him, Mrs Wallace?'

'Oh, I don't … other than what I've read about Sergeant Pilchem, of course.' She twisted the ring on her finger.

Dickens looked about. 'Is there anything else you think you might need, before I go? I've left the key for the cash box in its usual place.'

'Thank you. I need to buy another pair of shoes for Ida. She's outgrown her others already.'

'Has she, really?' Dickens tried to hide a smile. 'She's growing fast, Mrs Wallace.'

Ida Blenkinsopp had come to Urania Cottage shortly after the death of her friend, Frances Reilly. They had taken her in at Sergeant Pilgrim's request, even though she was a few years younger than the other girls. It meant she would have to stay with them longer, but the Matron knew that wasn't going to be a problem. Mr Dickens tried to hide it, but the girl had quickly become his favourite, perhaps because she was very close in age to his own daughters.

Dickens dithered at the door. 'If there's anything urgent you need, you know how to reach me.'

'I'm sure we'll manage, sir.'

She followed him into the hallway, and helped him find his hat and walking stick.

'Anything you need, anything at all. Do not hesitate to send me a note.' He waved goodbye to the girls as he walked down the path, and they all stopped what they were doing to wave back, except Isabella and Mary Ann, who were still chasing each other with the watering can.

Mrs Wallace watched him until he disappeared around the corner, headed in the direction of the omnibus stop, and then she returned to Kathleen. As she had feared, the girl had been too impatient to wait to plant her seeds and had upended the packet onto the soil.

Kathleen saw her disappointment. 'Weren't my fault, missus. They just fell.'

Mrs Wallace knelt beside her again to gather up the seeds.

'Missus Wallace!' Ida clattered though the gate, with Julia at her heels. 'Look! We've bought some lovely buttons.' She tucked an unruly red curl behind her ear and flourished a paper bag. 'They're perfect for that new jacket of Mary Ann's.'

The Matron handed the seeds back to Kathleen. 'Here you go. Try again. Remember, one at a time.' She stood up and turned to Ida. 'Bring them inside, let me see.'

In the hallway, Ida pulled a handful of buttons from her paper bag. 'They were only sixpence a dozen.'

'They're beautiful, Ida. I'm sure Mary Ann will love them.' She took the buttons. 'Now run along and put your apron on. It's pity to waste the sunshine.'

Ida turned, as if to run up the stairs, and then turned back to her. She smiled shyly. 'I'm so glad you're here, missus. I couldn't believe my eyes when I saw you, with your red hair and everything. Just like my poor Fran come back to life.'

Mrs Wallace's heart squeezed. *Frances.*

'You could almost be her sister,' averred Ida.

'Not her sister. I'm too old.' Bess Wallace smiled, and tucked a stray lock of hair behind Ida's ear. 'Her aunt, maybe.'

AUTHOR'S NOTE

An Act of Mercy is set in London in March 1850. History buffs and lovers of Dickens may have noticed that I've taken some liberties with history and biographical details for the sake of creating this imaginative piece of fiction. Dickens took a keen interest in the new police detective department at Scotland Yard, which was set up in 1842 and still very much in its infancy in 1850. His police stories, articles, and anecdotes on their investigations appeared in *Household Worlds* between 1850 and 1853. *Bleak House* was published in monthly parts between March 1852 and October 1853.

Charley Field, Adolphus 'Dolly' Williamson, and Dick Tanner were all real detectives in the new police detective department alongside Jonathan Whicher. Sir Richard Mayne and Sir Charles Rowan were Joint Commissioners of the Metropolitan Police. Although I've based all real-life characters on contemporary reports and descriptions, they have been fictionalized to suit the story

The murder of Louis Drake – the boy in the box – is based on a real case investigated by Detective Sergeant Jonathan Whicher in 1849. The real Sarah Drake had a less grisly fate than my fictional character – she was brought to trial and found not guilty, on the grounds of temporary insanity. In 1859, Whicher, by then an Inspector, also investigated a case of infanticide involving the

Reverend Bonwell; however, the two cases are not connected in the way they are depicted in *An Act of Mercy*.

I hope you'll forgive these liberties and trust they haven't spoiled your enjoyment of the novel. No offence is intended towards living relatives of any character whose name I have borrowed in the service of fiction.

CPSIA information can be obtained
at www.ICGtesting.com
Printed in the USA
LVOW12s2124200317
527869LV00001B/9/P